The room grew quiet. Too quiet.

Sydney glanced up. "What?"

Evelyn's normally carefree gaze had grown thoughtful, serious even. "He's never coming back, you know."

It was a good thing she owed Evelyn the world. Otherwise, Sydney might have ushered her best friend out the back door. "I never said I wanted him back," she whispered.

"Look at your life. Don't you think it's time to move on?"

"If you mean forget, no way." Sydney might have been divorced for years, but not a day had gone by since she'd signed the final papers that she hadn't thought of her ex-husband. Most days were OK. Most days she thought of him only once, or twice. Other days were bad. Sometimes they were so bad that she'd go to bed thinking about him, wake up dreaming of him and spend the next day plagued with memories. Sometimes she thought her heart was healed, and other times she could feel it tightening in her chest, breaking into a million tiny pieces all over again.

Why? That was always the question. Maybe knowing *why* he'd left her would give her some measure of peace.

Available in July 2008
from Mills & Boon®
Superromance

Blame It on the Dog by Amy Frazier
An out-of-control dog, a young son, and dog
trainer Jack Quinn. These are the males in
Selena Milano's life. The first two she loves.
The third? Well, he certainly makes life
interesting...

The Baby Doctors by Janice Macdonald
Single Father
Dr Matthew Cameron isn't looking for a
mother for his difficult teenage daughter – but
he might just have found one!

Dad for Life by Helen Brenna
A Little Secret
Lucas Rydall is looking for redemption. His
search brings him to Sydney Mitchell and the
son he didn't know he had. But his discovery
puts them all in danger and now Lucas must
become the man his family needs...

Undercover Protector by Molly O'Keefe

FBI agent Maggie Fitzgerald liked working
undercover...until Caleb Gomez's charms
reminded her she was a woman first, an agent
second!

Dad for Life

HELEN BRENNA

MILLS & BOON®
Pure reading pleasure™

First published in Great Britain 2008
by Harlequin Mills & Boon Limited,
Eton House, 18-24 Paradise Road, Richmond, Surrey TW9 1SR

© Helen Brenna 2007

ISBN: 978 0 263 86166 2

38-0708

Harlequin Mills & Boon policy is to use papers that are
natural, renewable and recyclable products and made from
wood grown in sustainable forests. The logging and
manufacturing processes conform to the legal environmental
regulations of the country of origin.

Printed and bound in Spain
by Litografía Rosés S.A., Barcelona

HELEN BRENNA

grew up the seventh of eight children in central Minnesota. Although as a child she never dreamed of writing books, she must have assimilated the necessary skills from her storytelling brothers.

With a degree in accounting, she started career life as an accountant and thought she'd end career life as an old accountant, but the decision to stay home with her kids made all things possible. After she won the Georgia Romance Writers' Maggie Award, her debut novel, *Treasure*, became a Superromance.

She continues to write away, living near Minneapolis with her husband, two children, two dogs and three cats, and would love hearing from you. E-mail her at helenbrenna@comcast.net or send mail to PO Box 24107, Minneapolis, MN 55424, USA.

Bloggers can chat with Helen and several other authors at ridingwiththetopdown.blogspot.com or visit her website at www.helenbrenna.com.

For Kelsey, the brightest star in my sky

Acknowledgements:

I could not have written this book without the tireless hand-holding of experienced medical anthropologist Susan Charles. She is a wonder, maintaining her sense of humour throughout my many episodes of idiocy. I only hope I did *your* beloved Peru proud, Susan.

Thanks also to my friendly neighbourhood FBI agent, but if I told you who he is then I'd have to shoot him!

And to Morse Caltabiano, *grazie*, from me. And Joe!

Many thanks to Tina Wexler, Johanna Raisanen and my beloved Princesses for their unflinching encouragement and support.

I've taken some liberties in this book and any mistakes are entirely my own. (Although I probably had a darned good reason for making them!)

CHAPTER ONE

THE AFRICAN MASK GLOWED with the mysteries of its ancient past. As Sydney Mitchell tilted it back and forth, its smooth planes and carved surfaces alternately caught and reflected the glaring fluorescent lights. "Legend has it," she whispered, "this mask has the power to summon a god more adept at the art of lovemaking than any woman can imagine."

"Really?" Evelyn Dahl leaned farther over the table, appearing to salivate at the thought.

"It was made for a fierce warrior princess who, by law, was not allowed to lie with any mortal man while her tribe was at war." Though they were alone in the stark workroom of her Seattle art gallery, Sydney let her voice take on the animated inflections of a storyteller. "Now, I don't want you to think the warrior princess wasn't a passionate woman. She was. But she also realized the need to stay focused for battle."

"She obviously needed her priorities adjusted," Evelyn added dryly.

"Her priorities were fine." Sydney scowled at her best friend. "The edict grew difficult to bear only after fighting with a neighboring tribe waged on for years."

"Years?" Evelyn muttered. "I should say so."

"Do you want to hear this story, or not?"

Evelyn motioned zipping her lips.

"Where was I?" Sydney paused. "Oh, yeah. The tribe's medicine man, understanding the princess's predicament, took pity upon her and made her this mask. He told her if she wore it at night in the privacy of her hut, a god of love would come to pleasure her."

"Sounds pretty kinky to me." Evelyn pointed to the covered eye sockets on the mask. "She couldn't even see this love god."

"The medicine man said it was for her protection. If she took off the mask and looked upon the face of the god, her eyes would explode, and she would die."

"Been there, done that."

"Evelyn!"

"All right. I'll shut up."

"At first," Sydney went on, "it wasn't dif-

ficult to leave on the mask. The love god plea-
sured the warrior princess so well nothing
else seemed to matter. But soon their trysts
involved more than mere physical delights.
They would lie in each other's arms, talk into
the morning hours, and the princess found
herself falling desperately in love. The mask
became a frustration beyond comprehension."

Evelyn shook her head. "How do you
make this stuff up?"

The answer to that question threw Sydney,
threatening to ruin the pacing of her story.
She didn't want to think about him, the man
who'd changed her love of art history into a
passion for antiquities. Or the way he'd
whispered his own stories, some real, some
fabricated, in the deepest, quietest part of
night, his arms wrapped around her, his soft
lips against her ear.

All at once, the ending to the story came
to her, a weight in her mind as real as the
mask lying heavy in her hand. "One night,
after they'd made love with the greatest
passion, the warrior princess simply had to
gaze upon the face of her lover or die from
despair. Die from looking, die from not
looking." Sydney held out her hands as if

weighing a matter of great importance. "The decision made, the warrior princess tore the mask from her face." She paused for effect.

"It was the medicine man," Evelyn said quickly.

"That old wrinkly thing?" Sydney chuckled.

"Who was it?"

Sydney grinned. "The ruling prince of the enemy tribe. He'd seen her in battle and yearned to possess her. So he struck a bargain with the medicine man in return for the promise of power if the enemy tribe eventually triumphed."

"What happened after she took off the mask?"

"The sight of the enemy prince filled her with rage. She took up her knife…and stabbed him through the heart."

"He died?"

Sydney nodded, satisfied. "Instantly."

"That's it?"

"That's it."

"No happily ever after?" Evelyn huffed. "No the warrior princess immediately regretted her angry outburst and in her despair thrust the knife into her own heart?"

"Nope." Sydney smiled. "In fact, with the

prince gone, the warrior princess conquered the other tribe in no time. She went on to live a full and rich life without the love god."

Evelyn's mouth gaped open. "That's pathetic."

Sydney shrugged. "Don't like my stories, make up your own."

"You keep spinning bummer fairy tales like that and your sales are going to tank." Evelyn threw her arms wide. "And this business…crumbles at your feet."

From the glass-enclosed workroom they could see the entire front gallery filled with artifacts and antique furniture, as well as selections of contemporary art. Many of the pieces displayed some form of ancient symbol carvings, a testament to Sydney's expertise in glyphs.

"My clients love my stories. I have more sales than I can manage and antiquities are hot." Sydney set the African mask back into its protective mailing material. "Besides, everyone's definition of happily ever after is different."

"Well, yours is as traditional as it gets."

Sydney grunted.

"And bitterness does not suit you at all."

"Sure it does. Ask my last date."

"That was a year ago, and you know darned well he didn't mean it as a compliment." Evelyn drummed nails polished pink to match the exact shade of her lipstick. "You should get out more."

"What's the point?" Sydney closed the box on the African mask and readied the label for shipment. "You fall in love. You come to know that there's no one else on this earth for you but that one man. Then everything falls apart. You turn around one day, and he's gone."

"You can't blame every man for one man's mistakes."

"Oh, yeah?" Sydney pulled a strip of tape across the package and sealed it. "Watch me."

"Some men are solid as rocks," Evelyn said. "I met this really nice accountant. He's not my type, but for you—"

Sydney groaned. "Not another blind date castoff." She slapped the shipping labels onto the package and set it on a nearby counter. Fatigue settled on her shoulders, now tight from a full day of selecting vases, sculptures, furniture and other odds and ends for Evelyn's newest interior design client. "Let's get back to the O'Neill house. I thought of a series of paintings that might work for the dining room." She crossed to the far wall and flipped through her inventory.

The room grew quiet. Too quiet.

Sydney glanced up. "What?"

Evelyn's normally carefree gaze had grown thoughtful, serious even. "He's never coming back, you know."

It was a good thing she owed Evelyn the world. Otherwise, Sydney might have ushered her best friend out the back door. As it was, Evelyn had been the first person Sydney had met stepping off that plane from Minnesota all those years ago. Sydney hadn't even known she was pregnant at the time. And when she did find out, Evelyn had been the only person to lend Sydney an attentive ear, a shoulder to blubber on, and a couch. Friends like that were hard to come by. Men like that, impossible.

"I never said I wanted him back," Sydney whispered.

"Look at your life. Don't you think it's time to move on?"

"If you mean forget, no way." Sydney may have been divorced for years, but not a day went by without her thinking of her ex-husband. Most days were okay. Most days she only thought of him once, or twice. Other days were bad. Sometimes they were so bad that she'd go to bed thinking about him, wake up dreaming of him, and spend the day plagued with memories. Sometimes she thought her heart was healed, and other times she could feel it tightening in her chest, breaking into a million tiny pieces all over again.

Why? That was always the question. Maybe knowing *why* he'd left her would give her some measure of peace.

"I will never forget him, but I have moved on."

"I'm not talking about this gallery." Evelyn shook her head. "Sydney, you're throwing your prime years away. You deserve a companion. Someone special."

"I have someone special."

"A little boy isn't what I had in mind."

"We've been through this a hundred times." Sydney flipped through the artwork at breakneck speed. The sooner she found what she was looking for, the sooner she could get Evelyn out of the way. "You're not a mother, so I don't expect you to understand. But take this as a given. Trevor is my priority. Spending time with him *is* my life."

"I understand more than you think. What

you don't see is that Trevor's getting older. He doesn't need you like he used to. Every time I come over with a date, he's all over the guy like jelly on peanut butter. He could use a little manly influence, if you ask me."

There was no doubt Trevor attached easily. He was such a trusting, giving child. All the more reason to shelter him. "The last thing he needs is a parade of men traipsing in and out of our lives." Sydney went back to the inventory of paintings. "Here it is." She pulled out the folder and gently laid the first painting on the table. "What do you think?"

"I think the real question is are you protecting Trevor—or yourself?" Evelyn paused. "Don't you want to know his name—"

"Blind date discussion's over." Sydney cut her off. "This is your newest, biggest client. Everything needs to be perfect. So what do you think of this painting?" She did her best to appear bright and cheerful. Resolved.

"All right. I give up." Evelyn released a long sigh. "The painting is marvelous. Let me see the rest in the series."

"I think I have three others." Sydney went back to flipping through her inventory.

The echo of their argument had barely settled when a soft chime announced the front door opening. Sydney looked up to see a man, one-hundred-plus feet away, stepping into her warehouse-styled gallery.

"Do you need to take care of that?" Evelyn asked.

"Janet's working reception, and I'm not expecting anyone." Although most of her clients were interior designers or corporate art collectors, the gallery floor received occasional street traffic. Even so, she kept her eyes on the man. Something about him struck a chord—

Oh, God! Lucas? The world seemed to tilt, and she nearly lost her balance. Her mind went blank as if the hard drive of her brain had crashed. She forgot to breathe. Think. Swallow. It couldn't be. Evelyn had voiced a well-known fact. Her ex-husband was never coming back. *Never.*

Sydney forced a deep breath into her lungs and her attention back onto the paintings. Last she'd heard he was in Bolivia chasing down Inca artifacts. Before that, Ecuador. And before that, coastal Peru and the high Andes.

Not that she wanted to keep track of him. His name simply popped out at her now and then in trade periodicals. She dealt in artifacts and antiquities. It was her business to stay informed, nothing more. So why would her subconscious conjure his essence, turning this stranger into something he wasn't? Maybe Sydney hadn't moved on as well as she'd thought.

Again, she caught herself glancing toward the front of the gallery. Though the stranger still stood a good distance away and had his back to her, something about his stance, the breadth of his shoulders, or the tilt to his head brought Lucas firmly to mind. She strained to see him more clearly, but a brief appearance of that shy Seattle sun glared through the windows.

He picked up an African terra-cotta statue to examine it, and a shudder ran through her. The guy knew his stuff. That hunk of fired clay happened to be the single most expensive piece on the floor. Gently, he set the statue back down and moved from the African collection to a display of modern Chinese art.

His hands. She needed to see his hands.

"Sydney, are you all right?"

Evelyn's voice startled Sydney back to task. "I'm sorry. You wanted to see what else I had by this artist, right?"

"Everything. This work is awesome."

"Umm. Were you planning on carrying the…Romanesque theme through the entire house?"

"Romanesque? No one said anything— What's the matter with you?" Evelyn's head snapped toward the front of the studio and she chuckled. "Rugged, but attractive. Do you know him?"

Sydney watched her assistant, Janet, approach the prospective client. "Never seen him before in my life." She forced her head down and refocused on the painting beneath her fingertips. Fingertips that had started shaking. "Do you have any ideas for the dining room furniture? Maybe we could import a few European antiques."

"That's a great idea. This client likes big. The bigger the better."

"I'll pull together a few examples and some pictures."

"Sounds great." Evelyn nodded. "Whatever we don't get done today, we can take care of in the morning."

Sydney found the other three paintings grouped together in the bin. She pulled them out and crossed the room, keeping her gaze upon Evelyn. She refused to watch Janet with the stranger. Refused to analyze his every move. Refused to make this day any worse than it had already become.

Janet's footsteps clicked against the tile floor, growing closer with every step. *Don't come to me. Don't come to me. Don't*— Janet stopped beside Sydney's worktable. "Sorry to bother you, Sydney, but the man out front insists on seeing you."

Sydney slowly looked up. Though he stood with his profile angled toward her, shadows blanketed every detail of his face. He was too far away. "What does he want?" She could feel Evelyn studying her.

"He wouldn't say."

Sydney sighed then, feeling downright silly. "Janet, would you show Evelyn some framing choices for these pictures?" She laid the art portfolios on the table and headed determinedly toward the front.

The stranger's back was to her as he examined a Russian vase, but the closer she got, the more hesitant she became. Everything about this man set her senses to full alert. His height. The cowlick at his neck. Even the way his black cotton shirt was tucked into his chinos, loose and comfortable. She followed the lines of his pants and settled on his feet. Barefoot with sandals. In January. Just like… *Oh, no.*

She stopped, eight feet from him, unable to bring herself an inch closer. The urge to turn and run threatened to overwhelm her. *Damn him!* She would not let these memories bring her to her knees. "What do you want, Lucas?"

The man grew still and then calmly rolled the vase from hand to hand. For a moment, she thought she'd been wrong. Then he spoke. "This is a spectacular piece."

A hundred-foot wave couldn't have knocked the breath from her lungs more effectively than the sound of that voice. It was a voice that had commanded authority in an auditorium filled with college students as easily as it had promised her the world in the quiet darkness of their bedroom so many years ago. It crashed through her now, inside her, draining her resolve.

When he turned around, time warped. She was back in Minnesota. Snippets of their life together flashed before her eyes as if she were drowning. A private look here. A touch there. Oh, how he had touched her. Her cheeks flashed hot with memories. And just as suddenly cold. The warrior princess inside her yearned for a knife. A big one. She should have pummeled his chest with all the anger that had festered over the years. Instead, she stood there paralyzed, staring at him.

"But then you've always had impeccable taste." He ran his fingertips over the burnished black surface of the vase. "At least some things haven't changed."

"Everything has changed." Speaking actually calmed her.

He set down the vase. "How have you been?" His voice was soft, intimate.

"If you think I'm going to stand here and have a gosh-how-ya-doing conversation with you, you're crazy." She folded her trembling hands in front of her.

"No. I suppose not." The right side of his mouth kicked up in that lopsided smile, the exact one that had set her heart fluttering the first time she'd laid eyes on him.

But there was something different about him today. At first glance, the changes seemed superficial. Shorter hair. A little graying at his temples and salted throughout. A few more lines furrowed the corners of his eyes and brow. His skin was darker, as if he spent a lot of time outdoors. His face was thinner. Still, he looked much the same. Except for his eyes. What she remembered, when honest with herself, were eyes filled with expectation and yearning. What she saw before her now were the haunted, steely gray eyes of a complete stranger. Time had not been kind to him. Good. He didn't deserve anything better.

"I'll get on with it, then." A muscle twitched in his jaw. "Do you recall our trip to Spain?"

Their honeymoon. How could she forget? "Vaguely."

"One morning in Madrid we stopped in a little shop off the beaten path."

The *Tesoro*. She remembered it like yesterday. The shop had been old and cluttered with junk, but he'd found a battered six-teenth-century seaman's chest that he'd simply had to purchase. Since then, she'd never underestimated the mystery of anti-quities.

"I found a sun god under the false bottom of a chest," he said, "and gave it to you."

"Sorry. Can't place it," she lied, hoping he wouldn't catch her at it. He'd always been so good at seeing inside her soul.

"Come on, Syd. Think. We both knew it

was special the first time we saw it. A small statue. Solid gold. It would fit right here." He held out his right hand, palm up, his fingers appearing as strong as ever. The remembered feel of them on her body, warm and purposeful, shot through her.

Seemingly frustrated at her lack of response, he looked around and grabbed something off a shelf. "It looked a little like this. Only smaller and much more simple in design. Do you remember?" He held out the gold-plated, quality imitation of a Mayan treasure.

"Maybe." She snatched the Mayan sun god from his hand, not wanting his touch on anything belonging to her. "Why are you looking for it?"

"Do you recall the legend of Manco Capac, the first Inca ruler?"

There'd been so many stories he'd relayed while she'd lain in rapt attention in his arms. How could he expect her to remember any of them? But she did. Every detail. "No. I've forgotten all of those ridiculous legends."

He looked away. Had she hurt him? Not nearly enough. For that, he'd need a few years of verbal lashings.

"I found the gold staff Manco Capac was said to have carried during his travels."

The staff of gold? Sydney's antiquity dealer's heart skipped in delight. The archaeological world must be standing in ovation. "So?"

His brow furrowed. "So…it's very…special."

"What does this have to do with the sun god?" She tried sounding as bored as possible.

"I believe the statue fits at the top of the staff, like a handle. It's the key to a project I've been working on for years. Without it I can never find—" He stopped abruptly. "Suffice it to say that without it I have nothing." He studied her, his eyes never leaving her face. "Do you still have it?"

"Oh, that sun god." The key to it all. She leaned back against a display case and casually crossed her legs in front of her. "No. Sorry." She pursed her lips and gripped her fingers around the imitation Mayan sun god. "I traded it in at a flea market for a set of dishes right after I left Minnesota."

He closed his eyes as if weary from a long, long journey. For a split second, she almost felt sorry for him. "Do you remember the vendor?" he asked. "The location? Anything?"

She shrugged and shook her head. "I was going to a lot of flea markets back then. I couldn't afford much else. It could have been in Olympia. Tacoma. I really couldn't tell you."

"This is important, Syd." He took a small step toward her. For one petrifying moment she thought he might reach out and touch her. Actually touch her skin. Fortunately, he seemed to think better of it and moved back again. "It's bigger than me. Or you. Bigger than the past between us."

"I don't have it, Lucas." She fought for equilibrium in the face of his intense scrutiny. "Now you need to leave. You shouldn't have a problem with that. You do it so well."

At that gibe, he looked away. She thought he might say something, but instead pulled a business card from his wallet. Before he flipped it closed, Sydney caught sight of a battered photo, the image so heart-wrenchingly familiar it was like being kidney punched. Their baby girl. Emily.

"I'm staying at the Alexis Hotel for a few days," he said. "Call me if you remember anything. It's important, Syd."

She reached out and took the card. Anything to get him to leave. And nobody called her Syd. Not anymore. "Sure. What-ever." She turned and moved one foot in front of the other, mechanically, until the doorbell sounded his retreat. She stalked past the workroom where Evelyn and Janet stood watching her, straight into her office, and leaned against the wall.

Evelyn charged into the quiet space. "Who was that hunk of burning love?"

"Lucas." Sydney heard herself say it as though disconnected from her surroundings. She felt numb, broken.

"As in ex-husband Lucas Rydall?" Evelyn stood in openmouthed shock.

Sydney nodded absently. She pulled Evelyn farther into the office, closed the door and locked it before crossing to the other side of the room. Along the way she dropped Lucas's business card in the garbage, and, for good measure, the Mayan sun god, too.

"I can't believe he came here," Evelyn murmured.

Sydney tilted the watercolor painting hanging behind her desk to reveal a small safe. She fiddled with the combination and opened the latch. Pushing aside the various documents and keepsakes, she removed a small, heavy box, lifted the lid and extracted a cloth-wrapped bundle.

"After all this time he shows up on your doorstep like nothing ever happened?" Evelyn strode across the room. "What's he want?"

"This." Sydney flipped back the fabric to reveal the solid gold sun god. "He wants this."

CHAPTER TWO

YOU CAN NEVER GO BACK.

Lucas Rydall stepped out of Sydney's gallery and onto the sidewalk, the truth in that old adage striking deeper than bone. If he'd been harboring any unconscious hope that there would still be something bordering on civil between him and Syd, it had been firmly squashed with the first look into her face. She hated him. Rightly so. He'd never been able to forgive himself for what he'd done to her, why should she?

He crossed a cobblestone plaza, one of many in Seattle's historic Pioneer Square district, and climbed behind the wheel of his rented SUV. No sooner had he slammed the door than a fat drop of rain splattered the window. The winter sky had clouded over while he'd been inside Sydney's gallery, and the abrupt change seemed, somehow, appropriate. The gray, bleak mass overhead certainly matched his current mood.

Any minute now, a deluge would begin, washing away the street grime and, he hoped, clearing the air, dispelling the scents of her gallery still clinging to his shirt. Maybe, if he let it, the rain could even cleanse his soul. Maybe it could numb the feeling threatening to break through the frayed edges of his armor. If he let it. That was the key.

Lucas wasn't accustomed to *letting* anything happen. He fought life every step of the way. And life sometimes fought back. Hard.

He put the keys in the ignition and sat there, contemplating the redbrick front of Syd's restored, turn-of-the-century gallery. The place had smelled lush and full of mystery, full of Sydney and her antiquities, and he'd been so sure the sun god would be there. Dammit! He needed that statue. Without it, this project screeched to a dead end.

The rain picked up, and his cell phone beeped to the timing of the droplets hitting his windshield. He flipped it open. "Rydall here."

"It's Max." His friend's deep voice sounded across the line, and Lucas pictured Max Wheatley sitting at his desk in the dark recesses of the Smithsonian administrative offices, surrounded by stacks of books and files. Though the image comforted Lucas in some small way, it didn't bring him home. Why should it? He hadn't felt at home anywhere, even in his own skin, for years.

"We've got problems," Max said.

Lucas jammed his index finger in one ear, effectively cutting off the outside sounds of rain and end-of-day traffic. "What's up?"

"Word on the street is that you have a lead on the Fountain of Youth."

"You're kidding, right?"

"Cochran's dead serious. He's already taking bids on the black market."

Although Phillip Cochran considered himself an art broker, the law-abiding world held no such illusions. The man was a thief, intelligent and sophisticated, but nonetheless heartless. Clients put in orders and Cochran filled them without care for anything or anyone in his way. Museums and homes had been violated, guards murdered and even a few individual collectors ransomed. International authorities had been after Cochran for years, but were unable to make any significant charges stick.

"Get this," Max continued. "That Huari

silver bowl you're looking for is going for twenty million."

The Huari people had been known to make some beautiful pre-Incan art, but that was a mighty stiff price, even for something once belonging to Manco Capac. "What makes Cochran think he can find it before I do?" Lucas asked.

"Last night several offices here at the Smithsonian were ransacked, hard drives and files stolen." Max sighed. "They knew what they were looking for and where to find it. Including your most recent project report about the sun god. One night of mayhem and Cochran's got five years' worth of your research."

"Could someone in your office be helping him?"

"Possibly. I'll keep my eyes and ears open. Oh, and your office was trashed worse than anyone's."

Apparently Cochran was taking this one personally. "Guess he didn't appreciate those two weeks in a Peruvian jail last month."

"I told you, Lucas, you never should have gotten involved."

"He almost kills a friend of mine trying to get Manco Capac's staff, and I'm supposed to turn a blind eye?"

"He's proved himself virtually untouchable through the years. Did you really think they'd lock him up for good?"

Lucas snorted. "I wonder how much that bribe set him back."

"He must know you're in Seattle for the sun god. Better watch your back."

Not that he had a back to watch. "It's a moot point, Max. Sydney doesn't have it."

Max almost choked. "What?"

"The project's over. Dead. She didn't have the statue."

"Now what?"

"I was hoping you might have some ideas." Lucas leaned back into the driver's seat and stretched his aching neck. Disappointment laced with exhaustion threatened to shut him down. Though for years now he rarely slept much more than a few hours at a time, a twenty-four-hour stint of flights from Lima to Miami to D.C. to Seattle was finally catching up with him. "The last five years goes right down the drain without that statue."

"You were so sure she'd keep it. What happened?"

"Get this. She traded it in for some dishes at a flea market right after our divorce."

Now Max laughed. "A flea market?"

"I told you, it wasn't an amicable divorce."

"You two never spoke during the process. Sounds amicable enough to me."

"Trust me. It wasn't." Lucas rubbed his hands over his tired eyes. How could she have gotten rid of it? *Their* sun god. The one she'd sworn she'd always keep close to her. He had to admit he'd allowed a minuscule part of himself to hope that she would tuck away what they'd had in a secret part of her heart and always hold it dear. Then again, he was the schmuck who had left her. It only made sense for her to slough off any symbols of their love, not to mention any memories of him.

"You've exhausted every possible lead in Peru," Max said. "Without the map, without the sun god itself, there's nowhere else to go, old buddy."

"I can't give it up."

"I know I shouldn't be saying this—and if you tell anyone I did, I'll flat out deny it— but maybe it's time to let it go. Why don't you take that professorship? Georgetown has been after you for years."

For an instant Lucas let himself entertain the notion, but in the end that was all it was, a notion, a dream. And he didn't deserve dreams. "No," he said with renewed determination. "There might not be any statue, but this can't be the end."

"Something isn't making sense," Max said. "Your ex sells a fair amount of antiquities, right?"

"And she's been pretty successful, by the looks of her gallery."

"Then she knows her stuff? She's more than a hack talking a good story and buying from five-and-dime exporters?"

"If her inventory is anything to go by, yes. In fact, I remember hearing about a Smithsonian curator consulting her a few years back about some newly discovered Mayan glyphs. Apparently, she's become an expert in ancient symbols, everything from Celtic designs to Egyptian hieroglyphics." Through the rain-streaked car window, Lucas pondered Sydney's storefront. "What are you getting at?"

"Seems odd she'd trade a priceless Inca artifact for worthless crockery."

Lucas remained silent, fresh doubts filling his mind.

"Maybe she actually sold the statue to another dealer," Max suggested. "You said she had every right to be angry. Maybe, out of pure spite, she doesn't want you to be able to track it down."

"Why wouldn't she have just ditched it?" Lucas posed the question, almost to himself.

"She'd have to know it was worth something."

"You'd have to know Sydney. With her, it's all or nothing. She'd have thrown it away before she'd profit from something like this. But a set of dishes? She'd use them every day, and every day they'd remind her of the sun god. Of me." Lucas tapped the steering wheel with his fingertips. "She's lying about the flea market."

Sydney had been the most honorable woman he'd ever known. Lying had been as foreign to her as walking a straight line had been to him. He'd always teased her that she should never try keeping the truth from him. He'd known her body so well, understanding its language had become second nature to him. If she'd been embarrassed, turned on, or hiding something, he'd been able to spot her signals across a crowded room.

His heartbeat quickened. Maybe it wasn't over. He replayed their meeting in his mind, recapturing her every motion. It wasn't hard. He doubted he would ever forget seeing her lovely face after all these years. Or taking in the graceful lines of her body once again. Long, slender neck, full breasts hidden neatly beneath a sweater he would have bet was pure cashmere. Narrow waist. Legs as long and straight as the North Dakota freeways he remembered from his child-hood.

And she'd crossed them. Yes! Right before she'd mentioned the flea market. *Oh, precious Syd.* In this jaded, dog-eat-dog world she still had to cross something before outright lying to anyone. He laughed out loud. "She still has the statue, Max."

"You sure?"

"She stuffed it away so she doesn't have to think about it."

"Can you get it back?"

"I'll try." Movement behind the glass front of Sydney's gallery drew Lucas's attention. "Gotta go. Sydney's shop's closing for the day, and I'm not letting her out of my sight. Not until I get that statue back." He snapped the phone closed.

From his angled vantage point, he could watch both the streetside front of the gallery and the rear lot where, presumably, employ-ees parked. The woman who had first greeted him upon entering Syd's gallery locked the front door and drew bars down over the storefront. He looked at his watch. Closing at 5:00 p.m. sharp.

He was glad Syd had no need to keep long hours. She'd done well for herself. Her store and offices were in an upper-crust business district. Her inventory was current and expensive. Though she didn't appear to have remarried—he hadn't noticed a ring on her finger and she'd gone back to her maiden name—she seemed to have gone on with her life. And life had been kind to her. Good. She deserved it.

After all these years traveling the world searching for peace, even while he'd beaten himself up for the asshole he'd been, maybe he'd made the right decision after all. She *was* better off without him.

The door at the rear of the gallery opened and two people stepped out. No Syd. After they'd each run through the rain to their respective vehicles and driven away, there were two cars left in the parking lot. A Mercedes convertible and a white Volvo sedan. He was willing to bet the Volvo was Syd's. She'd always been safety-conscious and sensible.

The rear gallery door opened again, and Sydney stepped out, holding an umbrella over her head in one hand and a briefcase in the other. The statue could easily have fit inside that case. She stood outside talking with another woman for a moment before walking to the Volvo. He smiled to himself. Syd had matured into one classy lady. Instead of her college uniform of jeans and sweat-shirts, her clothes were now conservative *and* expensive. She still wore her hair long, though she'd reverted to tying it up in back. He'd always preferred it down, enjoying the look of those wild, dark curls against her pale skin.

He yanked his thoughts back barely in time to see her pulling into the stream of traffic. He started his SUV and followed, keeping several cars between them. She maneuvered in and out of traffic, down side streets, and soon left the Pioneer Square neighborhood.

A few more minutes and Lucas shut off the windshield wipers. Hazy sun broke through the clouds. Sydney's Volvo climbed out of downtown and entered the Queen Anne Hill area. Tree-lined and charming with in-credible vistas of Puget Sound, it was exactly the type of neighborhood in which he would have pictured her. She pulled into the parking lot of an institutional building with huge white pillars marking the front door. He parked beside a truck a row away, hiding from view, and watched her walk inside. Was this a library, a large post office, what? He scanned the building and spotted the lettering above the front doors.

Coe Elementary. An elementary school? He shook his head and lowered his car window, needing fresh air to clear his head. What was she doing here?

Sydney came back out of the building with a backpack in her hand, holding the door open for a young boy, dressed in jeans, T-shirt and wearing a baseball cap. Lucas watched the little guy skip down the sidewalk and across the parking lot. He jumped to a stop near Sydney's Volvo and yelled excitedly, "Guess what, Mom! We get to have a pizza party on Friday!"

Mom. The little boy had called Sydney Mom.

"A pizza party!" she said, opening the car door and helping the boy buckle up. "How cool…"

Lucas's stomach lurched. She had a child.

Remarried, he could have handled. But this? Not after what they'd gone through. His pulse racing, his palms sweating on the steering wheel, he tried gauging the boy's age. But he'd been wearing a hat, and Lucas was terrible with guessing kids' ages. Babies he thought were six months turned out to be twelve months, teenagers he'd think were seventeen would be fourteen. Nevertheless, he ran through the calculations in his mind. The child was in school, so he had to be at least five. They'd been divorced for a little more than six years.

Could the boy be his son, or had she met someone else so soon after they'd split?

Sydney drove out of the parking lot, but he sat stunned, debating. The boy couldn't be his son. She would have told him. Then the memory of how she'd looked at Lucas in her gallery—angry, disgusted and frightened—sprang into his mind. Maybe she wouldn't have.

Lucas sped out of the school parking lot and caught sight of the Volvo before it turned down a side street. After several more ins and outs, the vehicle entered a driveway and pulled into a garage. He found an open spot along the street some distance back and parked, shut off the engine and sat there, watching. All thoughts of retrieving the statue trickled from his mind as the small, refurbished Victorian came to life before him.

First the lights went on in back, next in a front room, and lastly, upstairs. He tried to picture himself inside, but it didn't come easy. It didn't come without a price. Drawing on his own bittersweet memories, he imagined the home Sydney would have made for herself and her son.

It would be a home where a guest felt comfortable kicking off his shoes and propping his feet on the coffee table. Her travels would be noted with treasures hanging on walls, nestled in bookcases, and sitting on windowsills. They would be small and large, mostly inexpensive, always unique. Colors would be everywhere, nothing matching, but everything working together perfectly. And you wouldn't be able to look anywhere without knowing a child lived within those walls.

He made himself remember…sippy cups and diapers, high chairs and car seats. Blocks and stacking cups and messy fingerprints on the refrigerator door. But this child was bigger, older. Not a baby girl.

The imagined sound of a little boy's feet

pounding up and down the stairs filled his mind and an ache in his chest grew stronger with every beat of his heart. A TV blaring cartoons at full blast. Matchbox cars and action figures strewn on the floor. Backpacks and homework, snacks and bubble gum. Wet kisses, bedtime stories and tiny hugs strong enough to last a lifetime.

The sun god statue could wait. Lucas pushed open his car door. He had to know.

CHAPTER THREE

"Mom, can I have a snack?"

Sydney stepped through the back door and set her briefcase on the kitchen counter. Pre-occupied with its contents, she murmured, "Trevor, honey, we're going to have dinner in a little while."

"What are we eating?" Trevor dropped his backpack on the hardwood floor, kicked off his stubby Nike runners, and slid around the kitchen in his socks. When Sydney didn't answer, he stopped in front of her. "You're being weird."

"What?" She looked down at him.

"Focus, Mom." He threw her own tactics in her face. "You know? Dinner?"

She blinked. "No hats in the house." She snatched off his Seattle Seahawks cap. "What would you like?"

He snagged an airplane off the counter and swooped it through the air. "Kung Pao." The words squeaked from between lips pursed in preparation for engine noises. "Mom, are you listening?"

She stared at his face. At that moment, with his dark hair framing pale, dolphin-blue eyes and a quizzical expression, he looked so much like his father it was scary. Protective-ness surged through her. Trevor may have half another person's genes, but he was her son, through and through. She ran her finger-tips lightly across the freckles on his nose and cheeks and grinned. "I'm listening now."

"I said Chinese."

"Had it last night, bucko." She ruffled the stick-straight hair on his head. He hadn't in-herited a single strand of her curls. "How 'bout I make some spaghetti?" This would fill her quota of three home-cooked meals a week.

"Okay." He headed toward his room, swiping the plane through the air.

"Any homework tonight?"

"No," he yelled from halfway up the stairs.

She took a package of ground meat from the freezer, set it to browning on the stovetop, and slipped out of her sling-backed pumps. Her hand rested on the counter near her briefcase, near the sun god. She drew out the gold statue. Its cool surface quickly warmed in her hand, and, for a moment, the entire house seemed to grow silent, as if in deference to the little figure.

That was when she sensed it, the inexplicable connection she felt with Emily whenever Sydney held the statue. Emily had liked to play with it, and any time she did, she'd seem to feel better. Once upon a time, this sun god had smiled down upon her, upon all of them, embodying all that was beautiful in life. Now it seemed to laugh at Sydney, reminding her of the dire consequences of trusting, of believing. Of loving.

Without it I have nothing…the key to it all. Lucas's words echoed in her mind. If this statue was half as important as he'd implied, Lucas would be back. She should have given it to him in the first place and been done with him. He'd have vanished from her life as quickly as he'd traipsed back in. But how could she part with the one thing that provided her the strongest connection with Emily?

The doorbell rang and she jumped. She reached to return the sun god to her briefcase, and her hands stilled. They rarely had unexpected visitors. The bell chimed again. Lucas.

"I'll get it," Trevor said from the steps.

"No!" she yelled back and the briefcase dropped to the floor. "I've got it!" She stuffed the statue under several dish towels in the nearest drawer and sped ahead of her son through the family room.

"Who is it?" Trevor fell in behind her.

"Probably a salesman." She peered through the peephole in the door. She wasn't ready for this. She'd *never* be ready for this. The bell chimed again, and various escape routes zipped through her mind.

"Sydney, open up." Lucas's resonant voice carried softly through the thick slab of oak. Maybe he would simply go away. "I know you're in there."

Then again, maybe not. She slipped off the chain and cracked open the door. Seeing him the second time seemed no less a shock than the first. In some ways, this was much worse. He was outside her house. Her home.

"I hadn't planned on bothering you again." His eyes traveled from her face quickly down to Trevor's and back again, one hot question burning in their pale depths.

She nudged Trevor behind her. "What are you doing here?"

"Who is it, Mom?" Trevor edged back out.

"An…old friend, honey."

At the word friend, Trevor stepped into the open space. "Hi, I'm Trevor."

"Hey, Trevor. I'm Lucas." Lucas pointed at his T-shirt. "Seahawks. My favorite football team."

Much to Sydney's consternation, Trevor grinned back and glanced up at her. "Mom, can Lucas stay for supper? Please, Mom, please. We never have anybody over. Please!"

Evelyn's comment about Trevor needing a little manly influence reared its ugly head. Maybe he did, maybe he didn't. In either case, there was no doubt this was the wrong man. "I'm sure Dr. Rydall has other things—"

"I'd love to stay." He pushed through the front door and into Sydney's home.

Immediately, she felt violated. Lucas didn't belong here, not after what he'd done to her. Her instincts screamed to push on his large chest, to shove him back outside. The past needed to stay there. Where it belonged. Then reality set in. This wasn't going to go away. *He* wasn't going to go away. Not until a few things were settled, she resigned herself. He could visit with Trevor, play with him, share a meal with them. That didn't mean he belonged. Not here. Not ever.

She backed into the room and folded her arms across her chest. "Still like spaghetti?"

"My favorite." His gaze shifted to study Trevor. He could scrutinize all he wanted. It wouldn't change a thing.

"Well, come on in, then." She swung a hand toward the living room.

Trevor smiled expectantly. "Wanna see my Harry Potter collection?"

"I'd love to."

She watched her son ascend the stairs with her ex-husband trailing slowly behind, not a little anxiety thrumming through her. *This was silly.* She calmed herself and shut the front door. Lucas had most likely come here for more information on the sun god, but now he would probably be wondering about Trevor. Why he might care was beyond her, but the sooner the meal was over, the sooner he would leave.

In the kitchen, she went to work on dinner. Once everything was set to go, she opened a bottle of merlot, poured two glasses and downed one before filling it again. She carried the goblets up to Trevor's room and found the two of them sitting on the floor. Magic wands, Harry Potter figurines and other miscellany littered the carpet between them. Trevor had several casting stones in his hands, and he was playing a game.

Lucas had his back to the door, but she could see a framed photo in his hand. Her stomach clenched. She'd completely forgotten that picture was here. She held her breath, listening.

"That's my sister," Trevor explained. "Emily. She died before I was born. She had a brain tremor."

"Brain tumor," Lucas whispered.

"Yeah, that's it. She was only two, but even though she was really sick, my mom says she was really happy."

"She sure was." Lucas traced the outline of the little face with the tip of his index finger, and Sydney felt tears blur her eyes. "Em's smiles were bright enough to melt an entire foot of the coldest Minnesota snow."

"That's what my mom always says!" Trevor lost interest in his game and scooted closer to Lucas. "Did you know my sister?"

"I did." Lucas glanced up. "And I know she would have loved having a brother like you."

Trevor grinned. "My mom says she's in heaven now, watching out for us. She says if she concentrates hard enough, sometimes

she can still feel Emily's arms around her
neck and her chubby fingers poking in her
ears."

At that, Lucas looked away. He cleared
his throat and turned to put the photo back
on the bookstand. His gaze traveled up the
doorway and met hers. The sudden guarded-
ness there, almost cold in its severity, startled
her. She couldn't look at a picture of Emily
without softening in remembrance. He'd obviously learned to cope in a different way.
There was a man for you, tamping down the
pain as if that would make it go away.

But, in all fairness, she'd had Trevor to
help her heal. He'd had no one. For the first
time, pangs of remorse shot through her.
Refusing to give them purchase, she cast the
feelings aside. Trevor's welfare came first.
She'd done the right thing. Lucas had given
her no alternative.

"Some wine?" She stepped into the room.

"Thank you." He stood and took the glass.
"Trevor, your mom and I are going down-
stairs to finish getting dinner ready."

"Okay."

Lucas, none too gently, grabbed her elbow
on his way through the doorway and led her
down the stairs. She tensed, knowing what

was coming. For years she'd envisioned this happening, imagining what she would say, how she would say it. No mincing words. State the facts. The quicker, the better. When they reached the kitchen, he turned to face her, darts of accusation flying from his eyes. "Well?"

All the prepared statements flew from her mind. "Well, what?"

"Don't play games with me, Sydney. You know why I'm here."

"I told you I don't have the sun god."

"Screw the sun god," he said through clenched teeth. "Is he my son?"

Before a single word could leave her mouth, Trevor bounded down the stairs and into the kitchen. "When can we eat?" he asked. "I'm starving." He slipped his soft, small hand into hers and led her toward the stove.

She quickly pulled the meal together, and they sat down. All that had been left unsaid between Sydney and Lucas hung in the air like an electrical storm. Trevor, oblivious to the tension, chattered nonstop about everything and nothing through second helpings of pasta, salad and garlic bread.

Twice Sydney's gaze locked with Lucas's. He seemed such a stranger when he looked at her. But when she watched him listening to Trevor, devoting all his attention, he became the caring, charismatic man from her past. The man in the dreams she wouldn't admit she still had almost every night. The man from her college days whom she'd followed into his private office and devoured with her eyes, her hands, her mouth without a nanosecond's hesitation.

Followed? Who was she trying to kid? She hadn't *followed* anyone. *She'd* taken him by the hand and led him into his office. From that moment on, he'd never seemed happier. They'd made a family, once upon a time. A good one, despite all the heartache. She and Trevor and Lucas could have been a family, too.

Spaghetti lodged in her throat. Okay, that was it. Time to get this charade over and done with. She set down her fork and altogether stopped making a pretense of eating. She hopped up to put what was left of the meal away in the refrigerator before anyone could even think about third helpings.

"It's getting late, and Trevor has some reading to do." She began washing the pots and pans.

"Let me help." Lucas stood up from the

table. "Show me where I can find a towel, and I'll dry."

"In that drawer—" The statue! "I'll get it." She rushed over, pulled out the top towel and handed itto him.

He studied her for a moment, his brows drawing together, and then went about clearing the table and drying the dishes. When he wiped down the countertop, she would have sworn his gaze lingered longer than necessary on her briefcase.

Before long, but not nearly fast enough for Sydney, they were finished. "Time for some reading, Trevor." She hoped the comment would send a clear signal. "Head on up to your bedroom."

"Aww, Mom. Can't I stay down here until Lucas leaves?"

"He's leaving right now, aren't you?"

Lucas nodded. "Time to go."

Trevor took off for the stairs and turned midway. "Can Lucas read to me tonight?"

The request caught Sydney off guard, stirring up long-lost memories of Lucas in a rocking chair with little Emily snuggled in his lap. He'd seemed to extract such joy from being a father. But that was then. Whatever the hell had happened to him, she had a responsibility to protect Trevor. Dinner was one thing. Bedtime reading was an entirely different story. "Sorry, Trev. Dr. Rydall has an appointment to keep."

Lucas looked away. "Maybe some other time, Trevor."

"Aww. Okay." Trevor marched up the stairs.

Seconds ticked by, Sydney and Lucas squared off in opposite corners of the kitchen. Only the sound of the dishwasher churning in the background filled the uneasy silence. Finally, Lucas whispered, "I'm not leaving until I have an answer."

"You want an answer? Fine." She snatched the dishtowel from him, folded it over her clasped fingers and forced her statement out as tonelessly as possible. "He's not your son."

Lucas swallowed and turned his face away, but he wasn't quick enough. Sydney saw the kick-ass pain and, oddly enough, disappointment etch deeply into his features, nipping her satisfaction in the bud. She'd never imagined this reaction. Hadn't he told her after Emily he'd never have any more children?

"Who *is* Trevor's father?" he asked, his voice low and shaky.

"It doesn't matter. He's someone who doesn't want to be involved in our life, and I want it to stay that way."

He paced to the window and turned. "I want a blood test."

"Get a court order." She met his gaze as steady as possible. "And it's all yours."

"When's his birthday? How old is he? I have a right to know."

"You lost the right to anything the day you walked out on me. The day you left me standing in the cemetery with our baby girl's body in the cold, hard ground."

He pushed his hand flat against the counter as if to restrain his fingers from squeezing a response from her throat.

"Trevor is five," she caved. Time to finish this. "His birthday is June first. You do the math."

After a long, quiet moment, he lifted his face to the ceiling. "I guess it's just as well," he whispered.

She was right. He didn't want any more children, although, strangely enough, that knowledge didn't comfort her. She'd wanted to feel vindicated; instead, she felt drained. She hung the towel on the oven door handle. "Now we've had our little reunion, Lucas, and you need to leave. Don't ever come back."

He brushed past her as if he couldn't get out of her house fast enough, opened the front door and walked outside. "By the way. I thought of something after I left your gallery today. That's why I followed you home." He turned on the step. "Earlier, when you told me you'd gotten rid of the sun god at a flea market? You crossed your legs. You were lying, Syd. You still have the statue."

"I don't owe you anything, Lucas."

"I want the statue anyway." His eyes turned harder than she ever thought they could be. "And I *will* get it from you."

She watched him walk down the steps before closing the door firmly behind him. So what if she'd crossed her legs? He was only guessing she still had the sun god, and there was nothing he could do to make her cough it up. He'd already taken his best shot six years ago by walking out on her. He could never hurt her again. Retribution sure tasted sweet.

After setting the dead bolt and chain, she went upstairs to check on Trevor, planted a kiss on his forehead and plopped down on his bed. "What are we reading tonight?"

"A book from the school library." He seemed preoccupied.

"What's the matter?"

He shrugged. "Nothing."

She opened the book, but Trevor wouldn't look at the pictures. She kept quiet, waiting. He'd never been one to hold things in.

"Mom?" Sure enough, his soft voice broke the night's silence. "Why did you tell Lucas my birthday's in June?"

CHAPTER FOUR

LUCAS GROANED, the sound of the hotel telephone reverberating through his head. With a hangover he hadn't felt the likes of in several years, he pulled a pillow over his head and ignored the noise. The last thing he wanted was to talk. To anyone. The ringing subsided, presumably transferred over to the operator, and then started up again.

"Dammit!" he muttered into the pillow. It had to be Max. No one else knew, let alone cared, about his whereabouts. He untangled himself from the bedsheets and grabbed the phone. "What?" His voice cracked as he barked into the receiver.

"Were you sleeping?" Max asked.

Did an alcohol-induced stupor qualify as sleep? "Maybe."

"It's ten o'clock. Rise and shine."

"That's Eastern time. Leave me alone, Max."

There was a pause, then, "You said you were over her."

"I am," Lucas growled.

"Why do I detect undertones of a hangover when you haven't had more than a casual glass of wine in years?"

For that first year after he'd left Syd, Lucas had all but drowned himself in tequila. And beer, and whiskey, and vodka. Until one day he'd heard an obscure Inca legend from an old Quechua man and Lucas's life had again been infused with meaning.

He'd told Lucas the little known story of Ayar Kachi, Manco Capac's brother. Kachi, wanting to be king, promised the people he would do what Manco couldn't do, heal them of all illness. So he stole Manco's silver bowl, a gift from the gods and said to hold healing powers, and he took the sick and dying, many of them riddled with symptoms similar to cancer, into the Peruvian rain forest to erect a temple. The Temple of the Rain. In the cloud forests, *the brow of the jungle,* a boundary the Inca seldom crossed. There, the legend claims, they found relief, freedom from all sickness and pain.

Lucas could almost understand why Phillip Cochran had come to the conclusion

Lucas was searching for the mythical Fountain of Youth. Much like the Egyptians, the Inca had not only mummified the remains of important figures, they'd yearned for everlasting life, flirting with potions, *diccus que,* said to restore youth and ultimately defy death.

But Lucas had a different hypothesis. With what scientists knew today of these cloud forests, those minute ecosystems, each one unique, each one filled with botanical and ecological treasures, he had no doubt that if he could find that lost temple, if they could find Manco Capac's silver bowl and the exact cloud forest Kachi had discovered, then Lucas just might find valuable plant extracts hidden there. And those extracts might lead botanists to a cure for cancer. Now *that* would wipe his slate clean.

"Lucas?" The sound of Max's impatient huff over the line brought back the pounding in Lucas's head. "We don't have the time for you to fall apart."

"Leave it alone, Max."

"Right." He paused. "Does she have the statue?"

Lucas thought back to her response when he'd confronted her about lying to him.

She'd said she didn't owe him anything. Yet she hadn't denied still having the sun god. "Yeah, she has it, but I'm going to need some time to work on her."

"Your grant's running out in a few weeks, Lucas, and no one's likely to pick up the funding without significant developments."

"Tell me something I don't already know."

"If there's anything I can do from my end…"

"You'll hear from me." Lucas dropped the receiver onto its cradle and immediately regretted his hasty movement as the clatter echoed through the quiet room. He rolled over onto his back and stared at the ceiling.

Last night had been hell. He'd gone from Sydney's front door into the nearest bar. When that had closed, he'd hit the minibar back in his hotel room. If he hadn't puked it all up later, he'd probably be dead by now.

Maybe that wouldn't be so bad, being dead. It certainly seemed preferable at the moment to tailing Sydney until she forked over the statue. He'd probably be spending a lot of time at her gallery, even more at her house.

Their house. Sydney's and Trevor's.

The thought of them made his insides ache. Images of the home they'd made together mixed with memories of the past. January in her kitchen on Queen Anne Hill turned into January in a garden-level apartment on Grand Avenue in St. Paul. It was a quiet Sunday afternoon with two feet of fluffy snowflakes accumulating outside. Instead of standing there in Seattle listening to her tell him that Trevor wasn't his son, she was seven months pregnant taking a nap on a couch, her oversize T-shirt hiked up over her swollen belly, her hair mussed, her mouth hanging loose. She'd never looked more beautiful.

He'd pulled the rest of her hair free from that bun thing and accidentally woken her up. They'd made such tender love. The way she'd touched him, so gently, so slowly. The pace had been so different from every other time they'd come together. Things had usually moved so fast for them.

In fact, the very first time he'd set eyes on Sydney he'd wanted to touch her, to pull the clip from her hair and let it tumble over his fingers. She was a grad student, assistant to one of the art professors. His department shared the building with hers. His first week of work, she'd been walking down the hall and a coworker had introduced them.

She, all prim and proper, her hair back, tight. Her clothes nondescript and functional. Still, he knew right away. So did she. For the next few weeks they'd skirted around their physical attraction, spending hours talking in the halls, around campus, at the coffee shop. For the first time he'd been tied up in knots over a woman. All he could dream of every night was her wildness surrounding him, sweeping the surface of his skin. She'd consumed him from one sunrise to the next.

Then it happened. He'd been walking down a deserted hall toward his office. She'd come around a corner and their eyes had locked. His heart had started pounding like an African Djembe drum and his entire body reacted to that primal beat. As he stopped in front of his door and pulled the key from his pocket, she came behind him, silent.

He turned the key in the lock, swung the door wide and stepped back. He never said a word, never moved, only waited, breathlessly, for her to make up her mind. She reached for his hand and pulled him inside. When she turned and locked the door, he'd practically lost it right there. Their clothes had come off in two minutes, maybe three.

One month later, they were madly in love,

and she was pregnant. They were married in three months flat. Madness, that's what it had been, and he never regretted a moment of it. Except that for the next couple years he'd always felt he'd been living on borrowed time. Every day, he'd wondered if that would be the day the gods would look down upon him and laugh in his face, saying, "You thought you deserved this? Ha! You fool."

Then Emily had been diagnosed with an inoperable brain tumor and the gods had their perverted field day. The perfect life he'd had no right to had been swept out from under his feet. What fate hadn't ruined, he'd finished off later himself. He'd done a pretty good job of it, too. Messed things up real good, like his stepdad had predicted. The crazy thing was that if it hadn't meant ruining things for Sydney, Lucas would do it all over again.

He rolled over in bed, toward the weak sunlight pouring through the window, and thought of her opening up her gallery only a few blocks down from his hotel and getting on with her life, one that was full and rich and devoid of him. Isn't that why he'd left her in the first place, to let her pick up the pieces and have a chance at something normal? That's exactly what she'd built. A business. A home. A family. She'd found another man, someone she'd made love with, created a child with.

Oh, how Lucas had wanted Trevor to be his son. He hadn't known how much until Syd had told him so clearly, so matter-of-factly, that he wasn't Trevor's father, until the world had started to contract around him. In their house he'd felt as though he'd belonged. He'd even begun to envision a life for himself, not merely an existence. Trevor would have given him hope. Sydney would have grounded him.

Could she have lied about Trevor? Lucas had been distracted, emotional. Maybe he'd missed something. She'd been standing, her legs straight, one arm at her side, the other… holding a dish towel. Nothing about her body language gave him a clue.

The image of her in another man's bed swam in his mind. "Damn." He should have stayed in Peru, or Ecuador, or D.C., should have never come to Seattle. He reached for the half-empty bottle of Crown Royal on the bedside table and brought it to his lips. Oblivion was the next-best option.

"WHAT'S GOING ON HERE?" Sydney stared at the partially opened back door to her gallery, her heart thudding loudly in her ears. "Evelyn, did you see anyone around when you pulled up?" They'd agreed to meet in the parking lot first thing this morning and wrap up the proposal they'd been working on yesterday afternoon.

"I didn't see anything. I got here a couple minutes ago and waited for you in my car." Evelyn drew her cell phone from her purse. "I'm calling the police."

While they waited for officers to arrive, Sydney pushed on the back door, swinging it wide. She poked her head inside and sucked in a breath. From the looks of things, she might have believed a tornado had swooped in and churned for a moment or two within the confines of her gallery. Glass and every kind of debris imaginable littered the floor and countertops. Boxes had been hastily ripped open, their contents dumped. Cabinets stood ajar. Drawers hung from their rails.

Sirens wailed to a stop in the street out front and a squad car pulled into the parking lot behind them. Two police officers hopped out and hustled Evelyn and Sydney away from the back door. After they'd finished clearing the building, Sydney proceeded through the back storage rooms and into the break room, pushing aside debris.

"Looks like someone got a little angry." Evelyn pointed to the coffee stains marring one wall, the shattered remnants of the carafe strewn on the floor below.

"I can't believe this." Stunned, Sydney stepped onto the main floor and stared. Her collection of ancient writings and hand-picked artifacts that had taken her years and numerous trips overseas to acquire lay in various states of ruin at her feet. Display cases had been overturned. Pictures ripped off the walls. Vases smashed. Nothing appeared to have been stolen, only carelessly destroyed.

"Well, I think we can safely assume," Evelyn said, cocking an eyebrow, "that he came back looking for the sun god."

"He?"

"Lucas Rydall."

Considering Evelyn's accusation, Sydney glanced down at the purse in her hand, where she had stashed the statue that morning. "Lucas would never have done this."

"He shows up yesterday out of nowhere.

The next morning you find your gallery broken into, and you don't see a connection?"

"No." She refused to believe such violence could come from a man she'd once loved. "It's coincidence."

"Oh, Sydney, you can be so naive."

Sydney ignored her and crossed the floor to her private office, a sense of unreality fogging her brain. This couldn't be happening. This gallery was in a good part of downtown. She had a security system. She had safes.

Worthless safes, she noted on stepping into her office. The one she'd used to lock away the sun god for so many years stood wide-open and empty, its contents scattered on the carpet along with everything else from the top of her desk. She picked up pieces of broken wood from what had once framed a picture of Trevor on his first day of kindergarten. The photo itself was gone, probably shredded. About the only thing in the room that hadn't been demolished was the garbage can beside her desk.

"This was professional, Evelyn. Lucas wouldn't know how to disable an alarm system, let alone crack open a safe."

"Desperate men seek desperate solutions," Evelyn muttered.

Several detectives arrived, taking pictures, jotting down notes and asking questions. Sydney slogged through the next several hours, a massive headache brewing. After the last police officers left, her employees went about clearing away the damage. She'd be out of business until she could get new display equipment and replenish her inventory, but she had insurance. She'd be okay financially, at least. She was putting a Closed Due To Restoration sign on the front window when a man peeked through the door.

"I'm sorry, we're closed." Sydney blocked his way to the gallery and smiled. "We should be open again in a few weeks."

"This is terrible." The stranger, an athletic, sun-streaked blonde, looked around. "A break-in, huh?"

"Yes. Unfortunately."

"And I was hoping to find something unique for my wife. It's our anniversary this weekend."

"I'm sorry."

"Could I take a peek at what hasn't been broken? Your gallery came with only the best of referrals."

Sydney put her fingers to her temples. The headache threatening all morning came on full force. "Listen, I'm really sorry about your anniversary, but if I let you in and you hurt yourself on all this broken glass, my attorney will kill me."

"At least tell me this. Do you have any old Spanish things? From like…the 1500s? My wife and I recently saw an exhibit on Sir Francis Drake. She fell in love with these pendants that he apparently plundered from the Spanish fleets in the Pacific. Money is no object."

Sydney pressed her forehead. "If we're talking Sir Francis Drake, then chances are the artifacts weren't actually Spanish," she said, finding patience from God knows where. "They were probably Mayan, or Inca, or Aztec."

"Do you have anything like that? It doesn't have to be jewelry. Anything Sir Francis Drakish will do."

"No." Sydney moved to close the door, but the tenacious bugger held it steady with a forearm that looked to be made of steel. "Goodbye!" She pushed harder, and the man let go. He studied her from the other side of the glass, not angry or disappointed, merely curious. Oddly curious. She clicked the lock in place, and he turned to cross the cobblestone street.

"What's going on?" Evelyn came up behind Sydney.

"Did you hear that guy? What a jerk."

"Honey, go home. You've had a hard day." Evie reached up and massaged Sydney's tight shoulders. "Janet and I will lock up. You and I can finish putting that proposal together tomorrow or the day after. There's no rush."

Debating, Sydney glanced at her watch. Most of the debris from the break-in had been swept up and discarded, her inventory assessed, and insurance agents notified. Not much more could be done for the day. She had just enough time to go home and take a short nap before picking up Trevor from school. After barely sleeping last night, she needed it.

She left the gallery in Evelyn's capable hands and drove home. At her back door, the key poised at the lock, a sense of déjà vu assaulted her. The window of the attached garage had been broken. Returning her focus to the door, she grabbed hold of the knob. It turned smoothly without the key, and she threw the door wide.

Like her gallery, chairs were overturned and cupboards and drawers stood open, their contents spewed on the floor. Cushions were slit open, books torn from their bindings, tables tipped upside down. And again like her gallery, whoever had done this was long gone. No doubt they'd come soon after she'd left for work and had plenty of time.

A terrible sense of violation swept through her. Violation quickly turned to fear. And fear to terror.

Trevor. Oh God, Trevor.

CHAPTER FIVE

AN IMPATIENT KNOCK sounded on Lucas's hotel room door. Groggy and hungover, possibly not entirely sober, he rolled over on the bed. The knocking started again and continued, on and on and on. "Hold on," he yelled, and cringed with the pain pulsing through his head.

Knocking turned to frantic pounding. In only his boxers, he trudged across the room and peered bleary-eyed through the peephole. "What the hell?" He whipped off the chain and swung open the door. "Syd?"

Tears streamed down her face. Both fear and anger radiated from her like a wild badger cornered and ready to strike at any moment. "What the hell is the matter with you?" She pushed past him and into his hotel room.

"What are you talking about?"

"Where is he?"

"Who?" He shut the door.

She searched the room then turned, facing him. Impatiently, she swept back an errant lock of curly hair. "What are you involved in?" she asked, her voice trembling.

"What do you mean?" He grabbed a pair of rumpled jeans from the floor and yanked them on.

She gripped his arms and yelled, "Tell me where he is!"

"Syd, calm down. What happened?"

"You wanted the statue." She reached inside her purse and pulled out a cloth-covered bundle. "Here. It's all yours." She pushed it into his hand.

He unwrapped the fabric. The sun god seemed to look right at him, benign and smiling, as if it carried some age-old secret at the very heart of all that gold.

"Now," Syd cried. "Give him back to me." She marched into the bathroom, whipped the shower curtain aside, looked behind the door and began opening every cabinet and door in the hotel room.

"The statue?"

"My son!" She stopped in front of him and planted her hands on her hips. "Where have you taken Trevor? I want him back. Now!"

"Trevor?"

"Don't pretend you don't know anything about it."

Alarm spread through him. "Syd, I didn't take him."

Her glare of righteousness fizzled to uncertainty, and a tense blanket of silence fell over the room. "I thought he'd be okay with you, but if you don't have him," she said, her legs buckling beneath her, "who does?" She dropped down onto the edge of the bed and sobbed.

He knelt down in front of her. "Tell me what happened."

"My gallery had been ransacked when I got there this morning. I got a headache. Went home to rest. Someone had broken in there, too. Trevor. I thought of Trevor," she choked out. "I rushed to the school, but—" She clamped a hand over her mouth and sucked in a deep breath. "He was gone."

"The school let him go with a stranger?"

"They said I'd called. That I was in the hospital and a friend would be picking him up. When I got back out to my car, I found his backpack sitting on the front seat with this pinned to it." She held out a plain white envelope.

He opened it and withdrew a folded piece of paper. Inside were the hand-printed words:

You have the statue. I have your son. Contact the authorities, and he's dead.

"You thought I'd written this?"

"Who else knew I had the statue?"

Several people at the Smithsonian to start, due to all the status reports Lucas had been required to complete. But he could think of only one person who'd go to this extreme. "Have you called the police?"

"About my gallery, yes."

"What about Trevor?"

"No. I came right here. I really thought you—"

"You know me better than that." He clenched his jaw. "I would never do that to you. Or to Trevor."

She straightened her shoulders and wiped her eyes dry. "I don't know you at all, Lucas. Once upon a time, I thought I did. Turned out I was wrong. I won't ever make that mistake again."

Contempt oozed from her eyes, and he had to look away. What else could he expect? As much as he wanted to argue, he didn't have a leg to stand on. "I think I know who has Trevor. A guy named Phillip Cochran. Black market arts dealer."

"A thief?"

Lucas shook his head. "This guy's big-time."

"What did you pull us into?"

The hotel phone rang, and Lucas was afraid they'd soon find out. He picked up. "Rydall, here."

"Hello, Lucas."

The slow, arrogant voice was unmistakable. "This is over the line even for you, isn't it, Cochran?"

At the sound of the name Syd started pacing the room. Cochran chuckled on the other end of the line. "Do you have any idea how much investors are willing to pay for the Fountain of Youth?"

"It's not the Fountain of Youth, and you know it."

"People believe what they want to believe, and they'll pay every last dime they own for eternal life."

"So you kidnap an innocent child? One who had no connection to me just to get what you want?"

"No connection to you. Are you sure?"

"You need to brush up on your research skills, Cochran. Sydney Mitchell and I were divorced a long time ago. The only reason I'm here is to get the statue. She and the boy mean nothing to me."

"Lucas, please," Syd whispered, stopping in front of him. "Tell him he can have the statue. He can have anything. I just want Trevor back."

"He means nothing to you," Cochran repeated. "That's rather cold. For you."

"He's not my son."

"Funny. The boy has your dark hair and blue eyes. The likeness is unmistakable."

Lucas's thoughts raced as he tried remembering every detail of Trevor's face. Instead, the texture of his hair came to mind, thick and straight…like Emily's before chemo. Then came the memory of his eyes, as blue as the ocean…like…Em's. Lucas looked straight into Syd's face and, for the first time, saw through the fear in her eyes. Suddenly, he wasn't certain of anything.

Cochran laughed. "A little tongue-tied, Rydall?"

"Let me talk to Trevor," Lucas demanded, barely holding his anger in check.

"Hmm," Cochran murmured, apparently thinking it over. "All right. But I'll warn you, he thinks we're taking care of him while his mother's away acquiring for her gallery. Shatter the illusion and you'll only worry the boy."

"Is Trevor okay?" Sydney whimpered.

"They've told him you're heading out of town on business." Lucas held out the receiver. "Talk to him quick. Reassure him. Don't cry."

Sydney grabbed the phone, closed her eyes, and took a deep breath. "Trevor? You there?"

Lucas put his head near Sydney's and listened.

"Hi, Mom."

"Hey, honey, sorry for the short notice."

"That's okay. How come I'm not staying with Aunt Evelyn?"

Lucas strained to hear background noises coming across the line. An engine. Wind. They were outside.

"Um…Evelyn's coming with me, so she couldn't watch you."

"When are you gonna be home?"

"I don't know for sure. A couple days. Okay?"

Lucas signaled for Sydney to wrap it up.

He had to talk to Trevor himself, see if he could get some indication of where Cochran was holding him.

"I gotta go, honey," Sydney said, her voice nearly breaking. "I love you."

"Love you, too, Mom."

Lucas took the phone. "Hey, buddy. This is Lucas Rydall. Remember me?"

"Yeah," Trevor said. "Are you going with my mom?"

Sydney dropped to the edge of the bed and started rocking in place.

"I sure am. Watcha doing right now?"

"We're going fishing."

"That's cool. Where ya gonna fish?" No answer. "Trevor?" Lucas yelled. "Trevor?"

Sydney rocked even harder.

"Gimme that phone, kid." Cochran's voice sounded over the earpiece. "Why don't you go check out the Xbox?" He'd taken back the phone. "And you. Go play one of those games with him." Cochran was talking to someone other than Trevor. "Well?" He came back on the line. "Satisfied...*Daddy?*"

"This is crazy." Lucas shook his head. "Take Trevor back to school. We'll forget the whole thing ever happened."

An eerie quiet hung over the line. When

Cochran finally spoke, venom tainted his voice. "Do you have a clue what the inside of a Peruvian jail cell looks like? What it smells like? What happens there to white men when the sun goes down and the guards fall asleep?"

Lucas squeezed his eyes shut.

"But if this was all about revenge, Rydall, your son would already be dead."

"You hurt Trevor," Lucas bit out, "and there won't be a corner on this earth you'll be able to hide your weaseling damned ass."

At that, a cry escaped Sydney's lips.

"Then it's a good thing I have customer orders to worry about." Cochran laughed. "Meet me at the abandoned cannery dock on the south side of Vashon Island in an hour. And, whatever you do, don't tell the police. I want the sun god and the staff. If you don't have them both, I guess we'll all find out whether or not your little boy here can swim."

The line clicked silent.

Sydney watched Lucas hang up the phone, a mixture of trepidation and gut-wrenching terror coursing through her veins. "Is Trevor all right?" She stood up, clasping her hands together.

"First, you answer my question." He turned toward her, his eyes aflame with accusation. "Is Trevor my son?" When she didn't answer, he tossed the sun god onto the bed and grabbed her by the shoulders. "Tell me, dammit! Is he my son?"

"Look, we can hash this out later. Trevor's in danger!"

"The answer takes one second, Syd. We're not leaving here, until you—"

"Yes!"

Lucas exhaled as if she'd belted him in the stomach. He released her shoulders so abruptly she nearly lost her balance. "How could you do this to me?"

"Do this to you?" Righteousness welled inside her, a balloon of bile ready to burst. "You were the one who left me, remember? You were the one who said, and I quote, 'It was all a mistake. It was never meant to be.'" Her body shook uncontrollably, and she wrapped her arms across her chest as if that would hold everything together.

Those words, words he'd uttered so calmly, had decimated what little had been left of her after Emily's death. She remembered thinking that she couldn't have heard right. He couldn't possibly have meant what he'd said. He'd been distraught, confused. But then he'd left. His actions had spoken so much louder than any of his words.

Lucas groaned, shaking his head back and forth. "I probably did say that, didn't I?"

"I waited for you in Minnesota for two months, but when I didn't hear from you, I decided to pack up and start over. That's when I came out here to Seattle. That's when I found out I was pregnant."

"Did you file for a divorce before or after you found out?" When she didn't respond, he moved in front of her, barring her exit. She wasn't going anywhere. "Before or after?"

She glared at him. "Trevor deserved better than to wake up to an empty apartment one morning and find a cursory, evasive note on the pillow where your head had been. He deserved a father he could depend on, a father who would always be there, no matter what."

"That still doesn't answer my question."

"After!" she shouted, holding his gaze. "I went from the doctor's office to an attorney's office. There, are you happy?"

His pale eyes flashed with angry heat. Good. She wanted him to fight so she could fight back. Clear the air. Get this off her chest. Instead, she could see him mastering his emotion. The anger was pushed aside, stuffed down, ignored. Damn him. He hadn't changed a bit. Still making believe any undesirable feelings would disappear if he refused to acknowledge them.

She'd had enough of this. "We need to go. Now."

He dragged a T-shirt over his head and stepped into a pair of shoes. "First we need an alternate plan."

"No way." She shook her head. "We give him the sun god. We get Trevor back. It's very simple."

"Nothing's simple with Phillip Cochran." Lucas reached over and grabbed the phone. He called the hotel operator and asked for his car to be brought to the front. Then he reached back, grabbed the sun god off the bed, and marched into the bathroom. There, he wrenched a fluffy white bath towel off a pitted golden rod and proceeded to work the rod off its wall clamps.

"What are you doing?"

"Cochran requested the sun god *and* the staff."

She glanced at the rod again and this time noticed carvings on one end. "You've been using Manco Capac's staff as a towel rod?"

"I thought it was a pretty good hiding place. Come on." He turned on his heel and strode out of the hotel room.

"Lucas, I'm serious. No plan. Give the man what he wants." She followed him down the hall and into the elevator. "This is my son we're talking about."

Lucas turned on her. "*Our* son." In the confines of the elevator, his closeness was more than intimidating. "I know Cochran, and I say we need a plan."

The elevator doors opened and Sydney had no choice but to follow Lucas through the hotel lobby and outside. He gave the valet a tip and his claim ticket for his SUV and climbed behind the wheel.

Sydney stood on the sidewalk, her thoughts scattered. When she'd thought Lucas had taken Trevor, she was mad, but never thought he would hurt her son. Now, the reality of the situation hit her with full force. Trevor had been kidnapped by some kind of maniac and her ex-husband was flirting with disaster.

Lucas lowered the window. "Get in."

"I'm calling the police!" She paced back and forth along the sidewalk. "Or the FBI!"

"Don't!" he yelled. "Cochran *will* kill

Trevor." At that, several people walking by on the sidewalk turned their heads. "Sydney, listen to me." Lucas spoke with a clarity he was far from feeling. "We now have less than an hour to catch a ferry to Vashon Island. Do you honestly think we can explain this to the police or the FBI and make it to that cannery on time?"

She hung her head and closed her eyes.

"On the phone with Cochran I heard wind and an engine, and Trevor said they were taking him fishing. That means they're probably on a boat. And a boat means quick and easy getaway."

She stopped by the passenger window and met his gaze, finding it as unreadable as a glass of water and about as reassuring.

"If you want Trevor back—" his features softened almost imperceptibly "—you're going to have to set the past aside, Syd. And you're going to have to trust me."

CHAPTER SIX

LUCAS DROVE ACROSS Vashon Island, the pastoral setting outside his window an eerie contrast to the tension-filled silence inside their vehicle. He and Sydney had barely spoken a word to each other the entire ferry ride from Seattle. He didn't trust himself to speak to her, didn't trust himself to remain rational, and it gave him too much time to think, too much time to hash over what had happened in the past twenty-four hours.

That Sydney had kept from him her pregnancy with Trevor all those years ago he could almost—almost—understand. But last night, how had she justified outright lying to his face?

She fidgeted in the passenger seat next to him, glancing from her watch to the side window to the front and back again. One minute she spun Manco Capac's staff in her hands and the next she clenched it so tightly her knuckles turned white as the petals of a Peruvian Cattleya orchid. And he understood she was dying inside. The reality of losing Emily still burned in his soul, but no words had comforted him then. None would comfort her now. So he remained silent, packing his anger away and folding into himself. If they could get through the next hour, they'd be okay. They'd get Trevor back, and Lucas would figure out some way to get Phillip Cochran out of the picture.

Sydney glanced down at her watch. "We're going to be late," she said, breaking their silence.

"Cochran wants the staff and sun god. He'll wait."

She spun the staff around again and abruptly stopped. "Wait a minute." Slowly, she turned it in her hand and studied the decorative markings carved deep into the gold. She ran her fingers lightly over the largest carving.

"What is it?" he asked.

"Lucas, are you sure this is Incan and not Mayan?"

"Positive. We found it in a newly discovered temple near Lake Titicaca. It's not old enough to be Mayan. Why?"

"These markings. They look almost like glyphs."

He glanced at the staff. "Impossible. The Inca had no written language."

"I know, but these symbols. If they were merely decorative, they'd be more…repetitive." She shook her head. "There could be a Mayan influence." She pointed at the largest carving that was separate and above a row of three carvings, like a title. "I have no idea what this one means, but look at these." She pointed at one row of three symbols. "This is so similar to the Mayan glyph for the number three. And this one…looks like the symbol for a river. It could say…three…maybe… standing…no… pillars…on…a river. And this one." She pointed at the next grouping. "I'm just guessing, but maybe three… squares…frames… pictures…on…a mountain? What could that mean?"

Three windows on a mountain.

"Three-Windowed Temple on Machu Picchu! That's got to be where the staff is used to show the map to the Temple of the Rain." He blew out a breath. "You're right. They must be glyphs. Copy them down! Quick. Before we get to the cannery."

"Why?"

"I don't trust Cochran. We may need that information." He didn't want to voice his worst fear. What if they didn't get Trevor back?

She dug around in the glove box for a piece of paper, tore open an empty McDonald's French fry container, and scribbled down the markings as fast as possible. "I got 'em." She glanced up and pointed to the right. "Turn here. It's around the corner."

He cranked the wheel and pulled into the abandoned cannery parking lot. Sydney had stuffed the French fry box back into the glove box and was out of the SUV before Lucas had turned off the ignition. "Hold up." He hopped out of the car, a half step behind her. He grabbed her arm and took the staff from her hand. "I think you should consider staying back."

"Okay." She shot her eyes skyward for a split second as if she was giving his request some thought. "Umm. No." She took off for the pier.

"What if Trevor is there? What if he sees you?"

"Then he sees me. I am not staying in that car."

The overcast sky threatened to dump on them at any moment. They kept walking. In silence. Terrible, agonizing, silence. Between a row of weathered, unkempt buildings and down toward the water. Cochran had certainly chosen his location well. The area was deserted. Then Lucas saw it. A boat at the end of the pier with a man standing guard on the dock. It wasn't Cochran, as far as Lucas could tell, and with the realization they had a cigarette boat, his heart tripped faster. He hadn't wanted to be right about water being the quickest getaway.

"That's far enough," the man shouted when they came within thirty feet. Something about him seemed familiar.

"Wait." Lucas wrapped his hand around Sydney's arm and held her back. "We brought the statue and the staff," he yelled, and clenched his fingers around the long gold rod. "Let the boy go."

"I've got a better idea," the man yelled back. "Throw me that staff."

That's when Lucas recognized him. "Jason? Jason Kent?"

"You know him, too?" Sydney cried.

"He interned with Max at the Smithsonian this past summer. I can't believe this." Lucas had spoken with him on the phone quite often, but only met him a couple times. He was the leak. "Jason, what the hell are you doing here?"

"Nothing personal, Lucas." He shrugged. "It's about the money. Throw me the staff, and nothing will happen to your boy."

"You don't know what you've gotten yourself into, kid."

Jason pulled out a gun. "I mean it, Lucas."

Lucas tossed the staff toward the end of the dock. It rolled a few feet before Jason scooped it up and dropped it on the floor of the boat. "Now let Trevor go."

"First, give me the statue."

"Where's Cochran?"

"Toss me the statue," Jason yelled back.

"I don't trust him, Syd," Lucas whispered. Not that he would trust Cochran more.

"What other choice do we have?"

Lucas pulled the golden figure from his pocket and held it out. "Here it is. You want it, send Trevor walking toward us."

At that the boat engines roared to life.

"No!" Sydney screamed. She swiped the statue from Lucas and ran toward the boat. "Here. You can have it."

Lucas took off after her. "Sydney, stop!"

"Stay where you are!" Jason shot the dock at Lucas's feet.

Lucas froze and Sydney pulled up several feet short of the man. She held out the statue, her hands shaking.

Jason aimed the gun at Lucas's chest. "If everyone does what they're supposed to do, no one'll get hurt," he said, keeping his eyes firmly on Lucas. "Now, throw it here."

Sydney tossed it to him. "Please, give Trevor back to me."

The cigarette boat engines revved.

"No!" Lucas and Sydney sprinted down the dock.

Lucas lunged for Jason and caught his shirt, only to have it slip away. Jason sprinted the remaining distance and leaped onto the boat as it pulled away. Lucas barely stopped himself from careening over the edge into the water. "Dammit, Jason! Cochran! Come back!"

"Trevor!" Sydney cried.

Spray flew in the boat's wake, and Cochran appeared on the boat deck. "When I find the silver bowl," he shouted over the sound of the engine, "you'll get the boy back. And then, Rydall, I'm coming after you!"

Lucas sucked in several breaths and threw

his arm in front of Sydney, holding her back. The sound of the engine faded across the water, and she collapsed against him with unchecked sobs. "They took my baby," she choked out.

As the boat disappeared, Lucas fought to still the adrenaline rushing through his veins, to hold back the nausea rising in his throat. It had gone exactly the way he'd dreaded, and, in this case, he hated being right.

"I can't believe it," she cried.

Turning, he folded her into the circle of his arms, against his heaving chest, and rested his cheek against the top of her head. Beneath the fear, he smelled Sydney, real and alive. So many years ago he'd held her like this, comforting her, lying to her by telling her everything would be all right while their world fell down around them. He wanted to tighten his grip now. He wanted to hold on. He wanted to cry out his own frustration and talk about his fears. But where would he begin? The words piled up behind his teeth, cementing his lips shut.

For a moment, she clung to him, dug her fingers into his back and held on as if her knees might give way. Then she drew back, slowly, deliberately, and stared at him. "This is all your fault," she whispered. "If you hadn't come to Seattle, none of this would have—"

"I didn't mean for this to happen. I'll get him back."

"I don't believe anything you say." She pushed against him. "Why did you have to come here?"

Unsure, he kept his hands on her arms, automatically offering comfort. She struggled against his hold. "I hate you!" she screamed and smacked his chest. "I hate you. I hate you."

He wrapped his arms around her, holding her still. After a moment, she gave up struggling and went limp in his arms. "Sydney, please believe this. I'll get Trevor back for you if it's the last thing I do. I'm going to Peru. I'll find the Temple of the Rain before Cochran does. I'll get Manco Capac's silver bowl. I promise." He set her back from him and said, "Now give me the real sun god."

She took a deep breath and struggled to pull herself together, wiped her cheeks and the end of her dripping nose with the back of her hand. Then she unzipped her front pocket and pulled out the Inca statue.

He stuffed it into his jacket. Thank God, he'd managed to convince her to pick up the

Mayan sun god he'd noticed the day before at her gallery. A decoy for Cochran. It had been hiding in the garbage can in her office during the break-in. Another stop at a hardware store had secured them a wooden dowel. They may have surrendered Manco Capac's staff, but they now had something approximating its diameter and length.

They still had a problem, and it was a biggie. The only solution he could think of seriously troubled him. It put her directly at risk, and that was the last thing he wanted. Frantically, he racked his brain for any other option, but there was none. "One more thing," he said, resigned to the necessity of it. "You need to come with me to Peru."

"NO. ABSOLUTELY NOT." Sydney stalked through her kitchen, trailing behind Lucas.

"Man, oh, man." Lucas stepped gingerly over the debris littering the floor. "Cochran really did a number on your house." He passed into the living room and headed toward the second story two steps at a time.

As if she cared at the moment. Her son had been *kidnapped.* "What're you doing?" she yelled after him. "I told you, I am not going with you to Peru."

For over an hour while they'd taken the ferry back from Vashon Island and stopped at his hotel to collect his belongings, she'd been running off at the mouth trying to convince him she needed to stay in the United States, to stay close to Trevor. The entire time, he'd barely said a word. But he wouldn't physically drag her to the airport. Or would he? She heard him rummaging through her closet and bolted upstairs.

A small suitcase lay open on the floor and he was throwing stuff inside, pajamas, pants, sweaters and even underwear. She thought of being in a foreign country with him, of sharing intimacies fellow travelers were sometimes forced to endure, of spending time with him and working cooperatively with him. "I'm staying here. And you can't change my mind."

"You think I want you to come along?" He stopped in his tracks and spun around, glaring at her. "Going to Machu Picchu isn't a big deal. Tourists go there every day, but that's only the first stop. From there, we'll head three, maybe five days into the rain forest. We're talking jungle. Snakes large enough to strangle men and mosquitoes big enough to carry off small animals. You're only going to slow me down."

Her skin crawled. "Cochran wouldn't risk taking Trevor out of the U.S. If I leave with you who's going to find my son?"

"You're forgetting something." He paused, his gaze narrowing as he took the McDonald's French fry box from his back pocket and held it out. "I can't read hiero-glyphics! You can!"

"Give it to me." She snatched the box away. "I've already deciphered two of the three rows. If I can't figure out the last row by the time your flight leaves, I'll call you in Peru."

"That's not good enough." He went to her bathroom and stuffed various toiletries in her bag. "You said the second row of glyphs indi-cated the existence of pillars on a river, right?"

She studied the symbols. It looked like pillars, but something more. Maybe markers of a sort. "I won't know for certain without studying it more thoroughly, but I think so."

"What if the pillars themselves have more hieroglyphics giving directions to the temple? What then? I don't know anyone in Peru who can read these glyphs, and I don't have time to find another expert here in the States." He gripped her shoulders. "Sydney, you're the only one who can do this."

She looked away and stared at the street scene below. Cars driving peacefully past. People going about their business, life carrying on for them in only the most normal of fashions. Life for Sydney would never be the same. Her son had been kidnapped, her facade of safety irrevocably destroyed. She swallowed hard and looked him straight in the eye. "I'm calling the police."

"You can't." Lucas swallowed and glanced away. "Cochran has killed people before, Syd. If he gets wind that we've called the police, he won't hesitate to kill Trevor."

"How will he know? He'll be in Peru."

"He's not working alone. The police are too big a risk."

"I don't have a choice." She made for the phone on her bedside table. "He's my son. I'm making the call."

"Our son." He closed his hand over her wrist, and they glared at each other. "And I say our best option is to find the temple first, to get Manco Capac's silver bowl. It's what Cochran is after. We can use the bowl to bargain for Trevor."

"And leave Trevor here? Alone?" Her eyes welled with tears, and she bit down hard on the inside of her cheek. "Lucas, I can't do that."

Slowly, he released his grip on her wrist and sighed. "Sydney, you're not a cop, or a private investigator. How are you going to find Trevor?"

"I don't know, but I have to try."

He lowered his head for a moment, then his tension visibly eased. "Do you remember Joe Donati?"

"Your college roommate?"

Lucas nodded. "I ran into him a few years ago and did him a favor. He's an FBI agent now, and he owes me one. It's worth a shot." He pulled out his digital address book and located the number. "How 'bout it?"

It didn't take her long to think through their limited options. "Call him. He was a good guy."

He snapped open his cell phone and paced out in the hallway. Sydney quietly followed him, watched and listened. Lucas wouldn't look at her, kept his gaze averted. "Joe?" She held her breath. "It's Lucas Rydall. Yeah, I know it's late on the East Coast. I need a huge favor. No, I didn't do anything illegal, but it needs to be kept private. Can you do that? You're sure? Great."

Lucas went on to describe the chain of events and the culprit behind it all. "I have to go to Peru. Can you break away and take care of things from this end?" Then he smiled, and Sydney could finally breathe. "Thanks, man."

For the first time since he'd picked up the phone, Lucas looked directly into her eyes and gave not a fragment of his thoughts away. It was always so damned hard to tell what was going on inside that head of his. "Joe will be on the next flight to Seattle. He needs a contact when he gets here. Someone to give him photos and so forth. That's all he needs. Photos. Who's he going to work with?"

She stared back at him, silent. Six years fell away and she was at the hospital, outside Emily's room, leaning into Lucas, feeling his arms around her, letting him make everything all better. Only he couldn't fix things back then any more than he could fix things now.

Lucas covered the phone mouthpiece and whispered, "Sydney, he's a professional. You'll have nothing to do here. I don't want you to come any more than you want to go. But I can't read glyphs."

She dropped her face into her hands. She couldn't stay here and pretend everything was going to be all right. And she couldn't expect Lucas to do this alone. She had to do this *with* him. She had to go to Peru. "Evelyn Dahl," she said. "Tell him to contact Evelyn Dahl." Resigned, she recited phone numbers and addresses.

After relaying the information, Lucas hung up the phone. He stepped toward her and his arms lifted ever so slightly as if to embrace and comfort her. Immediately thinking better of it, he brushed past her and into her bedroom. "Joe's a smart guy," he said brusquely. "If he doesn't find Trevor within the next couple of days, we'll have our bases covered in Peru. We'll find that temple and the bowl before Cochran does."

Sydney followed him. "Will Joe keep this to himself?"

"He promised he wouldn't say anything to anyone. He'll take some vacation and work unofficially."

"That must be some favor he owes you."

"I got him out of a Guatemalan jail cell."

"Jail?"

"Want anything else packed?" He pointed at the suitcase.

"I'll get it." She took an inventory of what he'd already accumulated and set about filling the gaps, sifting through the piles of her clothing scattered about the room. "Jail? Guatemala? What happened?"

"He got picked up on vacation for a routine traffic violation. While he was yelling about missing his flight home and deserving a call to the U.S. embassy, I flipped a fifty into the guard's palm and opened the door."

"And what were you doing in a Guatemalan jail?"

"Actually, I was on my way out."

"Oh, it all makes sense then."

"You wouldn't understand."

"Try me." Something in the way he glanced sideways at her made her second-guess herself. She pushed the notion aside. "I really want to know."

"A bar fight. That one cost me fifty bucks, too."

That was hard to imagine. Lucas rarely even raised his voice. What could have pushed him that far? She studied him as she threw one last pair of pants into the suitcase.

"It was right after the divorce," he said. "I spent the first month moving from one Guatemalan bar stool to the next. The second month in the bars up and down the coast of Belize."

She tugged ineffectually at the zipper of her overstuffed suitcase. "Was that because of Emily or the divorce?"

"Both." He brushed her hands aside, pushed down on the flap and finished zipping the bag.

She'd always assumed the divorce had unburdened him. After he'd been served with papers, there'd been no offer of reconciliation, no explanations, no apologies. Nothing to give her any indication there had been any kind of remorse on his part at all. "I thought you wanted a divorce."

"You never asked, did you?"

CHAPTER SEVEN

TIMES LIKE THESE made Evelyn wish she smoked cigarettes. Or cigars. Or drank cognac, at the very least. There had to be something she could do to cap off the best sex she'd had in months. "Do you have any chocolate?" She threw her hands behind her head and stretched, luxuriating in 600-thread-count comfort.

"What?" This hunk of a man she'd known barely two hours looked at her quizzically.

"Chocolate. The real stuff. None of that candy bar crap."

He reached into the drawer of his bedside table and pulled something out. "Will this do?" He dangled a foil-wrapped prize over her head. Godiva. This man had a Ferrari parked in his garage. Owned a gorgeous neo-classic home in Magnolia overlooking Puget Sound. And stocked chocolate, real choco-late, by his bed, no less. What more could a woman ask for? Maybe she'd finally met Mr. Right. "That'll do." She nibbled on a corner of the truffle he slid across her lips.

Mr. Potential curled his warm, buff body next to hers and nuzzled his nose into her neck. He popped the rest of the chocolate into her mouth, and she bit down, letting the smooth filling run over her tongue.

"That was wonderful," she murmured.

"The sex or the chocolate?" He pulled away and angled a look at her face.

The first of Evelyn's warning flags flapped its little tail. "Both." She smiled, just in case.

"Are you saying I'm no better than chocolate?"

"Noooo."

"Then what are you saying?"

"You and the chocolate were both wonderful. Is there a problem with that? I really like chocolate."

"On a scale of one to ten, rate me."

She managed to stifle the groan rising in her throat, but couldn't keep her eyes from rolling back in despair. What was it with men? It wasn't enough to have their unit stroked, they had to get their egos stroked, as well?

"I don't rate men." She swung her legs over the bed and proceeded to step back into her clothing that had been tossed about the room. She noticed the Fabergé egg collection displayed on the bookshelf and sighed. Too bad. Fabergé might be a tad obvious, but it *was* truly expensive.

"Wait a minute." He jumped into his boxers. "When will I see you again?"

She stalked down the hall. "I'll call you."

One leg in his pants, the other out, he hopped after her down the spiral staircase. "But I never gave you my phone number."

Evelyn opened the massive front door. With a tiny wave to Mr. Too-Good-To-Be-True, she closed it behind her. "Whew!" Breathing a sigh of relief on the way to her Mercedes, she reminded herself that the jerk had actually shown his true colors within the first hour. She'd just been too blinded by lust to notice. Having come to the bar for happy hour with some friends, hadn't he insisted on driving *her* car to his house, citing some personal issue with women drivers? She must be a magnet for assholes.

Her cell phone rang. Pulling it out of her purse, she snapped it open. "Who is this?"

"Evelyn, it's me."

"Sydney? Where are you?"

"I'm at the Houston airport."

"What are you doing in Houston?"

"My flight's about to take off, so I don't have much time. You need to listen."

"You sound terrible. Where are you going?"

"Listen. Don't speak. Listen."

"I'm all ears." She did her best to clamp her lips tight as Sydney relayed all that had happened. "Trevor's been kidnapped?" Evelyn barely made it to her car. "You're going to Peru?"

"I don't have a choice."

"What can I do to help?" Evelyn slammed her car door and sat there, stunned. Trevor. Her precious little godson. It wasn't sinking in.

"There's an FBI agent named Joe Donati—"

The connection crackled with static.

"Sydney, talk louder. I can barely hear you."

"He's flying in…from Baltimore," Sydney yelled. "He'll contact you for information on Trevor. Stay awake, by your phone, give him anything he needs."

"That's all? Come on. You can do better than that."

"And don't let him go to the police or the FBI office."

"More."

"The flight attendant is standing right here. She's going to take away my phone." More static. "I gotta go," Sydney continued, rushed. "Dog his tail, Evie. Make sure he thinks of every angle, every possibility. I want my baby back."

"I'll be on him like salt on a margarita glass."

THE FLIGHT FROM SEATTLE to Houston had been uneventful, comfortable and short when compared to many of Lucas's recent excursions. This next leg of their trip would be an entirely different matter, but, with every flight overbooked, at least they'd convinced a couple to sell their tickets to Lima.

The wheels had no sooner left the airport runway, than Lucas stretched out in the first-class seat and cleared his mind, found comfort in the rhythmic beating of his heart and the slow rise and fall of his hands folded over his chest. It worked for about three minutes. Lucas had a son. A son. Now what?

Directly on his left, lost in her own thoughts, Sydney clearly believed he'd fallen asleep, and that was fine. Conversation with her or anyone else was totally unnecessary.

What would he say to her anyway? Hey, how about those Mariners? How's the art business? Or how could you, day in and day out for all these years, keep the existence of my child from me? Did you think about me once? Did you have any remorse?

Hour after interminable hour in between short naps, his thoughts jockeyed for control. One moment his heart would lift ever-so-slightly with joy and the possibilities the future held, and in the very next breath reality would crash down.

Occasionally, he caught glimpses of Sydney through half-opened eyelids. Most of the time, she either stared bleary-eyed out the airplane window or flipped restlessly through magazines. A couple times, he found her staring with glazed eyes at the glyphs she'd reproduced on the McDonald's French fry box. Once, she caught his eye, and the pain there, the uncertainty seared his heart. He never had been able to stay mad at her for long.

"Sleep," he said. "You're going to need it."

"How will Cochran get to Peru?" she asked.

He didn't want to tell her.

"Lucas?" she pressed.

"He'll hire a private jet." And get there hours before them. Their eyes locked, the only accompanying sounds the drone of the plane engine and hum of the overhead blower. "Trevor will be all right," he whispered. Misty tears sprang from her bloodshot eyes. He almost opened his arms, almost offered her what little comfort he could.

Crazy idiot. He turned his head and closed her back out. She'd cheated him out of the first six years of Trevor's life. That there might not be another six was unimaginable. He'd already lost one child. What kind of god would take a second?

Then again, who was he kidding? He hadn't been cheated out of anything. He'd walked away from it. Him and what the doctors had called his clinical depression. How he hated that word. Depression. It was so accurate, how low his life had sunk. Now, he had nothing. His current job was short-lived, at best. He didn't have a house, let alone an apartment. He moved from one country to the next, like a nomad. His personal possessions nearly fit in one carry-on duffel. To top it all off, his medical history meant his future was a total crapshoot.

Trevor's life, on the other hand, was stable and happy. He had a good mother who loved him with all her heart, a beautiful home, friends, school. Presumably, his life was full. What did he need Lucas for? That question haunted him for hours.

Around 2:00 a.m., and some ten-plus hours after they'd left Seattle, the airplane descended into Lima. Lucas sat up, tossing aside the tiny pillow and inadequate blanket.

"It's so dark," Sydney said, a sad smile touching those wonderfully full lips. "For such a big city, you'd think there'd be more lights."

The landing gear locked in place, and he glanced out the window. "There's a layer of pollution covering the city. Very little pene-trates it."

"Yuck," she said. "Spend much time here?"

"There are no Inca secrets in Lima. No reason to stay." There had always been another Inca ruin to investigate, another Quechua medicine man or woman to inter-view about Inca history and legends. Nothing took precedence over finding Manco Capac's Huari bowl and the Temple of the Rain. "Besides, Lima's one of the most crime-ridden stops in South America. And you won't find that in any tourist guide-book."

As he followed her off the large airliner and onto the tarmac, warm, humid air hit him full in the face, along with the familiar scent of dead fish and jet fuel. *Home sweet home,* he thought wryly.

Lucas saw a familiar face and led Sydney in that direction, steering her clear of the snarling police dogs, lunging and straining against their choke collars. While in Houston, he'd called ahead for a driver. With Sydney along, he wasn't taking any chances.

"*Buenos días,* Pepe," Lucas said, shaking the other man's hand. "Thank you for meeting us on such short notice."

The middle-aged Peruvian nodded and turned toward the airport terminal. "Whenever you need me, *Señor* Lucas, you call."

"Sydney, this is Pepe. He'll be our driver and bodyguard. Pepe, Sydney Mitchell."

"*Buenos días,* Sydney."

"Hello, Pepe." She turned to Lucas with a questioning look. "Why do we need a body-guard, and where are we going?"

"This city is *really* not safe for a couple

of unprotected gringos." He drew her along the barely lit tarmac. "We're going to the nearest hotel, sleeping for a few hours, and then catching the first flight out to Cusco in the morning."

After retrieving their luggage and a brief customs stop, they made their way through the terminal to Pepe's waiting car and drove to the Crillon, an ornate, colonial hotel. Pepe directed the bellman with their luggage and handed Lucas their room keys. "In the morning, I will meet you here."

Lucas nodded and led Sydney into the hotel.

She quickly glanced around. "A Super 8 wasn't good enough? We had to stay at the Waldorf?"

He came here so often that the Italian marble, Baccarat chandeliers and gleaming brass fixtures no longer registered. "It's a comfortable bed and safe," he said, "and, with the current exchange rate, costs less than a Super 8."

He found their rooms on the fifteenth floor, opened her door and swung it wide. She stood rooted to the spot, too tired to move, and an image of her, similarly alone and helpless, rushed over him. She was standing over Emily's hospital bed the night their little girl died, looking as if a wisp of a breeze might topple her. He'd stood next to her, unable to do anything.

Well, this time, he wasn't helpless. He might be lousy when it came to everyday tasks of husband and father, like sticking around, but he was a good hunter. He would find the Temple of the Rain and the Huari bowl, and he would keep Sydney safe.

"You have a couple hours, Syd. Get some sleep." He set her luggage inside the room and nudged her over the threshold. "Do not leave this hotel without me."

He pulled the door closed, stood in the hall. "Syd," he whispered. "Lock and chain it."

Protectiveness surged through him along with the answer to his dilemma about Trevor. Not every little boy needed a father. And this little boy would no doubt be better off without a father like Lucas. He listened as her dead bolt clicked and the chain slid in place, and he knew exactly what he had to do. He would get Trevor back to his mother. And when all this was done, Lucas would walk away. Again.

CHAPTER EIGHT

SYDNEY STARTLED AWAKE to the sound of pounding on her door. "Trevor?" she whispered, disoriented. The pounding sounded again, and reality slapped her in the face. Trevor's kidnapping wasn't a nightmare. Pound. Pound. Pound. Still fully clothed, she forced herself upright, rushed across the room and looked through the peephole. Lucas. She opened the door.

"I've been hammering on your door for a full minute." His hair was wet and he was freshly shaved. "You okay?"

She ran a hand over her face. "I didn't think I'd sleep." After he'd left her alone, she'd lain down on the bed, thinking she would only rest her eyes. Apparently, she'd done more than that. "Do I have time to shower?"

"Sorry." He handed her a travel mug of steaming coffee and grabbed her luggage from the very spot he'd left it several hours earlier. "Pepe's already waiting for us and we need to catch our flight to Cusco."

Bleary-eyed and hazy-headed, she followed him down the hall, outside and into Pepe's waiting car. "Any chance we can find a phone and call Evelyn?" she asked.

"Use this." He dug his cell phone out of his back pocket. "The public phones here are completely unreliable."

"What time is it in Seattle?"

"Two hours earlier than Lima." Lucas gave her all the necessary country codes and she dialed Evelyn's home.

Evelyn picked up on the first ring, sounding tired and more than a little disappointed that Joe Donati hadn't yet arrived. Sydney hung up.

Lucas patted her arm. "Joe'll get there as soon as he can."

A short while later, they'd made it through the mishmash of foreigners and *Mestizo* and *Indios,* what Lucas called the locals, at the crowded, smelly and humid Lima airport. She found herself seated next to Lucas on their one-hour flight to Cusco with Pepe across the aisle and up one row.

"Pepe doesn't talk much, does he?" she asked.

"Never has."

He was so unobtrusive he nearly melded into the background. "What's his story?"

"He's a former National Police officer, knows three languages, and now guides for a living. He's been my driver, interpreter and guard on every trip that I've made down here but one for the last five years."

Sydney glanced at what she could see of the man's muscle-bound shoulders. He might be several inches shorter than Lucas's six foot one, but the man was infused with quiet power.

"Would you mess with him?" Lucas asked.

"No."

"Anything happens to me you stick with Pepe."

They soon left behind the arid, coastal plains of Lima for the jagged, lifeless peaks of the Andes, but Sydney found herself still too sleepy to care about the spectacular view from her tiny oval window. The airplane had no sooner made its ascent than it began a slow descent to the smaller, more rural city of Cusco.

Lucas leaned across the aisle to Pepe. "Do you have the coca tea?" Pepe handed back two plastic water bottles. "Drink this." Lucas handed her one and took a chug from the other.

She glanced down at it. "What's coca tea?"

"It's made from steeped coca leaves."

"What's it for?" She tasted it experimentally, and it seemed mild enough.

"Cusco's at 3,300 meters. When we step off the plane, the altitude's going to hit you like a wall. The tea's a very mild stimulant." Several more swallows and he'd nearly finished.

"Is there cocaine in it?"

He chuckled and shrugged. "I suppose a miniscule amount. Not enough to dramatically affect you. Many Peruvians consider the plant sacred. Drink it. It'll help you feel better until we get out of Cusco and back down to a little lower elevation."

Sydney sucked down a few mouthfuls of the pale brown tepid liquid. Tea had always tasted like weed water to her, and this variety was no different. She glanced out the window, finally waking up. "I've never seen so many red-tiled roofs."

"They call Cusco the gringo capital of South America."

"Why?"

"It's the most common starting point for the Inca Trail. Most tourists coming to see Machu Picchu stay here."

She followed Lucas and Pepe onto the tarmac at Cusco's regional airport. "It's cooler here than Lima." She pulled a sweatshirt over her arms and immediately felt dizzy from the motion. She stopped and took a deep breath, but jolts of nausea still rocked through her stomach.

"The altitude's hitting you." Lucas went to her side while Pepe continued on. "Drink the rest of your tea."

She swallowed as much as she could hold. Before she knew it, the airport was behind them and she was seated between Pepe and Lucas in an old, white Chevy pickup, a fresh bottle of coca tea in her hand, their luggage stowed in back. By the time Pepe drove them northeast out of Cusco, a dull ache had started at her temples. "Where are we going?" She zipped up her sweatshirt and tucked her cold hands between her legs.

Lucas adjusted the heat. "Through the Valley Sagrado, the Sacred Valley of the Inca. To a village named Ollantaytambo."

The words barely registered in Sydney's sleep-deprived, altitude-shocked brain. What *did* sink in was visual. "Guess we're not in Washington anymore."

She rubbernecked, her mouth hanging slack. No Puget Sound and forests of ever-greens. No distant and untouchable Mount Rainier visible only on the clearest of days. This was high-altitude rain forest with wild orchids dripping from the trees. These mountains were incredibly steep, green-spired, cloud-enshrouded. And they were right there, as if she could reach out the truck window and touch them. The entire land-scape was dotted with Inca walls and ruins and freely roaming pigs and cattle.

As they drove through the deeply incised valleys, Sydney felt daunted and awe-inspired by the magnitude of all that sur-rounded them. "I wish Trevor could see this," she said. To keep from breaking down, she focused on the map in her lap. "Ollantay-tambo." She pointed to its location.

"That's it," Lucas said.

"So we'll be about…forty-two kilome-ters from Machu Picchu? We're going there now, right?"

"Wrong." He glanced at his watch, then studied her tired face. "It's almost one o'clock. Too late."

"But Cochran probably arrived here hours ago." She felt a surge of panic.

"You wouldn't make it."

"Don't worry about me." Even as she said it, she pushed her palm against her throbbing temple. Her stomach pitched, her head ached. "If we don't get to Machu Picchu before Cochran does," she urged, "we might find him waiting there for us."

"I'm aware of that."

"Lucas, I'll do what I have to do. Please."

Beside her, he took a deep breath. "Look." His voice softened. "The legends say that Manco Capac's staff will somehow show the way to the Temple of the Rain. I don't know exactly how it's going to work or how the sun god figures into the picture, but we need to be in the Temple of the Three Windows on Machu Picchu at noon. Theoretically, on summer solstice."

"So we're too late for today."

He nodded. "We have to wait until tomorrow. We're a little late in the summer season, but we'll make it work."

"What about Cochran?"

"We have to assume he knows about being there at noon, as well. He couldn't have made it there today, either."

"He'll make it tomorrow."
"Let me worry about that."

EVELYN PACED, nearly wearing a tread in her antique Persian rug. She stopped at her condo's floor-to-ceiling windows and stared out at Puget Sound. It was one of those perfect Seattle mornings that occurred only when the Pacific breezes came from the south, or Jupiter was aligned with Saturn, or some other astronomical nonsense. And she barely noticed. The FBI agent was late, and it wasn't due to the fickle Seattle fog.

Frustration, anger and, definitely, fear, bubbled up. What if the FBI guy never showed? *Trevor. Oh, Trevor.* She clenched her fists, hoping the bite of her long nails would refocus her attention. Instead, tears tickled the back of her throat, and sweat coated her palms.

No, no, no! She would not fall apart.

The doorbell rang. "Well, it's about time," she muttered, letting irritation override panic.

Unfortunately, the scruffy vision of the man through her door's peephole did nothing to assuage her concerns. FBI brought to mind suits, ties and military-style haircuts. Not several hour delays and five o'clock shadows heavy enough for grazing herds of cattle. "Who is it?"

"FBI, Miss Dahl." The man's voice was deep, his diction slow. "Special Agent Joe Donati."

Another glance through the peephole produced a clear view of his badge, and she swung the door wide. The full image of the man only made matters worse. With blue jeans, tight black T-shirt, and a tattoo fully encircling his left bicep, this guy had to be either scheduled for a photo shoot or working undercover in a drug ring. He certainly didn't look capable of finding a kidnapped child.

He studied her in return, smacking his gum with every movement of his jaw. "Are you finished?" she asked. "Or would you like further inspection?"

Rather than appearing contrite, his smirk blossomed into a full-blown smile, and two adorable dimples dented his cheeks. Definitely not a photo shoot. The man wasn't nearly sullen enough. "Maybe later." He dropped a worn leather duffel inside the door and marched into her condo. "Right now I'm hungry and need a shot of caffeine."

He stopped in her kitchen, studied her cabinets and managed to find a coffee cup behind the first door he opened. After reaching into her refrigerator for eggs, milk and orange juice, he found a frying pan, again on the first try.

So what? It was a kitchen. "Look, Agent…"

"Donati," he filled in. "Call me Joe."

"Okay, Joe, you were supposed to be here hours ago."

He eyed her while cracking several eggs into a bowl. "I caught the first open flight out of Baltimore, but they had to deice the wings of the plane three times."

"You could have found another flight."

"I can pull a lot of tricks, Evelyn, but I don't have Air Force One at my disposal." He made himself a full-blown breakfast, cleaning up as he went, then sat down at her countertop and devoured his plate of food.

So he had a legitimate reason for being late. She still didn't like the feel of him, or the way he'd charged into her space and taken over. He finished his last bite, rinsed off his plate, and set it in her dishwasher. The kitchen didn't look the slightest bit worse for wear. Wasn't he Mr. Perfect?

"Now I'm ready." He offered her a piece of peppermint gum, popped some into his mouth, and rubbed his hands together. "Give me everything you've got. Pictures, video-tapes, anything that helps identify the kid, his habits, his routines."

Her stomach flipped at the thought of Trevor. Kidnapped. "The *kid's* name is Trevor, and first I want to know what you do at the FBI. Are you a paper pusher, or do you have actual field experience?"

"Every FBI agent's a paper pusher." For a moment he looked as though he wasn't going to give her a gram of satisfaction. "I work organized crime."

"So you've never done a child kidnapping case before?"

"Child, no. Kidnapping, yes."

"Aren't you going to get into trouble for this? Working on a case without your superiors knowing about it?"

He grinned. "No."

"Bullshit. For all I know, there's a car full of agents waiting outside."

"I gave Lucas my word."

"I don't know Lucas or you from the old couple down the hall."

"Why would I put a little boy's life in danger?"

"Because that's the way the FBI works. By the book."

"Really? Here all this time I thought I was supposed to use my training, logic and instincts. Thanks for enlightening me."

"Don't try to pretend you're some hotshot renegade agent—"

"Renegade, oooh. I like that. Can I use that sometime?"

She tried ignoring him. It didn't work. He was too big. Too real. Too…hairy. "If I knew anyone else to call, I'd be on that phone in a heartbeat."

He took a quick look at the door and glanced back at her. "Want me to leave?"

"Sydney told me I had to work with you. That doesn't mean I have to like it."

"You're something else. You know that?" He shook his head and laughed. "Who is this kid to you?"

"My godson." Much to her chagrin, her voice cracked. "I'm not taking any chances."

He studied her for a minute. "Well, you're right. Most agents would get in deep shit working a case unofficially."

"There. Told you."

"But *I* won't."

"What makes you so special?" Apart from that damned gum-chomping smile.

"Well, it's simple, *amica mia. Io parlo Si-*

ciliano." The foreign words flowed off his tongue like a balm and a sexy one at that. "I'm one of only three agents in the entire country who can speak Sicilian. As long as there's Italian Mafia, I can do damn near anything I want and get away with it."

From the look in his eyes, she had no doubt. "One more thing, and it's important." Her muscles tensed. "Are you going to find Trevor?" She didn't want to hear any statistics, any false promises, any platitudes. For once in her life, she wanted commitment from a man.

"Yes," he said softly. "I'll find your godson."

"Okay, you're on the job." She told him everything about Trevor she could think of, moving from one picture to the next. And she had a lot of pictures. Sydney and Trevor were the only family she knew anymore.

"He has a sleepover with me every month. Dinner and a movie with my favorite guy," she said, grinning at the thought of sleeping bags in front of the TV and popcorn strewn on the floor. He was the only person she knew who could sleep with a smile on his face. "The next day we always go on an outing. The aquarium, the zoo, a drive to

Mount Rainier. Last summer we went to Pike Place Market, and I convinced him to eat sushi."

She picked up a photo from the past winter of the two of them at Stevens Pass. "And he talked me into snowboarding. Me! Can you imagine?" She looked into Agent Joe's face, and damned if she didn't see compassion. Without warning, she puddled up. *Shit!* Where was the man's sarcasm and innuendo when a girl needed it?

And, just like that, his smirk was back in place. "You in a furry ski bunny suit?" He eyed her up and down. "Yeah, I can imagine that." His voice sounded suggestive, but the look in his eyes clearly said, "Take the cue, Evelyn. Take the cue."

She sniffled and snagged several tissues from a nearby box. "I don't do furry." Female blubbering crisis averted.

"Didn't think so." Agent Joe snapped his notebook closed. "Now, take me to Trevor's house, okay? I'll look the place over for clues and then I'm off to Tacoma."

She tossed the tissues and came to full attention. "What's in Tacoma?"

"Phillip Cochran grew up there."

"You think Trevor's still in the area?"

"Flight records indicate that Cochran came in from San Francisco yesterday on a private jet full of men. He left Seattle yesterday with only one man."

Now we're getting somewhere. "So even though we don't know for sure what happened after Vashon Island, they didn't take Trevor out of the country. He's still in the States?"

"Exactly." Joe nodded. "I've got a buddy staking out Cochran's Carmel Beach compound, but I don't think he's going to see any activity. Cochran's men stayed back. Most likely with Trevor."

"Near Tacoma."

"Probably not. But that's where I'm starting."

"You mean *we*."

"No. I mean me."

"I made a promise, too. You're not leaving my sight."

Tough guy crossed his arms. "You sure ask a lot."

"Can't handle it?"

"Oh, I can handle it." He picked up his leather duffel by the door. "First I need to get a hotel room and change."

No hotel. "You can change here." She led

him to the guest room down the hall.
"There's a bathroom off the side."

A short time later, the guest bedroom
door opened. "All set," he said from the hall.
"Let's go."

The man's metamorphosis could not have
been more complete. Designer suit, crisp
white shirt and a power-striped tie replaced
black T-shirt and jeans. And he'd shaved.
Evelyn was dying to find out if his cheeks
were as baby soft as they looked.

"Are you finished?" he asked. "Or would
you like further inspection?"

If she wasn't careful, she might fall for
this one.

"Let's hit the road, Evelyn. You're
driving."

Then again, careful might not be good
enough.

CHAPTER NINE

SOME DISTANCE from Ollantaytambo Pepe pulled his truck up to a small stucco home with a red-tiled roof. Sydney hopped out, stretched her legs and glanced around. The first things she noticed were the new black Toyota Land Cruiser under the adjoining carport and a satellite dish on the roof. Next, the chickens freely roaming the yard and the alpacas grazing on the short grass in a nearby fenced area.

As Lucas slammed the pickup door a man came out of the house and gave Lucas a bear hug. "If I hadn't seen your sorry ass last week, I'd say it was good to have you back." Though shorter than Lucas by a good six inches, the man had breadth to his frame, lending him an uncommon presence.

"Good to see you, too, Miguel."

The Peruvian studied her from head to toe

with keen, so-dark-they-were-nearly-black eyes. "You're Sydney."

Lucas frowned. "Enough with the medicine man mumbo jumbo. You're not impressing anyone but yourself."

"Medicine man. Humph."

"Sydney Mitchell." She held out her hand.

His hair, black enough to shine silver in the late-afternoon sun, was cropped short. "I'm Miguel." He stepped close to her, wrapping both his warm palms around hers. "We won't bother with the rest of my name. You wouldn't be able to pronounce it anyway."

His teeth sparkled white against the backdrop of his dark skin. If he hadn't been an inch or so shorter than her with a face as welcoming as a puppy's, she may have been intimidated by his invasion of her personal space. As it was, she wanted to sit even closer with him and talk in whispers. There was no question he would listen, no question he would understand.

He stepped away, and Sydney immediately felt how cold it had gotten outside. For the last couple hours they'd traveled down into the Sacred Valley out of Cusco and into the deep shade of the valley floor. Miguel glanced behind her. "*Buenos días,* Pepe."

"Don Miguel." Pepe nodded.

"Come." Miguel led the way into his home. "You look ready to fall over."

Pepe and Lucas, dismissing Sydney's offers of help, grabbed all the packs and deposited them inside the small house. One large room greeted them with the aroma of roasting meat and potatoes, and, despite queasiness and a tenacious headache, Sydney's stomach growled. She hadn't eaten since Houston.

"Do you wish me to stay?" Pepe asked Lucas.

Lucas shook his head. "*Muchas gracias,* Pepe. I'll send word into town if we need you."

"Well then, *adios.*" Pepe disappeared back out the door.

Sydney glanced around Miguel's home, hoping for a phone to call Evelyn. Though sparsely decorated with any feminine influence decidedly missing from the decor, the place had a warm, kick-off-your-shoes kind of feel. There was no sign of a phone in the kitchen area off to the right, so Sydney focused on the living area to the left. A huge sectional couch upholstered in red plaid and two overstuffed chairs formed a conversation area by the hearth in the far corner. Thickly woven wool rugs were scattered here and there and alpaca blankets had been thrown over the chairs and couch. As inviting as the room looked, she still couldn't relax.

"I don't want to be rude," she said, "but do you have a phone?"

"Yes. Over here." Miguel walked to the table by the couch and pulled a charger unit out from behind a lamp. "It's a satellite unit, so you should be able to call anywhere. Lucas will help you." Miguel quietly disappeared into the kitchen.

Lucas helped her with the country codes, and she tried all of Evelyn's numbers again. Though there was no answer on Evelyn's home phone, her friend had left an informative greeting on her machine. "No news yet, Sydney, but superagent man is here and we're working on it. Leave me a number." After leaving Miguel's number on Evelyn's machine she hung up the phone.

"Anything?" Lucas asked.

Disappointed and near tears, she shook her head and described Evelyn's message.

"Give Joe some time." Lucas squeezed her shoulder. "He'll find Trevor." They went together into the kitchen.

"Sydney, you don't look well." Miguel

stepped toward a large oak table. "Come. I have something for you."

Small, green leaves, similar to ficus, only darker, lay fanned out on the table in three sets of three. Miguel picked up one set, softly blew over them, murmuring something Sydney couldn't understand before presenting them to her. "A *kintu*. Coca leaves for your body and soul."

She looked to Lucas. "Miguel blew life into his prayer," he explained. "Now he offers you love, health and prosperity. Go on. Like Catholic communion."

Sydney took the leaves. As Miguel's touch flowed through her, as his gaze connected with hers, she immediately felt a sense of renewal and even a modicum of peace. He *was* a shaman. She placed the *kintu* on her tongue.

"You chew them," Lucas offered. "Then tuck them between your cheek and gum. It'll help you feel better, like the tea, only stronger."

The leaves were cool and mild in flavor.

"Now." Miguel smiled at her. "*You* must feed Lucas. Then Lucas feeds me."

Sydney hesitated and reached for the second set of leaves.

"Not necessary," Lucas interceded, and

without ceremony stripped the coca leaves from the stems with his teeth and started chewing, tossing the stems into the garbage.

Under different circumstances, she may have felt slighted, but as it was she couldn't help feeling he'd done her a favor. Sharing the benevolent, yet intimate gesture with him would have seemed too much.

"Lucas, Lucas." Sighing, Miguel shook his head. "I will let you feed me, Sydney."

"What do I say?" she asked.

"Anything you want."

She picked up the leaves and blew on them. "Live long and prosper."

Chuckling at the *Star Trek* reference, Miguel accepted the leaves. "Now I will get you two something substantial to eat."

"May I help?" she asked.

"No, no. You are my guest." Miguel brought over two mugs. "Warm coca tea," he explained.

"Sit before you fall." Lucas held out a chair for her.

She plopped down and finished half the cup in one gulp, not realizing how thirsty she'd been. As the stuff kicked in, her back unwound, her stomach settled, but, without news of Trevor, she couldn't completely relax. She distracted herself by studying the

surroundings. Miguel's house was comfortable, but rustic without any modern conve-
niences.

Miguel seemed to spot Sydney's curiosity.
"When I left the U.S., there was only one
thing I missed. A refrigerator." He laughed
from where he stood at the counter by the
stove.

"Miguel was born and raised here," Lucas
explained, "but he went to college in
Boston."

The label on Miguel's jeans said Eddie
Bauer and his boots were The North Face.
"Internet shopping." He grinned. "Who
would have thought all these companies
deliver to Ollantaytambo?"

Lucas stood up, opened a cabinet and
brought silverware and napkins over to the
table. Then he picked up a loaf of bread and
set it on the table with a cutting board and
knife. He'd obviously spent enough time at
Miguel's to know where everything was kept
and felt comfortable poking about. He went
back for a large brown bottle, poured two
fingers worth of the clear liquid into a small,
thick glass and handed it to Sydney.

"*Pisco*," he said. "Peruvian brandy." He
set the bottle on the table and drank only his

coca tea. "Between that and the coca leaves, you should feel much better."

Sydney had almost forgotten what it was like to have someone take care of her after so many years alone with Trevor. As a single parent, there had been no one else except her to cook the meals. No one else to do the shopping. No one else to make any kind of arrangements. She should have enjoyed sitting back and relaxing. Instead, it bothered her that she was too sick to carry her weight. She'd not only grown accustomed to self-reliance, she now thrived on it.

Tomorrow, she promised herself, *back on your own two feet.* She took a taste of the *pisco* Lucas had poured for her. Two more sips and her tired body turned to jelly.

Miguel ladled something into bowls and brought them to the table. "Soup," he said, sitting down. "Your stomachs won't handle anything heavier for now."

Sydney glanced at the creamy concoction. It smelled wonderful, but her stomach was still flip-flopping.

"Eat," Lucas ordered. "Before you slide out of that chair."

She forced her hand to pick up the spoon and scoop up the hot liquid, keeping the coca leaves tight between her gum and cheek. The flavors of potato and bits of chicken simmered in her mouth and made her want more. Before she knew it, she'd finished most of the bowl.

"So, Lucas," Miguel said. "You found the sun god."

"Yeah, I found it."

"Surprised to have him show up at your doorstep, eh?" Miguel smiled at Sydney. "But you have come to Peru with him. This is good." At that Sydney lost her appetite. She set down her spoon. "What?" Miguel threw up his hands in apparent dismay. "What did I say?"

"Phillip Cochran's selling the idea that we're after the Fountain of Youth. Bidding's up to twenty million." Lucas explained the kidnapping in brief. "He's holding Sydney's son hostage until he finds Manco Capac's bowl."

"This is terrible." Miguel bowed his head and stared at the roughly hewn tabletop. "I'm so sorry."

"It's not your fault."

"If I hadn't told you about the legend of the sun god..." His voice trailed away.

"You're not responsible for Cochran."

"But I always thought you should abandon your search for this temple. And now you cannot."

Voices outside and a soft tapping on the rough wooden door drew everyone's attention. The door swung open and a young woman in a brightly colored woolen poncho stepped inside Miguel's house. In her arms she held a small baby, a fleece Patagonia hat warming his tiny head. Inconsolable, the child screamed. Miguel took the baby. "Shh," he whispered. The mother smiled politely and set two large bottles of what looked like more *pisco* on the table. She bobbed her head up and down, speaking in a language Sydney couldn't understand.

"Quechua," Lucas answered her unspoken question. "These people are believed to be directly descended from the Inca," he explained. "And Miguel's the only doctor within many days' journey for these people. They pay him with whatever they can. Sometimes a chicken or guinea pig. Sometimes *chunu,* tiny potatoes they grow."

"Guinea pig?"

He shrugged. "A traditional Peruvian dish."

"They eat guinea pigs?"

Miguel grinned back at her. "Don't knock something you have never tried." He took the baby and mother into a room off the kitchen, and the crying stopped. Only Miguel's deep, soothing voice carried through the thick door.

"He's a doctor? You called him a medicine man."

"I was kidding." Lucas stood up and began cleaning the kitchen. "Miguel's as legit as they come. He got his medical degree from Boston University and worked several years at Boston General before moving back here. Gave up a couple hundred thousand a year in the States for a few bottles of maize beer, chickens and potatoes."

"He seems to be doing okay financially." Feeling marginally better, she stood and helped him clear the table.

"It never hurts to inherit a few bucks." At her questioning look, he explained. "A wealthy doctor from Massachusetts did a mission stint down this way when Miguel was about fifteen. Miguel was beating him in chess within a few hours and assisting him in examining rooms in a matter of a few days. The doctor sponsored him in college and left Miguel most of his estate. Now, he's doing his best to spread it around. Did you notice the little hat on the baby?"

"Patagonia?"

"That's Miguel. Food for this family. Clothing for that one. A new cart or livestock, here and there. Occasionally, a new house. What he can't buy here in support of the local economy, he brings in from elsewhere. Everyone knows Don Miguel." Lucas's eyes softened, and Sydney found herself mesmerized by the change in his countenance. For that brief moment, he almost looked like the man from her past. Her husband. Emily's daddy.

In that instant it dawned on her. "You're not searching for the Fountain of Youth. What is it, then?"

"It's called the Temple of the Rain."

"I've never heard of it or Manco Capac's silver bowl."

He said nothing, merely gazed back into her eyes with something akin to distrust.

"Lucas, tell me."

"Most people have heard the legend of how Manco Capac and his sister sealed their brother, Ayar Kachi, in a cave, but an old Quechua man finally told me why they did it."

"Why?"

"Because they couldn't kill Kachi." He

covered his face in his hands. "Several Quechua elders verified the details of the legend, but you're going to think this is nuts."

"No. I won't."

He let go a long sigh, and then continued. "Ayar Kachi wanted to be king, but the people followed Manco Capac. So Kachi, thinking he would win over the hearts of the people, stole Manco's silver bowl. Kachi then convinced many sick and dying Inca and a Kallawaya, a physician to the kings, to travel with him deep into the Peruvian rain forest and search for the Temple of the Rain." He paused and looked straight at Sydney. "Where the tears of the gods were said to fall from the heavens. Anyone who drank those tears from Manco's bowl would live forever."

"Sounds like a fountain of youth to me."

"But the legend goes on. Kachi found the temple, drank from Manco's bowl and returned for the throne, claiming to have healed his followers, and, indeed, they were said to have visited their relatives in dreams, happy and healthy. Manco Capac and his sister were enraged at Kachi and his false promises, but try as they might, they could not kill him."

"So they sealed him in a cave," she finished for him. "And the bowl?"

"Kachi left it in the temple, fearing betrayal."

"So that's what Cochran is after? A silver bowl and tears from heaven?"

Lucas nodded.

"What do you think is there? At this Temple of the Rain?"

"I'm not sure, but I'd planned on bringing in an ethnobotanist to collect plant specimens from the surrounding area. And hope to find the silver bowl or other *qeros,* or ceremonial vessels, that might have held healing tonics or medicinal potions."

"A cure for cancer," she murmured. "You're looking for a cure for cancer."

The room fell silent for a long time. The pain and agony of loss were still etched on his face after all these years. Time melted away and he was her daughter's father all over again. She remembered so well the conflicting emotions, the responsibility for a child that only a parent can feel, coupled with the complete and utter helplessness to do anything to save her life. "Lucas, Emily dying wasn't your fault."

He looked away. "But Trevor's kidnapping is."

CHAPTER TEN

BY THE TIME Sydney and Lucas had finished cleaning the kitchen, the sun had set below the horizon. Miguel had no sooner taken care of the little baby than another local woman came to the door, this one pregnant and in need of a checkup. While they remained behind closed doors in the other room, fatigue settled on Sydney's shoulders.

"Come on." Lucas picked up their bags and walked down a hall toward the back end of the house. "We need to get some sleep if we're to head out first thing in the morning."

"We're staying here?" she asked.

"Miguel wouldn't have it any other way, but there are only two bedrooms. That one is Miguel's." He nodded toward the right. He walked through the doorway of the room on the left and threw her bag on the only bed, a double. "If you want, I can sleep on the couch."

She thought of him stretched out in that airplane seat. "It's okay. You take the…left side. I'll take the right," she said, reversing the pattern they'd shared while married. Admitting she still slept on the left seemed too personal.

"I thought you'd want the…" He paused, as if he, too, remembered. "Never mind." He tossed his bag down and dug through it. "There's a bathroom at the end of the hall. I'll wash up in the kitchen."

She pulled out toiletries and fresh clothes, locked herself in the bathroom and brushed her teeth. Far past an overtired state, her mind buzzed with all that had happened in the last two days. How Lucas could have any energy at all after more than a day and a half of travel was beyond her. Of course, some of that had to do with the fact that he'd been unconscious much of the time. While sleep had eluded her during the interminable flights, it had claimed Lucas as though it owned him. She'd caught herself watching him several times. He hadn't looked any more at peace with his eyes closed than he did fully awake and operational.

At one point, he'd awakened and caught her gaze upon him. Understanding had flowed from him like a summer breeze after a long, cold winter, cocooning her in warmth. "He'll be all right," he'd whispered.

At that tired, strung-out moment, Sydney had wanted nothing more than to reach out and hold his hand, or, better yet, cuddle up in front of him. She would have found peace with his arms enfolding her and his body curled around her. There, sleep would have easily claimed her.

When Emily had been dying, Sydney had sought solace in so many places. Friends—they meant well. Church—please. Her mother—not in this lifetime. The only peace to be found had been in Lucas's arms. Arms so strong and giving, they could have comforted the entire children's wing of the hospital. He'd always known what to say, when to say nothing, and when to cross a room to hold her. Even making love with him, whether gentle or frantic, had refilled Sydney's cup in a way nothing else could.

Good thing on that airplane he'd finally lowered his head and fallen back into oblivion, eliminating any possibility of her making a complete fool of herself. How could so many years of bitterness dissolve in less than thirty-six hours? Her anger had been her armor. Now, she felt vulnerable and defenseless, and it scared the hell out of her. She was tired, she reminded herself. Her armor would be back in place, good as new, following a restful night's sleep.

After washing her face and changing into a T-shirt and boxers, she padded back to the bedroom. Though dark, she could make out Lucas's form under the covers, his bare shoulder contrasting sharply with the beige-and-white quilt. Thankfully, he faced away from her.

She scooted as far to her edge of the bed as possible and lay quietly for a moment, getting used to the mattress. She couldn't get comfortable. This was too weird, sleeping in the same bed with her ex-husband. She flopped onto her back. It didn't work. The look of his tanned skin against the pale bedding had been etched into her mind. She bunched up the soft down pillow and turned onto her side. Nope. Fifteen minutes and several adjustments later she was still awake. So was Lucas.

"Are you cold?" he asked.

"A little." With the sun gone, the mountain air felt downright chilly.

He unfolded a heavy, red alpaca blanket

from the end of the bed and smoothed it over her. The added weight and warmth felt good, but she could think of a different kind of heat that would have felt even better. The back of his fingers grazed her cheek, and she found herself leaning into him, seeking comfort from his touch. She wanted him, and she didn't even care that he knew it.

He lingered for a moment, then pulled away with a long sigh. "Try to relax. You'll sleep."

"Spoken by the man who can sleep practically anywhere." She tried to lighten the mood. "God, I envied you on our flight down here. Other than to get that blanket, you haven't moved a muscle since I came into the room."

"You've been shifting and grunting enough for both of us. If you lie quiet—" he dropped his voice to a low hush "—and listen to the night sounds of the mountain, bet you'll be asleep in minutes."

Under normal circumstances, he would have been right. But this situation didn't come close to normal. She stared at the white, stucco wall, her eyes unfocused. And, she knew with a sinking feeling in her stomach, there was only one thing that would calm her.

Still, she gave it a valiant effort, taking a deep breath and exhaling slowly, closing her eyes and listening. Miguel moved quietly through the house. Some kind of animal, maybe a cow or pig, made a soft snuffling noise outside. Instead of calming her, the sounds seemed to grow in intensity, setting her on edge. She fidgeted, adjusting her pillow, moving positions, pushing aside the blanket, then pulling it back.

"Oh, for crying out loud," Lucas muttered. He rolled over and in one swift movement tucked her against him and into his arms. "There. Now we can both sleep."

At first her spine stiffened, then the sensation of being held by him again after all these years, the heat of his body against her backside, the heavy weight of him, his muscles hard and yielding at the same time, came over her like a balm, settling her. The warm, soft skin of his inner arm soothed her cheek, and, with every breath he took, her tension slipped away. Lucas fixed everything.

She closed her eyes and sighed, her muscles melting into him, her body wanting him. Good thing she was too tired to do anything about it.

SHE WAS OUT. Dead to the world.

Lucas carefully maneuvered his arm out from under her head, sat up and glanced down at her face. A thin line of starlight angled across her patrician features, softening them, making her appear tranquil and completely at ease.

He touched the tip of his finger to her full upper lip and yearning ignited inside him. It had been six years since he'd had Sydney's body beneath his hands, six years since any woman had touched him with tenderness. How tempted he was to put his mouth to her neck, to breathe her in, to wake her and become a part of her again. In her arms, in her life, all would be set right for him. But at what cost to her?

Too much. He would always cost her far too much.

Quietly, he stood and left the room. Needing a physical outlet, he went directly to the shed in back where Miguel let him store all of his gear. He yanked out a tent, sleeping bags, pads, lanterns, a stove, huge packs to store supplies and everything else he thought he might need for the trip ahead.

Every time Sydney's image came into his mind he did his best to blot it out, working harder and faster, shoving gear into packs and lugging them toward the carport out front. Back and forth, over and over.

A pack slipped off the shelf and a revolver fell onto the ground. Lucas picked up the gun—his gun—and stared at the smooth black metal, the weight strangely comfortable in his hand. There was a time when he had considered it an answer of sorts, a time when he believed it would have put him out of his own misery and protect everyone else from his inevitable mistakes.

He rested his forehead against the flat of the barrel and closed his eyes. The image came out of nowhere. It always did, blindsiding him. His father lying dead on the ground, a semicircle of blood surrounding his head, brain matter spattered against a wall. There had to be something different out there for Lucas. Something he was missing. He grappled for anything to hold on to, anything that gave him a reason for being.

Trevor. He was the key. Lucas had to get him back home to Sydney. He had to stay focused in order to find the temple and Manco Capac's Huari bowl and make everything all right again. He took a heavy breath and let the gun lie flat in his palm.

Miguel's footfalls sounded in the darkness. He came up beside Lucas and took a long, silent look at the gun in his hand. "I thought I might find you out here. You should be in that bedroom with your wife."

"She's not my wife anymore." Lucas went back to the business of packing.

"A piece of paper can't destroy bonds of the heart, the soul."

"You always were a romantic."

"And you always did, as you Americans say, have your head stuck up your ass."

Lucas clenched his jaw. "Stay out of it, Miguel."

"I've done all I can. You want to ruin your life, I won't stop you."

Lucas swallowed. "I still need you to do something for me."

"Name it."

"Cochran can't make it to Machu Picchu tomorrow morning."

"Consider it done." Miguel picked up a pack and started walking with Lucas back to the house. "You will be long gone before he sets foot on that sacred ground."

"One more thing." Lucas stopped and looked off into the distant night. "I need weapons. Several guns. And whatever ammunition you can get your hands on."

Miguel glanced at the gun already in his hand and said quietly, "Do you think that is wise?"

Sometimes he wished Miguel didn't know so damned much about him. "It's for Sydney's protection. But I still wouldn't think twice about putting a bullet in Cochran's head if I get the chance."

"Lucas, my friend, you are an archaeologist, not a soldier. A teacher, not a killer."

"Trevor is my son, Miguel. *Mine.* What would you do?"

MOST OF THE DAY Evelyn had been one step, both figuratively and literally, behind Joe Donati. Though they'd visited more than twenty bars, businesses and homes in the Tacoma area, they were no closer to finding Trevor. Few people remembered Phillip Cochran, and those who did wouldn't have thought twice about turning him in to any authority wanting a piece of his sorry butt. Even Cochran's parents.

Finally, they'd called it a night and returned to Evelyn's well after dark. "I need to grab my bag, then I'll head to a hotel." Joe walked toward the guest room.

"I'd rather you stayed here."

He glanced back, an eyebrow raised. "Whaddya got in mind, Evie?" All day he'd been doing this, picking her up with funny anecdotes, distracting her with come-ons.

And all day she'd let him. "Don't get your hopes up, big guy. You're staying in that guest bedroom. Alone."

"We can do better than that, can't we?"

She followed him down the hall. "Don't you have more work you can do?"

He tossed his suit coat into the guest room and turned toward her, loosening his tie. "Not much more I can do tonight. We might as well…unwind."

Sex, sex, sex. He was worse than her. But they were not happening as long as Trevor was out there. She didn't even want to think about where he might be sleeping. "Look. Let's just call a spade, a spade, okay. I'm not jumping into bed with you tonight."

"How 'bout tomorrow night?"

She shook her head, chuckling. "Never give up, do you?"

"Not when I see something I want."

"Trust me, Joe, I wouldn't be any fun right now, but after you get Trevor back…you and me…best night of your life."

He ran his palm over his mouth, then

smoothed down the day's growth of stubble on his cheeks. "You worth the wait?"

"What do you think?"

He chuckled. "Truth is, I've met women before…*kidda fimmina bella. Pari na baruna.*" His voice, wary yet laced with longing, melted like warm honey down her neck. "They have classy clothes, perfect makeup, expensive jewelry. They're all wrapped up like a package, pretty and seductive."

He skimmed the neckline of her sweater and let his index finger linger near her collarbone. "They make you think you'll burn your fingertips by touching them." He pulled his hand away as if he'd been scalded. "You get them into bed and turns out all they care about is what a man can do for them." He looked her up and down, assessing her. "No offense, Evie, but you strike me as that kind of woman."

No doubt she was most of the time. "It won't be that way with you."

"Prove it."

Staring straight into his eyes, she backed him against the wall, leaned into him and settled herself over his leg. He splayed his hands at his sides, a silent promise not to touch her even as the muscles of his thigh stiffened beneath her.

Heat and need rushed from the ends of her toes to the tips of her lips as she kissed his neck, softly, deliberately. Then she moved to the corner of his mouth and dipped her tongue into him. He groaned as if her touch truly burned him and bent his head, allowing their kiss to deepen. He tasted of that peppermint gum he was constantly chewing, of promise and patience, and, amazingly, she wanted more.

Only not tonight. She pulled away.

"Maybe I was wrong about you." His hands were bunched in fists against the wall, and his chest rose and fell a little harder and faster. "Want to wait until this is over, huh?"

"The sooner you get Trevor back, safe and sound, the sooner you get to find out just how worth it I am."

"Safe and sound. I can do that."

She closed the door to her bedroom, putting an inch and a half of six-paneled cherrywood between them. Seconds later, she heard his fingers flying over his laptop keyboard.

CHAPTER ELEVEN

SYDNEY AWOKE EARLY to the sound of Lucas moving quietly about the room. She remained still, not even cracking open her eyes. Man, did that bring back a few loaded memories. She'd usually slept later than he had during most of their first year together. Probably had something to do with her being pregnant and him teaching early classes at the university. He'd come to her before he left and put his ear to her stomach. Run his hands through her hair, kiss her neck. So many times he'd ended up undressed and back in bed.

Rebelling against the memories, she snapped open her eyes. Mistake. He was less than six feet away, naked except for a pair of boxers, but thankfully oblivious to her awakened state. She should have closed her eyes, given him privacy, but the sight of his body, highlighted by the first rays of sun filtering through the window, fascinated her. The husband she remembered had a healthy, attractive physique, but the man standing here now was stronger, leaner. The professor had been replaced by an active archaeologist.

He slipped on a pair of hiking pants, stretched, then ran his hands through his sleep-tousled hair, causing his shoulder muscles to bulge and flex. He pulled a sweater over his head and covered his chest, but longing already stirred inside her, low and deep. She'd learned every nuance of his marvelous body, and he'd awakened hers to slow pleasures and intense sensations. While their nights had been filled with fun explorations and fiery passion, their mornings had been steeped with sleepy, raw emotion. He'd always said such lovely things at daybreak, leaving her feeling cherished for the rest of the day.

Now, he sat on the edge of the bed, nearly close enough to touch, and bent down to tie his boots. When he straightened, his gaze caught hers and held. She fought to turn away, but the look in his eyes kept her locked in place. He remembered, too. He stood and brushed his hand over the top of her head. The touch seemed so innocent, so nonchalant, and still it sent a tremor down her spine. "Stay," she almost said.

"We'll be heading out as soon as we finish breakfast." Thank heavens he left the room.

She dressed quickly, ate even faster, and they were out the door and on their way to Ollantaytambo in Miguel's old pickup. By the time they made their way to the market square Sydney was wide awake, and there was a lot to see. The entire village was so old that a few of the buildings were ancient Inca stonework and many had been built over Inca foundations. She studied every cobbled street and narrow stone-walled alleyway, absorbing each glimpse of unusual architecture.

They passed a market displaying bushels of fresh carrots, potatoes, bananas and peppers where villagers were already running about their day's business. It was cloudy and chilly yet, and while some of the younger women wore sweatshirts or jackets, a few of the older women wore bright, multicolored wool. "The women's ponchos are so beautiful," she said.

"Men wear ponchos." Lucas yawned. "Women wear what's called a *manta.*"

"What's with the hats?" she asked. They

were black and red and curiously inverted. Trevor would have gotten a kick out of them. He loved any kind of hat.

"It indicates they're villagers of Ollantaytambo. In Chinchero, it might be fedoras. In Lamay, it could be alpaca stocking caps with a traditional woven pattern."

They left the village center and pulled into a parking lot. "From here we take a train to Aguas Calientes at the base of Machu Picchu." After grabbing a duffel bag containing the makeshift wooden staff and the sun god, he hopped out of the truck.

As she followed him toward the station, a sense of loss overwhelmed her. She wished she'd come to Peru for a different reason than finding an ancient temple. She wished she could have stayed for a day in Ollantaytambo. She wished she could explore. With Lucas and Trevor. The thought made her dizzy. She dragged several deep breaths into her lungs.

"Altitude still bothering you?" he asked, turning toward her. "Don't worry, you should acclimate by this afternoon."

Right. She would never acclimate to anything with him nearby. "I'll be fine," she said, waving him on.

She spent the entire train ride to Aquas Calientes, the tiny village at the base of Machu Picchu's mountain, focusing on the symbols from Manco Capac's staff. She was fairly certain of her original conclusions on the first two lines, but the exact meaning of the last line, while it also had something to do with a river, was unclear. The meaning of the main glyph, the most complicated of all, heading the three rows, eluded her. She would have guessed it would signify the Temple of the Rain, but the picture of the profile of a disfigured face over a box with four evenly spaced circles, made no sense.

When the train stopped, she stuffed the fry box in her pocket and jumped down onto a dirt platform along with Lucas and several other tourists. The locals called out and held up their wares, brightly woven blankets and ponchos, attempting to entice buyers. Lucas sped past them and headed toward a line of buses. They joined a throng of tourists paying fares and climbed aboard for the remainder of their journey.

"Are there always this many tourists?" she asked.

"Believe it or not, today appears to be a light day."

Though the bus was as modern as they come, they made slow progress on the gravel road, forced to wind back and forth on switchbacks tighter than any Sydney had ever experienced. She kept quiet and faced forward. One look out the window and the steep drop, coupled with leftover altitude sickness, and she had little doubt she would have tossed her cookies on the spot.

"We'll be there soon," Lucas reassured her. Before long, they pulled into a gravel parking lot and everyone filed off the bus. "It'd better clear up, or we're in trouble." Lucas took off on a footpath leading them even higher up the mountain and directly into the ancient city of Machu Picchu.

If the clouds hung any lower, they'd end up hiking through them. They needed sunshine to find the map. A gust of wind blew several tendrils of her hair free from her clip. "Maybe the wind will blow the clouds clear."

"Or we'll be back tomorrow."

"And so will Cochran." She struggled to keep up with Lucas, but once again the altitude slowed her down. "How high are we?"

"About eight thousand feet. It's not as bad as Cusco."

Well, that certainly made her feel better. She struggled for air and trudged over the stone steps that had been laid by Inca hands more than five hundred years earlier. One after another, agricultural terraces lined either side of their path. They climbed even higher to find a row of little stone houses with replicated thatched roofs. Just when she thought she could handle no more, Lucas stopped. "This is it."

She found herself surrounded by row after row of stone walls, houses, terraces and temples. A lone tree stood sentinel in what may have been a central gathering court.

"We need to be in the Three-Windowed Temple."

As if he knew the layout of this place better than the back of his hand, he strode across the ancient village. Had their trip served a different purpose, Sydney would have dawdled for the entire day, pondering this incredible spectacle, picking his brain about the different dwellings and other structures, but not today. Today she hiked after him and barely looked around.

Once inside a stone enclosure, across an open area and up a series of steep, narrow steps, he stopped again. "It doesn't look like much, but this was probably one of the most sacred Inca temples." Unusually large windows faced east, framing Huayna Picchu, Machu Picchu's mountain sister, and the mountains beyond a vast river valley. He dropped his bag on the ground, took out the wooden dowel, handed her the sun god, and walked around the site looking for something. "We're early. We've got some time for the sky to clear. Did you decipher any more of the symbols?"

"No. Do you know what to do with the staff?"

"Miguel told me about the legend, but he didn't have specifics. I was hoping we'd find some clue when we got here." He shook his head. "We may need Gonzalo."

"What's a Gonzalo?"

"Not what. Who." Lucas smiled for the first time since they'd arrived in South America. "Gonzalo's a Machu Picchu shaman. He'll be around here somewhere if we get desperate."

Sydney looked around the stone enclosure. They were alone. They had the sun god and the staff. All they needed was sun. She folded her hands over the little statue, looked up into the sky, and said a prayer to God, to the powers that be, to anyone who would listen.

"You here again, my friend." A Peruvian, his straight black hair blowing with the breeze, walked slowly into the temple.

Lucas glanced up. "Well, speak of the devil. *Buenos días,* Don Gonzalo."

The man smiled at Sydney. "This is your first time at Machu Picchu?" He spoke the name with a reverence she had never before heard, enunciating the syllables like an actor on a stage. "You came here with our Lucas?"

"Yes."

He cocked his head. "You, too, have come here for answers."

"I'm not sure what you mean."

"You have been called. Like most who come here." He nodded, studying her face. "I tell most to look toward Mother Earth for their answers. Not Lucas. All his answers are inside." He held a hand over his own heart. "But he doesn't listen." He saw the sun god and reached out with both hands.

Lucas nodded, so she handed it to Gonzalo.

"Inti Titi." He smiled and beheld the statue with softened eyes and open hands. "Where did you get this?"

"Madrid."

"Ahhh, booty of the mighty conquista-dors." Gonzalo grinned, exposing amazingly white teeth. "Inti smiled upon you. Yes?"

"Once upon a time. Maybe," Sydney said.

"He will smile on you again." He looked over his shoulder. "And on Lucas."

"Gonzalo, give it a rest." Lucas shook his head.

"Do you think you will find what you are looking for today?" he asked Lucas.

"I think this is finally it."

"And if not, then what?"

"Then I start all over again."

Gonzalo mulled over the response. He looked down at the statue, back at Sydney, and finally rested his gaze on Lucas. "You have the staff?"

Lucas nodded. "I have something that simulates the staff's general length and diameter."

He strode a few paces in to the far wall, eyed his position, and said, "It goes here. At noon."

A thought occurred to Sydney. "Gonzalo, if you know where to find the Temple of the Rain, why don't you go there yourself?"

"You're barking up the wrong tree, Syd." Lucas shook his head. "He has no interest. Neither does Miguel."

"The Quechua do not need physical evidence of our past to understand its secrets," Gonzalo said. "This is a gringo's journey." He took several more steps, stopped at the middle of the temple, and looked toward Lucas. "This will show you a path, Lucas. And while you may not find all the answers you seek, you *will* find a truth. If you look hard enough."

"Sydney, show him the symbols."

She held out the French fry box. "What do these mean?"

"That, I do not know."

"Three pillars on a river? Does that mean anything?"

Gonzalo nodded. "Three markers along the path. That is the legend. The last marker leads to the temple."

With two of the lines figured out, the other line and the title might begin to gel. "Now we need the sun," Sydney said.

"Can't help with that." Gonzalo shrugged. "I'm not a miracle worker."

"Ha." Lucas chuckled. "Changing the weather is one of the first things an Andean shaman learns when he's initiated *pam-pamesayoq*." As Lucas said it, the wind picked up. In seconds the wispy low-lying clouds cleared and the sun glared through each of the windows, immediately warming the rock enclosure.

She glanced at Gonzalo, his easy manner spooking her. "What about the sun god?"

"Inti Titi?"

"What do we do with it?"

Gonzalo shrugged. "You do not need him to find the temple. All you need is the staff."

"Miguel said—" Lucas stopped and clenched his jaw.

"Don Miguel knows what questions you need answered. Better than you do yourself." Gonzalo disappeared through the narrow entrance to the temple and out of sight.

Lucas's eyes flashed. "Miguel's got some explaining to do."

"Does that mean all of this was for nothing?" she cried. "You came to Seattle, and Trevor's been kidnapped for nothing?"

He shook his head. "I didn't know. I'm sorry, Sydney."

"Quit apologizing, all right?" She shook it off and looked at her watch. "It's noon. Let's do this and get out of here." Though there was no denying the power of Machu Picchu, there was nothing magical about the place for Sydney. In fact, it was downright spooky.

Lucas pulled the staff from his bag in quick, angry movements and stood where Gonzalo had been. The sun was close, but not directly overhead this time of year. The staff projected a shadow against the temple wall, and Lucas studied it. There was nothing to see, merely a dark, straight line of shadow against the light rock wall. "This doesn't make any sense."

Sydney stepped closer. As the sun shifted, the shadow bent ever so slightly to the right. She touched the wall. "Look at the shadow," she said. "Do you see the way the contour of the wall bends and twists it with the angle change of the sun?"

"So what? It doesn't mean…"

They both watched as the sun moved a bit more and the shadow of the staff shifted more abruptly. "Where would the sun be if it was summer solstice?" she asked, keyed up.

"Right about there." He pointed at a spot a tad higher in the sky. "That means to compensate, we need to put the staff…right about here." He moved the staff a few inches to the right. Nothing changed on the face of the wall. Then the shadow slowly shifted again, eventually bending more than sixty degrees and dramatically altering its original position. "That looks so familiar."

"Do you know where this is?" Sydney sounded desperate. She knew it, and she didn't care.

"Wait a minute! It looks like…it's a river! The Urubamba." They'd found the map.

Excited, Sydney pulled out her map of Peru, attempting to identify the area. "Where's this Uruwhatever?"

Lucas's eyes never strayed from the wall. "East and north of Cusco. Through the valley," he spoke absently.

"I can't find it."

"Forget that map! Come here and hold the staff. Quick! Before the sun moves." She grabbed the staff. He moved to the wall, studying it intently. There was a pattern to the indentations and cracks in the rock face. Someone had taken great pains in laying out the design. From what Sydney had seen so far of the walls and buildings at Machu Picchu and in Ollantaytambo the Inca were nothing if not meticulous.

"I think I know where this is." The pattern came together. "If the shadow of the staff is the Urubamba River, then see this ridge in the rock face that hits the shadow at a perpendicular angle? And the opening the shadow passes through? That's the Pongo. Pongo De Mainique. A canyon. The only break in the Vilcabamba mountain range. And this spot here, where this indentation joins the shadow? That's where the Timpia River joins the Urubamba."

He stepped back and the river and their map disappeared. The sun had moved only minimally, but because of the abrupt changes in the wall face, the shadow returned to its straight-line shape.

"It's gone," Sydney whispered. "Did you see enough?"

"Shh." He took out a notebook and sketched the map from memory. When he finished, he held it up. "What do you think?"

"It's perfect. But the three pillar markers. Did you see them on the wall?"

"No. I was too focused on identifying the river location." He walked to the wall and ran his hands over the section where the shadow of the staff had created their map. "Feel this."

She crossed to his side, and he put his hand over hers, directing her touch. One. Two. Three. She felt them. High points on the face of the wall. "Can you remember where they were on the map?"

He stood back. "No. Dammit! But I think the first one was here. Near Timpia."

"Gonzalo? Should we find him again?"

"He won't know. And we can't wait another day for the sun to pass in this exact spot again."

"So now what?"

"Now we head for Timpia." He left the Three-Windowed Temple and went to the ruin's edge. "And we find the end of the staff."

"And where is that?"

"Over there." He pointed northeast. "A pilot can fly us to Timpia, but from there, we're on our own down the Urubamba."

The face of the cliff they stood at dropped some eight hundred feet to the river below. Green mountains rose like giant, pointy tombstones from the base of the valley. Some were so high they were shrouded in clouds. The valleys themselves were covered in a wilderness so thick there didn't seem to be any passageway. It looked impenetrable, impossible. And it was the only way to find the temple. And the silver bowl.

For Trevor.

CHAPTER TWELVE

THE MINGLING SCENTS of bacon and freshly brewed coffee woke Evelyn the next morning. Her thoughts flew to the man in her kitchen and their encounter at her bedroom door the previous evening. She rubbed the spot near her collarbone where his fingertip had settled against her skin, remembered the way his eyes had assessed her, and a hunger that had nothing to do with breakfast assaulted her. Pots and pans weren't all Agent Joe Donati was stirring.

With a soft sigh, she hopped up, crossed to her bathroom and assessed herself in the mirror. Normally, she had rules about appearing *au naturel* in front of men, but she was guessing Joe would actually appreciate the look of a fresh-from-bed woman. Gathering her hair into a messy bun, she slipped into an apricot silk robe and adjusted the neckline to expose a bit of cleavage. Thought she was all show and no action, did he? She couldn't wait for the chance to prove him wrong.

Padding barefoot out to the kitchen, she found Joe seated at the breakfast bar, his laptop positioned in front of him. A half-eaten plate of scrambled eggs and bacon sat off to the side, along with toast and orange juice. He glanced up when her feet slapped against the cool Spanish tiles of the kitchen floor, and all thoughts of seduction instantly flew her mind. Gone was the flippant, sexy agent at her bedroom door last night. In his place sat a tired and stressed-looking man. Dark circles marred the pale skin under his bloodshot eyes, and concentration furrowed his brow and set his lips in a thin, stubborn line.

At once, pangs of guilt set in. Here was a man who had selflessly dropped everything to jump on a plane and come to the aid of an old friend, risking maybe not tremendous, but at least modest ramifications in his job.

She opened her mouth to ask him what he was doing when the transformation in his face as he scanned her full length finally registered. His pupils darkened, and his lips eased into a grin. Lack of sleep apparently hadn't dampened his libido. His gaze settled on the cleavage she'd so artfully displayed, and his intensity gradually shifted from work toward a different, yet no less purposeful goal. Sex. The low-down dirty kind.

A cozy feeling swelled in her chest as she realized she'd been right. He did enjoy the look of her, bed-head and all. She poured herself a cup of coffee. "Good morning, Joe."

"Yes, it is." His grin deepened.

At the more arrogant than normal tone to his voice, she spun around. "You found something."

"It wasn't easy. Followed a trail of five different Cochran-owned subsidiaries in and out of their various holdings, but I finally got it."

"Tell me." She dropped into the chair across from him.

"Cochran owns a lot of property in the Pacific Northwest." He tossed her two pages worth of real estate holdings.

She scanned the list and found everything from mountain hideaways near Spokane to coastal investment property. "It'll take a week to check out all these locations."

"We can narrow it down."

"How?"

"There had to be a reason Cochran met Lucas and Sydney on a boat. Why he chose Vashon Island as an exchange point." Joe flipped his laptop closed. "You don't get seasick, do you?"

"WHAT ARE YOU GOING TO DO?" Sydney jumped out of the truck and followed Lucas into Miguel's house.

Ignoring her, he searched every room, his movements sharp and hostile.

"Let it go, Lucas," she said after him. "Let's just pack our stuff and head out to this Urubamba river."

"We can't until morning," he grated between clenched teeth. "It's too late in the day to cross the mountains."

Finally, he stalked out back and they found Miguel in a small barn, showing a group of villagers how to use some new equipment for shearing alpacas. Lucas grabbed the front of Miguel's shirt and backed him up against the nearest wall. "Why? I want to know why." The surrounding village men surrounded Lucas. Sydney got the impression that one word from Miguel and Lucas was dead meat. Lucas didn't seem to care. Miguel signaled for the men to back off.

"Lucas, relax." Sydney walked up and touched his shoulder. "He didn't mean any harm."

"Our son's in danger because he lied to me."

"I was wrong," Miguel said, his dark eyes clouding with remorse. "I'm sorry, dear friend."

"Sorry? That's it?"

"It's good that you are angry with me. I am angry with me." Miguel's voice grew quiet. "I should have told you yesterday, but you know why I did it, Lucas. Do you really wish me to speak of it with everyone present?"

At that Lucas let go his grip on Miguel's shirt and released him entirely. He paced for a few minutes, his head bent, and then he pulled the sun god from his jacket pocket, took one quick look at it and let it fall to the ground. "That sun god is worthless. Always was. Always will be."

Sydney watched him stalk away and disappear up the path toward an ancient terrace. Typical. Still holding down his every emotion with an iron fist. He had done this with everything from teaching his classes to dealing with an irate driver on the freeway. Still controlling himself, measuring his responses, weighing his reactions. In every one of his dealings.

Except for one. The way he'd loved her. That'd been the only time Lucas had ever seemed to let himself go, let himself—and her—feel his raw, unchecked emotions. Sometimes it had even been too much, it had been so strong. If his emotions had hurt *her*, how had they affected Lucas?

The possible answer to that question stunned her. She thought she'd known him, understood him, tied up all the loose ends and stuffed him in a box. Maybe she'd been wrong again.

Uncertain, she turned to Miguel. "Why did you tell him he needed the sun god?"

Miguel sighed and readjusted his shirt. He said something in Quechua to the men around him and they quickly dispersed, leaving Miguel and Sydney alone. "I've known Lucas many years, shared many experiences, been like brothers, and still I have a feeling that I do not know the real man."

"You and me both."

"But I've been lucky enough to catch glimpses of him." He sent away the alpaca he'd been shearing and cleaned off the tools. "Most of the time Lucas is…all business.

Places to go, people to see, things to do. Only a few times have I seen someone different. Right here. Around a late-night fire." He pointed toward the fire pit off the side of the house, where chopped blocks of tree trunks were arranged in a circle as makeshift seating. "Not a drop of *cusquena* or *pisco,* and he has opened up. I have seen a man who laughs often and easily from his belly. A man who lifts his face to the flames of the fire, to the midnight moon and sky full of stars and opens his arms, his heart, to the world." He paused, staring at her, and when he spoke again, his voice was quiet, almost a whisper. "You had to have known this man, Sydney. This man loved you."

She remembered. She'd tried to forget in the wake of the pain Lucas had caused her, but the truth always hung in her heart, never letting her forget. The man she'd met, the man she'd fallen in love with, wasn't the man who'd left her.

"I think," Miguel said, continuing, "that the real Lucas is not like most men. He feels too deeply. He experiences everything with much force, much clarity. He cannot be simply happy, he is ecstatic. When he is sad, he is not merely unhappy, he is despondent, inconsolable. And when he loves, it is with passion and strength, with his full heart engaged."

Sydney looked away. That love had been hers. Pain erupted all over again, as if it was only this morning she'd woken up to find him gone. "What's this have to do with the sun god? With me?"

"You must know."

"No, I don't. I don't know Lucas anymore."

"This is true." Miguel studied her. "I have seen only bits and pieces of your Lucas. All the time I have known him he has kept that man locked up, immersing himself in shadows and gloom." He packed the last of the tools into a case and closed the lid. "I think he hopes the darkness will temper him, protect him. Instead," he said, throwing the equipment onto a shelf and turning, "it's killing him."

"Why are you telling me this?"

"Because *you* are his light."

Sydney snorted. "Well, then, he must not have told you. *He* left *me*."

"He told me. He tries to be honest." Miguel nodded. "But sometimes when he speaks the truth you must hear around the words and listen with your heart. Sometimes our Lucas, he's like the llama. Raise your hand to pet him, to cuddle his ears, and as much as he craves your attention, he spits at you."

She said nothing, trying to make sense of what he was saying.

"So one night, a few months ago, when he told me about finding a sun god statue on your honeymoon and that you still had it—" Miguel walked toward her "—I lied. Told him it was the key to his quest. Which is true, in a way. I did not know there was now another child. I'm sorry."

She picked up the sun god where it lay discarded in the dirt, and brushed off the dust. The shaman may have been wrong about this spirit shining down upon them, but she couldn't get herself to leave it behind. Holding the benign little figure in her hand made her want to find Lucas, to go after him and get some answers.

"I need to talk to him." She started toward the path up the mountain.

Miguel touched her arm. "I think that would be unwise."

"Why?"

"One day Lucas will learn how to stay and

fight." Miguel turned her around and directed her toward the house. "Today is not that day."

CHAPTER THIRTEEN

THE RICH, BUOYANT SOUNDS of Peruvian music hung in the early evening air, floating up the hill toward Lucas on a cool mountain breeze. He sat alone on a rock at the edge of a steep gorge not far from Miguel's house and listened to the locals celebrating. The soothing call of the *antara,* Andean panpipes, mixed with the folkish strains of an acoustic guitar and the quiet backbeat of a single hand drum.

He only listened, distant and separate, feeling no more a part of what transpired behind him than he felt a part of life in general. That was his usual story, after all, standing on the outside looking in, the last six years of his life, anyway. He breathed. He ate. He slept. He may have done it while traveling the world, but that didn't change the fact that he woke up and went through it all over again, day after day.

Normally, that routine was fine with him, an existence with no highs or lows, no edges, seams or breaks. It felt reassuring in its emptiness. Yet a small part of him knew there was something treacherous in that comfort, as if daylight had spilled through a thin crack, giving him a split-second glimpse of what he'd once been and what he'd become.

The mountain air suddenly felt cold on his neck, and he flung his head back to stare at the sky. Only high in the unpopulated Peruvian mountains could one see this kind of spectacle, the blackest drop cloth imaginable brilliantly dotted with never-ending pinpricks of light.

Behind him, the music quieted and Sydney's laughter drifted up on a gust of wind. The sound of it, alive and real, mixing with the music and conversation and permeating the still night air, drew him around like a beacon on this dark, lonely night. He sat there quietly and watched her, sitting near the campfire with Miguel and several others.

Apparently, Miguel had healed an important elder in the community, and they'd built a bonfire at the edge of the yard in his honor. Not that any of it mattered to Lucas. All he cared about at the moment was the way

Sydney's face looked bathed in the flickering yellow-orange firelight. A bottle of *cusquena* dangling from one hand, she looked genuinely relaxed for the first time since he'd reappeared in her life. Her mouth curved in a smile as Miguel delighted her with some anecdote.

He found himself wanting to make her laugh like that, wanting to be a part of what was happening around that fire. Life. A real one. What would it feel like after all these years? Before he could change his mind, he unfolded his cramped legs, stood up, and headed down the hill, keeping his sights on Sydney.

Halfway there, a noise in the brush made him pause. It might have been an animal. Or, a thought struck him, something worse. Cochran. No, he couldn't have found them this quickly.

When Lucas reached the group surrounding the fire, the chatter stalled. A few of the locals glared at him uneasily, clearly protective of their Miguel.

"Lucas!" Miguel stood and greeted him with a hearty slap on the back. "I knew you would come."

The locals eased and went back to their

conversations and the group of musicians started a slow, melancholy song. Lucas took the bottle of water Miguel extended and sat on the tree stump on the other side of Sydney. "You must be starving," she said.

"I'm fine. I'll eat in a bit." Lucas exposed his chilled hands to the heat of the fire.

"I'll bring something out for you." She began to stand.

"Ah, ah, ah." Miguel settled her back down. "You are guests at my house. I will get him some food."

Sydney chuckled as Miguel disappeared. "Guests. Right. He wanted you and me to be alone."

"Already you know Miguel well." Lucas grinned. "A little misdirected at times, but he's a good man."

"And an excellent friend."

The look in her eyes was so pure, so honest, so naive. Miguel had been right. Lucas never, ever, would have gone back to her. Shame and guilt had kept him away all these years, would have kept him away forever. If not for Miguel and his fabrication about the sun god, Lucas would have never known he had a son.

He stared down at his hiking boots and

whispered, "Tell me about him. Tell me about Trevor."

At first, the light went out of her face, as if he'd flipped a switch bringing her back to reality, then her eyes softened. Had a small part of her forgiven him?

"Your son," she began, "is the smallest eternal optimist you will ever meet. He wakes up every morning with a smile on his face and a bounce in his step. He skips more than any little boy I know."

"Must have gotten that from you."

She laughed. "I'm not so sure about that. As much as I hated to admit it—before," she quickly added, "there's a lot of you in him."

"Don't say that." He stared into the fire and shook his head.

"Why not? You have many redeeming qualities."

He looked to see if she was crossing any body parts. "Name one."

"All right." She chewed on her lower lip while giving it some thought.

"Don't break anything while you're reaching for those straws." He grinned, in spite of himself.

"I have one. You're adventurous."

"Only one?"

She swatted him on the shoulder. "You were always ready to hop on a plane at a moment's notice or make love on a deserted beach." She paused, only just realizing what she had said and awkwardly turned her face to the fire.

The beach in Fiji. A blanket on the sand, moonlight overhead, and no one around for miles. The memory could still get him going.

"I guess I always did enjoy new restaurants," he said, hoping she—and he—would recover with a change in subject. This conversation felt too good to be over so soon.

"Exactly!" She beamed. "You were the one ordering the most exotic thing on the menu."

He used to order some pretty questionable stuff, but if memory served him right, it was so *she* could have a taste. "Yeah, but kids don't like different food."

"Trevor does. He'll try anything at least once. Spinach, pad thai, carrot juice. Evelyn even got him to try sushi."

Lucas chuckled. "What's his favorite?"

"Anything Chinese. The spicier the better. Even spicy salsa with chips. Anything chocolate. No nuts. Almost any kind of fruit or veggie." Sydney groaned. "But he wasn't always a good eater. When he was little, he wouldn't eat anything except peanut butter crackers and strawberries. I know, I know, allergies. But that's all he'd eat."

Trying to picture Trevor as a toddler and thinking of all the years they'd lost had Lucas falling into gloom. Thankfully, Miguel chose that moment to return with a plate full of saucy, diced meat and avocado and tomatoes.

"See what I mean?" She pointed at the plate. "You're going to eat that, no questions asked."

"That's our Lucas." Miguel rubbed him on the back. "Always trusting the world. It may not always treat him fairly, still he trusts it all the same."

"So I'll ask for him." Sydney shrugged. "What is it?"

"Nothing exotic like hamster." Miguel grinned. "Trout smothered in garlic sauce." He turned to the group sitting near Lucas. "Come, I need help with some food inside."

Several locals followed Miguel into the house, leaving only a few musicians, playing quietly near the fire. Lucas took a forkful of the meat spiced with peppers and onions. "Does Trevor collect anything?"

"Harry Potter stuff and he loves hats. I

swear he has a cap for every professional baseball and football team."

"What about friends?"

Sydney took a swig off her bottle of beer. "Oh, he's very social."

"Gets that from you," he said. She didn't argue, and he found himself wanting to laugh again. Damn, it felt good.

"His best friend is Nathan. Three houses down the block. We had eight boys over at his last birthday party." A shadow of what looked like regret passed over her face. "His real birthday is in March. He's in first grade."

Whether it was Lucas's imagination or not, the night grew silent for a moment. "That means you were about two months pregnant when Em…when I left."

"I hadn't had my period for several months before she died. Stress, I guess. I didn't think I could get pregnant."

"I remember that. You lost so much weight." He balanced the nearly finished plate of food on one hand and brushed his hand up and down her arm. "What does he like to do? For activities or sports?"

Sydney stared at him, as if she'd lost her voice. "Most men wouldn't…wouldn't trust anything I've said, especially after the way I lied to you. Aren't you mad at me, at all, for keeping Trevor from you?"

"I was." He set his empty plate on the ground. "You did what you had to do for good reasons."

Her eyes misted. "You're alike in that way, too. Trevor never holds a grudge. He can be mad as a hornet one minute and hugging the breath out of me the next."

Her voice held a note of incredulity. He was too much a pessimist to believe it could be respect, but maybe she didn't hate him. Not entirely. As the tiny seed of hope sprouted in his heart, his gaze slipped down her face, from her eyes to her lips. They glistened in the firelight, wet and soft.

"Me?" she said, sounding slightly breathless. "I can stay mad forever."

Slowly, he shook his head, clearing his mind. "Not forever. Life's too short, Sydney." He really wanted her to be happy. She deserved it. He turned away from her and flicked a twig into the fire, focusing on the bark sizzling in the flames.

"I want him back." Her voice cracked. "I miss him." A tear fell, darkening the dirt at her feet.

He reached out, folded his hand over hers,

and squeezed. "Sports, remember. Tell me about the sports Trevor likes."

She sniffled and drew in a shaky breath. "Soccer in the summer, basketball during the school year. He's naturally athletic and co-ordinated. Once again, like you. Except for that one time," she said, "he fell off his skate-board and broke his arm. It was pretty bad and I thought it might heal funny, but the doctors have said it's as straight as can be."

At the mention of doctors, Lucas stiffened. A dimness passed over their bonfire that had nothing to do with clouds passing under the full moon or night shadows from the woods surrounding them. How many times had he wondered if the cancer had been genetic? "Has he ever had any symptoms…like Emily?"

"Oh, no, Lucas," she whispered. "No."

This time it was her hand that squeezed his. Emily's death was still an oozing wound. It was obvious Sydney had accom-plished much of her healing through Trevor. There was nothing either of them could do to give Lucas that same opportunity. Those first years of Trevor's life were gone.

"Lucas, I'm sorry."

"You're a good mother." He let her hand go and sat back.

Sydney studied him for a moment, her eyes narrowing with concentration, as if a private battle waged on in her mind. Finally, she took a deep breath and spoke. "It was a Tuesday at 11:36 a.m. at Harborview hospital," she began. "Trevor was born on a gorgeous morning…."

She went on to detail every moment she could remember of Trevor's life, the way only a mother could. From the first time he slept through the night to his first word to his favorite subjects in school. She described how scared she'd been with his first headache and how relieved she'd been when a phone call in the middle of his first sleep-over had been a wrong number.

He laughed, he smiled, he felt his eyes dampen, and Sydney went on and on and on. He absorbed every seemingly mundane tidbit, thirsty for a sense of his son. Somewhere along the way, he glanced absently around to discover the remaining musicians had quietly disappeared, leaving him and Sydney alone at the fire. Miguel at work once again.

"You've done a good job raising him," he said when she finally ran out of things to say, and he, questions to ask.

Lucas had been right. Trevor was one little boy who was doing just fine without a father.

Loud, urgent footfalls sounded behind them, and Lucas spun around to find Miguel coming from the house. All the locals were filing out, as well, heading home. "I just got off the phone," he said.

At that they both jumped up. "Trevor?"

"It's Gonzalo."

"The shaman at Machu Picchu?" Sydney asked.

"He's in the Cusco hospital. Beaten badly. Witnesses say a *tourista* with some *Indios* got at him."

Sydney covered her mouth.

"Cochran?"

"Sounds like it, and he's already hired himself a handful of thugs."

"Is Gonzalo all right?"

"He'll live."

"How did Cochran know about Gonzalo?" Sydney asked.

"If you have questions about Machu Picchu everyone around here knows Gonzalo's the man." Lucas cringed. "I should have warned him that Cochran would be coming."

Miguel put his hand on Lucas's shoulder. "You didn't know this would happen."

"What did Cochran get out of him?"

"Everything."

Lucas paced a step or two away. "That means Cochran knows we're here."

Miguel nodded. "And he knows about the Urubamba. There were chalk marks on a wall near Gonzalo. Sounds like your map."

"Syd, go pack your bags," Lucas said. "We leave tonight."

She ran for the house.

"I need Pepe."

"Already sent for him." Miguel sighed. "I can probably get you a flight to Timpia, but once you are there, my friend, I can do little to help you."

Miguel's influence was great, but it didn't extend to the Machiguenga Indians of the rain forest. "You've done more than enough already." Lucas headed toward the carport and double-checked the gear he'd already packed.

"When you arrive in Timpia find Don Estevao. He might lend you a river canoe." Miguel nodded. "Need anything else, any more gear?"

"No. We're set."

"Can you use a portable satellite phone?" Miguel handed over a small leather bag.

"You and your toys."

"Hey, you never know when you might need one."

The moment grew heavy with unspoken thoughts. "Miguel, I'm sorr—"

"No." Miguel held up his hand. "You have done nothing wrong, my friend. Accept that and stop running from yourself."

Lucas set his gear near the door and followed Miguel into the house. Miguel grabbed the phone and spoke in highly charged Quechua, presumably arranging their flight to Timpia. Lucas found Sydney in the bedroom frantically throwing together their belongings. He gripped her arms and stopped her, slowly rubbing his palms up and down. "Shh. It's okay. Everything's going to be okay."

"We still haven't heard anything from Evelyn."

"Miguel gave me a satellite phone. We should be able to contact her from anywhere in the rain forest."

"Are you sure?"

"Positive." He brushed her cheek. "Let's go." He swung the backpacks over his shoulder and headed down the hall. Pepe was waiting for them at the door.

Miguel finished his call and turned to them. "You're all set. A pilot will take you to Timpia as soon as you arrive at the Cusco airport." He handed Lucas a thermos of coffee and a cooler of fresh supplies.

"Thank you, Miguel." Sydney extended her hand. "For everything."

He ignored her hand and hugged her before turning to Lucas. "I do not feel good about this leaving at night, Lucas. You know how dangerous the mountains can be. Maybe Sydney should stay—"

"No," Sydney said before Lucas had the chance to respond. "I'm going."

"This is where it gets rough, Syd. You sure?" Lucas asked, studying her eyes for any sign of uncertainty. What he saw surprised and fortified him. She had his back. They were doing this together.

"I'm sure," she said. "I spent some more time tonight on the glyphs, but I'm not certain about the last line."

"Then maybe morning would be best."

"No can do, Miguel." Lucas set off for the truck and signaled for Pepe and Sydney to follow. "The only thing we had going for us was time. It just ran out."

"WELL, THAT WAS A COMPLETE and total waste." Evelyn threw her purse onto the kitchen countertop and stood with her hands on her hips. They'd spent the entire day investigating Phillip Cochran's various real estate holdings by boat, including a run down the Oregon Coast, and all she had to show for it was windblown hair and chapped cheeks.

"The day wasn't a complete bust." Joe plugged his laptop into the outlet off the counter and sat down, back at work despite the fact that he had to be beat.

"How do you figure?"

"We know where Trevor's *not* being held." He typed away on his keyboard. "Let me check e-mails. I've been waiting to hear back on a couple things. Maybe something else turned up."

"Like what?"

"Like this."

Evelyn hurried to his side. "What is it?"

"One place we haven't checked out." He grinned. "An island in the San Juans."

"Cochran has property on an island?"

Joe looked up. "He owns the entire island."

CHAPTER FOURTEEN

AN OVERLAND TRIP across the rugged and wild terrain between Cusco and Timpia would have delayed Sydney and Lucas several days. Their pilot, though less than enthusiastic about a flight over the Vilca-bamba mountain range in the dead of night, landed them on Timpia's small runway within several hours.

Upon arrival at the Machiguenga Indian village, Sydney helped Lucas and Pepe carry several loads of supplies and equipment down to the river. Pepe had refused to stay in Cusco, insisting he would get them safely onto the Urubamba before heading home.

The village itself, still deep in slumber, was little more than a small airstrip and a grouping of thatched huts set alongside the sandy shores of the river. After the last trip, she quietly followed Lucas and Pepe down narrow dirt paths illuminated only by a three-quarter moon looking for Don Estevao's hut. "Shouldn't we wait until morning?" she whispered, a few steps behind him.

"We need to move out as quickly as possible."

"What we need is sleep."

"The sooner we head downriver, the better. Cochran will be right on our tail."

"How can that be?"

"I didn't want to worry you, but a car might have been tailing us on the way to Cusco. And then at the airport, there was an *Indio* hanging a little too close for my comfort."

"One of the men who beat up Gonzalo?"

"Possibly." Lucas nodded. "We'll be all right once we're on the river. Hard to track us on the water." He stopped next to Pepe at a hut a bit larger than the others.

"Don Estevao." Pepe whispered the shaman's name.

The simple wooden door opened when they knocked and a leathery-skinned old man dressed in jeans and a T-shirt appeared from the black depths of the hut. His eyes seemed alert and knowing for such a late hour.

"I am sorry to awaken you," Lucas said. "We

come from Don Miguel's in Ollantaytambo. Can you lend us a river canoe and motor?"

Pepe translated for Lucas and Don Estevao.

"Come back when it is light," Estevao said and started to close the door.

"It's an emergency."

"You go *now* to the river?"

"Yes." Lucas nodded.

The man spent a long moment sizing them up before stepping out of his hut and closing the door. "Come." He led the way back to the river. At a lean-to near the shore, he stopped and indicated a large, sturdy canoe. Lucas and Pepe hoisted it out and down to the water.

After mounting a motor and loading several tanks of gas and their supplies, they were ready to shove off.

"Thank you, Pepe." Sydney extended her hand.

"You're more than welcome, Sydney." He shook her hand and then, turning to Lucas, pulled him into a tight embrace. "Stay safe, my friend."

"*Gracias,* Pepe. Thank you for everything." Lucas turned to the old man. "*Gracias,* Don Estevao. How can I repay you?"

He chuckled, an unexpectedly booming

sound for such a scrawny frame. "You can beat Miguel in five-card stud the next time you're in Ollantaytambo."

"Now *that* might be difficult." Lucas laughed and shook the other man's hand. "Luck and Miguel go together like poker and cards."

Estevao nodded his agreement and his expression turned serious. "What takes you downriver in the middle of the night?"

"You're better off not knowing."

"Hmm." The old man considered the answer. "Others will come looking for you?"

Lucas nodded. "Don Miguel can delay them in Cusco a day, two at the most, but they will come. Pepe, please, go back in the morning. Cochran will have too many men with him for you to try and slow him down alone." Pepe reluctantly nodded, and Lucas turned to Don Estevao. "And I wouldn't ask you to endanger your village to protect us. Give those who follow what they need."

"Then be careful, Miguel's friends," said the shaman, and he sent them off with some unintelligible Machiguengan phrase.

Sydney chose to think his words some sort of blessing as they shoved off into the night, a blessing that would help them save Trevor.

The river current grabbed their wide canoe, pulling them along, and Pepe and the shaman's shadowy forms slowly faded into the backdrop of the jungle.

The moon and a floodlight at the front of the canoe provided all the light they needed to track the intermittently sandy shoreline, but Sydney'd never much liked rivers to begin with, and traveling on one at night was especially frightening. Lucas kept the motor on low speed, conserving gasoline, he explained, and the murky waters of the slow-going river barely rippled in their wake. They'd need most of what gasoline they had for the more arduous trip back upstream after they'd found the temple.

"Keep your eyes out front," Lucas ordered. "Yell if you see anything floating in the water."

She sat up a little straighter. "You mean, like, snakes or something?"

"Nothing so dramatic. Wood or debris that might mess up our one-and-only motor."

For several hours, the going was clear and uneventful and they managed to cover a lot of water. While Sydney struggled to keep her eyes open, she concentrated on the black surface of the river, alerting Lucas to even blacker shadows that might indicate floating objects. Eventually, they ran into fog, not the garden-variety lacy mist she was used to driving through in Seattle. This Urubamba river fog was thick, heavy. Her rain poncho beaded moisture within seconds.

He cut the engine to the lowest possible gear allowing him to steer while the current took them. After a nerve-racking ten minutes of being unable to see more than a foot in front of them, he said, "I don't know this river well enough to keep going, Syd. We're going to have to land and wait for this to burn off." They found a spot of shoreline clear enough to land. After hauling the canoe out of the water and into the woods, hiding it from view, they pitched a two-man tent behind some taller bushes and climbed inside.

Sydney spread a sleeping bag out beside Lucas and plopped onto her back. She rolled onto her left side, back onto her right, repositioning herself on the narrow camping mat and in the process bumping her leg into Lucas's knee. There couldn't have been more than a few inches between them. "Two-man tent, my foot," she mumbled while bunching her thick, fleece sweatshirt into a makeshift pillow and trying to relax.

It wasn't going to happen. All evening, there had been problems demanding immediate attention: deadwood in the water, snakes around the corner, mosquitoes to swat. Now, in the quiet darkness of the tent, there was nothing to help her forget that more than two days had passed and Trevor was still in the hands of a kidnapper. He could be dead. Not since Emily had such terror gripped her heart.

She rationalized that the kidnappers would never hurt Trevor until they found the temple and the silver bowl. Evelyn and the FBI agent were hot on Trevor's trail. They may have even found him already. Nothing helped. And crying was not an option. She was not going to make Lucas take her into his arms again like last night. Tipping her head back, she held off the tears.

"Hey," Lucas whispered. "You okay?"

"I'm fine."

"No, you're not." He rolled over, hesitated for a moment, and then drew her into his arms, settling her back tight against his chest. She didn't even bother to stiffen up this time. He felt so right against her. Her cheek against his bare arm, the scent of him, fresh air and water, surrounding her. Her fear over Trevor didn't disappear, but it did lessen, as if Lucas had taken some of it upon himself.

He'd always known what she needed, when she needed it, and the realization she was still so transparent to him shook her to the core. It had always been that way between them. He could read her mind, and she never had a clue what he was thinking. Of course, there was a distinct reason for that. She let him in. Constantly. She talked and dumped, blew gaskets and yakked. He barely said a word. What was really going on inside that mind of his was anyone's guess. It made her mad, suddenly, that he had shared so little of his life with her.

As if he sensed her thoughts once again, Lucas pulled her even tighter against him. He stroked her back and neck, flicking away the tension. As she relaxed, her guard came down and as her guard came down, tears came up. She sniffed and closed her eyes. *Be strong. Stronger.*

He leaned in close, his mouth near her ear. "Legend has it," he whispered, "that Inti, the Inca sun god, created woman from his tears."

"That's not true." She turned her soggy face toward him. "Huiracocha, their most powerful god, created the first woman. She rose as sister queen to the first Inca king from the waters of Lake Titicaca."

Softly, he brushed a hand across her cheek, drying it. "I thought you'd forgotten all those ridiculous legends."

His lips were mere inches from hers. "I lied."

"Why?"

"Because I wanted to hurt you." She glanced up, into his dark eyes. "Did I?"

He nodded. "Does that make you happy?"

"No." The realization surprised her.

"Well, you're right," he went on, his voice a little sad, a little hopeful. "Huiracocha created a *queen*. But Inti? He created a *real* woman." The way he'd said the word *real,* drawing it out, low and sensual, sent a shiver across her back. "Have you ever heard of a cloud forest?" And just like that he'd moved on, forgiven her.

"No. Never heard of one."

"They form where rain forest meets mountain, like the eastern side of the Andes here in Peru. Warm, moist air meets colder temperatures creating ever-present mist and clouds." She snuggled deeper into the crook of his arm and let his voice rumble through her, recreating a magic lost but never forgotten. "Like a never land," he continued, "it's cool, quiet. Mystical. It was said the cloud forests were Huiracocha's private oases. He would go there to be away from the people and other gods, replenishing himself.

"One day, Huiracocha was sleeping in the yawning branches of a vilca tree when Inti yelled down from the heavens. 'Come out. Come back. We need you.'

"'Go away,' Huiracocha yelled back. 'I'm resting.'

"Inti waited. And he waited. The longer he waited, the more interested he became in Huiracocha's fascination with these cloud forests. Impatient and curious, Inti called his son, Kon, god of the wind, to blow the clouds away.

"Kon blew and blew. After every breath the clouds would roll away, revealing the vibrant colors of the precious orchids, the dewy softness of the moss and ferns, the richness of the fertile black earth and trees more magnificent than any Inti had ever seen in his sunny, dry domain. But when Kon inhaled the clouds would roll back, even heavier than before."

In no time at all, Sydney slipped into his enchanting world and reality faded away. Within their tent all was right. Trevor would be safe. Evie and Joe would rescue him. A smile on her lips, she leaned back into Lucas, into his embrace, where tonight she felt she belonged more than any other place on earth.

"'Go away,' Huiracocha ordered, sick of the noise and wind.

"'I want to come down,' Inti cried. 'I want to see what you see.' In frustration, he reached his lacy fingers into the mist, and the clouds evaporated. Inti's bright light shone into the forest, and having never before felt those clear, strong rays, the tender plants shriveled and died.

"Huiracocha became angry, and he banished Inti to the eastern coast. For years, Inti paced the peaks of the mountains, crying. His great tears are said to have created many of the mighty rivers of the Amazon basin. The Rio Urubamba, the Ucayali and the Huallaga."

Suddenly, she became aware of Lucas's left hand moving absently along her back, his chest hairs tickling her arm, and how her own fingers had become interwoven with the fingers of his right. She thought about pulling back, but it felt so natural. So right.

"With Inti's long absence," he said, returning to his legend, "Huiracocha saw the rain forests shriveling and dying, yellowing from too much water and not enough sun. The coast, on the other hand, was turning dry and barren. He made a deal with Inti. 'Fix my rain forests and you can return to roaming the country as you see fit.'

"'And the cloud forests?' Inti asked.

"'You must never return,' Huiracocha replied.

"Inti hovered over the dying forest, hesitating. Finally, he cried three last tears. The first one created woman's legs, long and strong. The second, her hips, breasts and arms, loving and gentle, imparted with a healing touch. The third, her head, beautiful, intelligent and proud. With black hair, long and thick like yours. The kind a man could lose himself in." At that he took a wisp of her hair, scrunched it between two fingers and brought it to his face, closing his eyes for a moment.

"He bade her walk through the forest, and she did. Everything she touched turned green with life and grew as never before. Soon the cloud forests were healed, and the heavy mists returned, hiding her from Inti."

"That's sad."

"Not entirely. Every November and December Inti returns to the edge of the cloud forest and cries for her."

"Their rainy season." Sydney smiled.

"That's right."

"So why does their rainy season end?"

His hand stopped gliding along her back, and he stiffened. All at once, he wasn't a friend offering comfort. He was a man, alive and burning. "Why do you think?"

She didn't want to think. She wanted him to take her away. To a place with no past, no future, only the two of them and their bodies, wonderfully alive in sensation.

"The woman finally comes to him." His soft breath tickled her ear. "She makes love to him, whispering to him all the delights of the cloud forest. When she moves over him, loving him, he becomes one with her and he sees all through her eyes. Inti cries no more tears. He's happy again."

She rolled onto her back and looked up at him. "Is that a real Inca legend?"

"Does it matter?"

"Yes."

He hesitated. "I made it up," he said aloud. His eyes said, *Tonight. For you.*

Reaching through the darkness, she lightly ran her fingertips over his lips. Instead of pulling away as she'd half expected, he leaned into her hand and shifted his head back and forth, spreading her touch over his face. Then his mouth was on hers, warm, wild. Infinitely soft. As if neither could believe what was happening.

She opened to him as she'd done hundreds of times in their past, and their tongues met as if finding home again. She trembled and drew away, the sensations too raw and powerful.

He hovered above her, his breath fast, his chest heaving with restraint. "That was *not* a good idea."

"No."

"No more legends." He fell back down beside her. "Go to sleep." Though his arms remained around her, his muscles tightened like steel beneath her hands. He was holding himself rigid, holding himself back.

The courage—if one could call it that—to finish what she'd started drifted away. She laid her head down. As tired as she was, it didn't take long for the cacophony of the jungle to distract her, for the feel of his arms slowly relaxing around her to lull her to sleep.

Lucas wasn't so lucky. Only after he knew for certain that she was completely oblivious did he allow himself to rest his cheek against the curls at the crown of her head, to breathe in her scent. Remnants of the bonfire at Miguel's still clung to her hair, mixing with fresh air and her earthy, warm scent.

As Inti's cloud forest woman had done for Inti, so Sydney could do for Lucas. She would bring him happiness, peace, joy. He breathed her in and tightened his arm around her, let his fingers trail down her bare arm. Let himself remember the last time they'd made love. They'd known the end was so near for Emily and had sought solace in each other's arms. Brief shelter from the storm kicking up around them.

Emily had died the next day. For the first time since the funeral, he let himself miss his little girl and noticed the pain had miraculously dulled. When he allowed himself the freedom to miss Sydney, the ache was still as fresh and heart-wrenching as the day he'd walked away.

For so many years he'd tried to forget. Now he let every precious moment come back to him uncut. He pressed his lips to the top of her head. "I have always loved you," he admitted to the darkness a truth he'd denied himself for years. "I never stopped." The memories were all he would allow himself. He closed his eyes and let himself dream.

CHAPTER FIFTEEN

SYDNEY FLOATED DOWN a black river in a canoe only large enough for her to sit at the base with her legs stretched in front of her. Sleepy and sluggish, she leaned back and rested her arms along the canoe's edges, and let it mold to her frame like a pod surrounding an overgrown pea, cocooning her in its warm embrace and rocking her gently downstream. Electric-pink clouds drifted overhead like cotton candy in the dismally gray sky. Waves crashed and rapids appeared, and still the canoe kept her safe and dry.

It understood her desires, the canoe. She'd think "slow" and it dawdled in the current. She wanted to go in a certain direction, and it steered exactly where her thoughts intended. She wanted to spin, and it took her for a hair-raising ride.

The canoe laughed then, a sonorous, rumbling sound that vibrated through her, *massaging her muscles bone deep. Her insides warmed, spiraled into sexual aware-ness. She stretched and wriggled deeper. It was such a great canoe, and it made her feel so good.*

Then Trevor materialized on the shoreline beside a great sand castle and her con-tentedness evaporated. She sat up, alert and wary. "Trevor!" she yelled. Squatting and absorbed in the task of shoveling sand into a bucket, he paid no attention to the river, to her. "Trevor!"

She willed the canoe to shore, but it wouldn't listen. The current grabbed hold and pulled them downstream. The sides of the canoe tightened. A bit too much. What before had felt safe and inviting swiftly turned into something binding in its posses-siveness. Needing to break free, to get to Trevor, she drew up her legs only to find two dark eyes bulge from where her feet had been and a nose protrude from the floor of the canoe.

This wasn't a canoe at all! It was the African mask she'd been showing Evelyn in her gallery.

That meant the mouth— Oh, no, he was going to swallow her. She scrambled up the sides, and they turned into arms, holding her. First her toes, then her feet and ankles dipped inside the black mouth. It lashed at her feet with its thick, sticky tongue. Whipped them raw. "I'll swallow you whole," it groaned.

The mask morphed into Lucas. Back to the mask. Back to Lucas. He stood up in the river and held her steady, the current of cold water rushing by them on either side. She curled into his arms, into his warmth. "It's all right," he mouthed against her cheek and walked toward shore.

Every step he took drained him of strength, until her weight seemed too much for him and he nearly lost his balance in the swift current.

"Put me down," she warned.

"I can make it. Two more steps." He stumbled to shore and sprawled onto the sand.

She reached out and caressed his cheek, but instead of easing his tiredness, her touch turned his skin to wood. She leaned over and ran her fingers through his hair, leaving a trail of twigs. "I never stopped loving you," she said against his lips.

He turned hot beneath her fingertips and his heat transformed her. A pool of arousal, every nerve ending awakened, she slipped within him, whole. She was lost to the sensations swirling around her, inside her.

All at once, the gentle tones of his voice turned into laughter, sick and twisted. Again, he became the mask. Only this time she was trapped inside him, looking out. Now she'd never make it back to Trevor. She pounded against the wooden walls and thrashed against his hold, a grip that grew tighter with every breath.

Let me go!

SYDNEY SNAPPED OPEN her eyes. Lucas's face, softened by sleep and the first pastel rays of dawn, rested only inches from hers. Caught between the real world and the haze of her dreams, she thrashed back and forth inside the sleeping bag.

"Easy." Lucas awoke and tightened his arms around her. "Shhh. You were dreaming."

"More like nightmaring." She froze as she remembered. "Did I say anything?"

"Let me think." He brushed his hand over his face and scratched the back of his neck, coming around quickly. "Was the 'Oh, baby, baby! Give it to me,' part of your dream? Or mine?"

She felt her eyes widen in alarm and the heat of a body blush slowly creep up her face. Her heart stopped as she retraced the foggy dream, frame by frame.

"Oh, Sydney, honey." He laughed. "I was sound asleep." He looked rather surprised at this revelation. "Dead to the world. I didn't hear anything."

Sometime during the night, she'd ditched her own sleeping bag for his, and all at once, the placement of his body in reference to hers became clear. Her bare toes against his hairy calves. His arm heavy across her waist. His hand cupped at her back. The signs of his own awareness of her growing and bulging in his boxer shorts, hard against her groin. His gaze moved from her eyes to her lips then back again. "Tell me you were dreaming about…me."

She parted her lips, and her breath passed through in a rush. Then his mouth was on her, covering her. No time to stop. No time for reservations or thought. Only primitive need. Want. She wrapped an arm around his shoulder, a hand at his head, buried her fingers in his coarse hair. Then she lifted her leg over him, tightening around him, rocking against him.

"Oh, Syd," he groaned against her mouth, slanting his head, deepening their contact. He flattened his hand on her backside and pressed, bringing her tight against him.

She whimpered and shifted, yearning to feel him even closer, deeper, inside. Now. All timidness from the previous night disappeared in the pale light of predawn. She ran her hands over his bare chest and shoulders. Yes! This was what she wanted. To begin again. To rediscover the feel of him.

His chest heaved with her touch and soon his hands slid down to the hem of her shirt, dragging it over her head. Her hair came free, falling in long, curly folds down her neck. He buried his hands there, and then shifted to her breasts, cupping them, stroking her nipples. "Where do I start? Where do I touch you first?"

"Everywhere," she groaned. "All at once."

He tried. Moving over her. Covering each breast with kisses, lingering and licking her belly. Then he pulled off her pajama pants and moved to her mouth, devouring her even as his hand slipped between her legs. As if time had never separated them, she opened to him. All the heat of the years spiraled inside her.

"Mmm," he moaned long and low against her mouth.

She tugged on his lower lip with her teeth and moved to touch his erection. He jerked, his sharp intake of breath cracking through the quiet morning air. He pulled his mouth away and grew still. "Don't…move."

She inched toward him, trailing soft kisses down the side of his cheek.

"It's been…forever. Too…fast," came his answer, breathless and shaky. She felt his heart thumping in rhythm with her own. "This is…how…trouble to begin with."

"I don't care." Her words came out on a soft breath. "I want you. I've never stopped wanting you."

He pulled himself away and fell back, his eyes black with need. The sight of him in her dream, flat against the sandy shore, filled her mind. "One more touch, Syd, and everything changes. Be very sure what you want."

There was no doubt. She reached out for him. An instant before contact, he rolled away. A split second later, he'd grabbed his clothes and was out of the tent.

For one minute, maybe five, she lay there numb. Her hand fell to the ground, and she shivered as the cold fingers of reality doused her fire. What was she thinking? He'd walked out on her and six years later, she's naked in his tent, gladly willing to take any scrap of attention he's willing to dole out. For the moment. For the next month. For as long as he was willing to stick around. And when he left again, then what? How could she care so little for herself?

The sound of him rummaging around their small camp, his movements quick and quiet, drifted through the thin fabric of the tent. The truth was she didn't hate Lucas any longer. Six years of anger and bitterness had somehow melted away, softening her edges. Maybe it wasn't that she didn't care about herself, but that she cared so much for him. What she'd dreamed was true. She'd never stopped loving him.

The realization didn't come with great gladness, as it should have, as it did that first time so long ago. This time there were no easy answers. This time she had Trevor to think of. This time she doubted Lucas's love for her.

With a resigned sigh, she sat up and pulled on her camp pants and a long-sleeved shirt. By the time she climbed out of the tent, Lucas had already dragged the canoe down to the water and was brushing away any sign of their presence from the sand. It couldn't have been much past six.

"Grab something to eat and let's start breaking down the tent," he said, his tone curt, all trace of their shared intimacy wiped from his face. "We have a long day ahead of us." He was a mask. Unreadable. Untouchable.

IT WAS A GORGEOUS afternoon on the Sound for January. No fog. No rain. No wind. Only sunshine, deep blue water and an awesomely powerful speedboat. Evelyn pulled her jacket closer around her and glanced at her FBI agent—since when had she begun thinking of him as *hers?*—as he bent over a map of the San Juans. "Are you sure you know what you're doing?" She gave him the look.

"Last time I checked I was the FBI agent and you were the interior decorator."

"Designer, not decorator…and how do you know what I do? I haven't told you anything about myself."

"You're thirty-four years old. Never been married. Graduated summa cum laude from the Art Institute of Seattle. Got your first driver's license from Montana." He looked over his shoulder at her and smiled. "And you're a natural blonde, so why you dye your hair that bleachy platinum color is beyond me."

Her natural shade *was* prettier, but the bottled color gave her distance. "You did a background check on me?"

"On everyone. Most incidents involving children are either directly or indirectly related to their parents. I wanted to know who I was dealing with."

"What did you find out?"

"The only questionable person is Phillip Cochran. And even that's only by association."

"How far back did you go?"

"Why? Got skeletons in your closet?"

"Do you always answer a question with a question?"

"Make you nervous?"

"No." She turned away. She just didn't like people digging into her past. "So where is this island you're looking for?"

"Changing the subject. Fine by me. The GPS unit says it should be right around this point." When the boat cleared a large island with several homes on it, he slowed and hugged the coastline. "Take the wheel. Keep it slow. That smaller island over there is Cochran's. Keep your distance."

Evelyn took his place. "What are you going to do?"

They were several hundred yards to the north of Cochran's island. "I want to get a good look at what we have over there without rousing suspicion," he said. He pulled a set of binoculars from his bag and crouched under the canopy to study the layout.

"What do you see?"

"Very little physical activity. One, two guards. A couple outbuildings. Three, four guards. A main house. Okay, now take a wide turn around the other side." The binoculars remained practically glued to his face. "Keep your distance!" he said over the sound of the engine. "Move out! If you get too close, they'll see me. Now speed up. This side's undeveloped. Head back to the big island. Where you first took the wheel."

The entire cruise back, he didn't take his eyes from Cochran's island. "Slow down a little," he finally said when they came close to the coastline of the larger nearby island. "Stop. Okay, I see something. He's looking back. Damn. We don't have much time before they get suspicious."

"Did you see Trevor?"

"No, but with all this security, we gotta be

at the right spot. Head toward that pier on the big island." Evelyn pretended to dock the boat. "Wait a minute. That's weird."

"What? Who do you see?"

"Inside the tree line. Partially hidden. One of the men…with a baseball glove on. Wait a minute…that could be…"

"Trevor?"

"I don't know." Joe pulled out a photo from his jacket pocket. "Straight dark hair. Pale skin." He picked up the binoculars again. "It's him. Trevor's playing catch with one of the guards."

THOUGH TREVOR WAS NEVER far from Sydney's thoughts, the views of this strange and wonderful rain forest kept her from completely obsessing about him. The river was much wider and the trees much larger than she'd expected. The water, a deep murky brown, flowed swiftly past sandy banks scarred by massive tree roots. A jungle. She was in a real jungle, and for the first time since arriving in Peru she was glad she wasn't twiddling her thumbs back in Seattle. Here, at least, she was doing something that, in the end, might save her son.

Intermittently, Lucas would track their progress on the map he'd drawn of the river at Machu Picchu. When the river permitted, she spent time analyzing the carvings on Manco Capac's staff. The designs were almost too simple when compared with the more complicated Mayan hieroglyphics system, but now that she was on the river, getting a feel for the environment, the last row began to gel.

They'd stopped briefly for lunch and taken a few breaks to stretch their legs, but for the most part, they'd motored down the Urubamba for the past fourteen hours, putting as many miles between themselves and Timpia—and Phillip Cochran—as possible.

It had been a quiet day, marked mostly by the hum of the small boat motor or the sound of squirrel monkeys squawking a warning through the treetops at their approach. "We could take this all the way to the Amazon," was one of the few things Lucas said all day. Both of them had been, thankfully, lost in their own thoughts, silently agreeing to leave alone what had happened in the tent that morning. He'd been introspective and thoughtful, yes. Angry, no.

They'd had to pull out paddles several times, with Lucas giving Sydney a few cursory training tips on how to navigate through a series of rapids. Less rainfall than normal was the only thing making the river passable this time of year.

Though he'd explained he'd only been on the river a few times, he pointed out sights of interest to break the monotony of the day. The clay licks captured Sydney's attention more than anything. Macaws, vibrantly colored red-and-green birds, gathered with blue-headed parrots and hooked their sharp talons into the cliff side. They hung, some-times by the hundreds, licking minerals off the steep riverbank.

As the sun fell below the treetops, they started looking for a campsite. This became a difficult endeavor as the tree line had moved closer to the river's edge, leaving fewer spaces open enough for a tent, yet secluded enough to remain hidden from the water.

"The bend in the river up ahead looks like the general location of the first marker." Lucas pointed at the map before tucking it back into his pocket. "Have you figured out that last row of glyphs yet?"

"Not for sure."

"Let's pull over and take a look for that

pillar anyway." He steered them toward the eastern shore, killed the small engine and reached for a branch.

"Wait a minute." It had occurred to her earlier in the day that several of the symbols very likely represented directions. She pointed at a particular glyph, the profile of a face with many swirling lines coming out of the mouth. "I think this one could mean north. See the water, turbulent and flowing, presumably coming from a god's mouth? The Urubamba does flow north, right?"

"Yes. But if that's north, what is this?" He pointed to another symbol with swirling lines on the right side and what looked like a four-petaled flower on the left. "It looks like it's using the river as some kind of guide, too. Maybe that one's north."

"I think the flower symbolizes the sun. The sun rises in the east. Lucas, I think we need to be on the other side of the river."

"That's your call?"

She nodded.

"Okay." He maneuvered the canoe to the other shoreline and ran her aground. Three stops later, tired, dirty, and full of mosquito bites from punching their way through thick vegetation, they'd found no sign of the Inca pillar.

"This is going to be harder than I thought," she muttered, swabbing her sweaty brow with the shoulder of her T-shirt.

"This jungle takes over everything." He studied their surroundings and took a deep, discouraged-sounding breath. "An Andean shaman would use a sacred medicine plant to find the markers or possibly even the temple itself."

"How would that help?"

"While under the influence of the plant, his visions would show him the way."

"You're serious?"

"Completely." He nodded. "I've seen it done. One of the single biggest Inca sites in Peru to date was found by a Peruvian archaeologist under the influence. He's the one who helped me find Manco Capac's staff. I've spent the better part of six years here and have only begun to scratch the surface of this country's mysticism."

"Well, barring sacred medicine plants, what exactly are we looking for?"

"Most likely a vine-covered tree that looks unnatural in shape when compared to its surroundings. Something relatively close to shore. Something tall—"

"Something like that?" Sydney pointed behind him.

He spun around. "Exactly like that."

CHAPTER SIXTEEN

SET A FEW FEET from the shoreline, a tall, vine-draped column rose above the low jungle foliage growing to the water's edge. Lucas brushed past Sydney and pushed his way through bushes and between trees. Pulling up just short of the curious object, he peeled away a section of clinging vines and scraped at the moss-covered surface to reveal a smooth gray stone.

"The first marker," he whispered, clearly in awe. "This is incredible." He touched, studied and contemplated, turning into the young archaeologist she remembered, so passionate about his work, so animated.

And Sydney couldn't stand it. She wanted him to be the asshole she'd envisioned for years. She wanted him to be cold, distant. Instead, he was still Lucas, the man she'd loved so long ago.

"Well," she said, interrupting him and his

communing with the Inca. "Did you find any glyphs?"

He glanced around. "They're here," he said. "More symbols."

She made her way to his side and studied the area he'd scraped clean, running her hands over the stone. Though the carvings were weathered and worn, there was no doubt the main symbol on the pillar matched the largest carving on the staff, the one she had yet to identify. There was also another row of three glyphs.

"I was right," she said. "These are directions to the second marker. West side of the river again. But I don't know what this one is." She pointed to the middle symbol, small circles surrounding a grouping of lines spiraling inward. She pulled out a pencil and the French fry box and copied down all the markings, exactly as they appeared on the pillar. "Are there any more?"

"No, and you look exhausted. I think we should camp here for the night."

"Don't worry about me, Lucas. If you want to continue on, I'm game."

"This spot is as good as any we've seen along the river."

After they'd hidden the canoe, Lucas

pointed at a fallen tree. "Sit down and relax. I'll set up the tent."

"I can help."

"Sit," he ordered.

A little consideration was one thing, pampering was another. "I'm not a china doll, Lucas. You don't have to keep taking care of me."

He studied her face and grinned. "No, you're too dirty to be a china doll."

"What?"

"You have smudges all over your face."

She wiped at her cheeks and felt a layer of grit rub off. "Why didn't you say something earlier?"

He reached out and brushed at her forehead. "Maybe I liked it." His voice turned husky as his fingertips grazed her upper lip. The topic they'd avoided all day, their encounter in the tent that morning, leaped between them like a full-blown fire. He drew his hand away and backed up. "I'm heading to the river before it gets too dark. Set up the tent yourself, huh?"

She watched him disappear through the bush, feeling confused and unsettled, but glad to have a task. She raised the tent, arranged his sleeping bag and pad inside, and when she pulled out her own sleeping bag, the sun god thudded to the ground. When she picked it up, an easy calm settled over her. It was time to resolve a few things. She stuffed the statue into her pocket.

After she'd drawn the rain flap over the tent and secured it, Lucas returned, his hair wet from an apparent washing at the river's edge. He tossed her a clean wet cloth, dropped a fish onto the ground and proceeded to gut and clean it.

"How did you catch that?" She drew the cloth over her face.

"With my bare hands." He winked at her.

"Really?"

Chuckling, he held up a line and hook. "With this."

The fish, about a foot long with a wide, dark gray body, looked a little too familiar. "Is that a piranha?"

"Black-finned Pacu."

She dropped down to sit on a rock and watched Lucas start a small fire. He wrapped the fish up in several damp palm leaves he'd laid out in front of him and set it over the flames. "We have to talk," she said.

He kept his head down. "About what?"

"Us."

"There is no us."

"Lucas, you can't pretend what happened this morning—"

"Nothing happened this morning. At least nothing important enough to talk about."

"How can you say that?"

"Look." He glanced up. "A man and a woman. Alone in a tent. That's a risky situation even in the best of circumstances. You were close. And it's been a long time for me. That's all."

How could she make him acknowledge something she wasn't sure she wanted to acknowledge herself? He pulled the fish out of the fire and folded back the palm leaves. Aromatic steam rose from the cooked fish, and she realized she was starving. She reached for a pack and supplemented the meal with some *gallentas,* biscuits Miguel had supplied, and what remained of their bananas. Soon, their meal was finished, and they faced each other, the fire between them.

Everything had changed. All day, her revelations from the morning and her feelings for Lucas had eaten at her, little insidious nips between thoughts of Trevor and beautiful diversions in nature. Before, it hadn't seemed to matter, the reasons for Lucas's abrupt disappearance six years ago. Best to let sleeping dogs lie and all that. Explanations were for reconciliations. They had a past, no future.

But that had been when she hated him, when anger had sheltered her heart. That had been when she'd known with certainty they were finished, over, history. Now she wasn't sure about anything. She felt inside her pocket for the sun god, Emily's sun god, drawing strength from it. "I don't understand you, Lucas." His face was illuminated by the flickering flames of the fire. "Why?" she whispered. "Why did you leave me?"

For a split second, he looked into her eyes, and then, as if her pain was too much for him, he glanced away. "This isn't a good time."

"Like there ever will be?"

"This *really* is not the right time for this."

"You owe me an explanation."

"Yes, I do. But not now. Not today." Agitated, he jumped up and paced off the small perimeter of their camp.

"I've waited long enough. Now's as good a time as any, Lucas. I need to know why at the deepest, darkest moment of my life you weren't there for me."

"I *can't*. Not yet." He turned and slowly

walked toward the thick of the rain forest, grabbing a machete on his way.

"So that's it," she yelled after him. "You're on the hot seat, cornered, and you're going to leave. Again. Don't you know how to do anything else?"

Head down, he stepped away.

"Lucas! Catch!" He turned and she tossed him the sun god. "You need this." More than she did.

He disappeared into the brush.

"THAT SATELLITE NUMBER you gave me can't be right." Evelyn spoke into her cell phone while pacing a hallway in the Seattle office of the FBI. She'd previously called the Ollantaytambo number Sydney had given her and had spoken to a man named Miguel. Now, she'd called him back. "I've tried it three times and no one's answering."

Miguel asked her to recite the number. "Yes, that's correct," he said. "They may not hear the ringing. Rapids on the river. Forest noises. The phone may be stuffed under a pack. Be patient," he said. "She will answer."

Who was he, the freaking Dalai Lama?

Evelyn snapped her cell phone closed and waited for Joe to resurface from the head

FBI honcho's office. Occasionally, a stern word or two reached her ears through the closed door. Official words like *protocol, warrants,* and *just cause.* There were also a few not-so-official phrases like *Goddamned imbecile* and *Who the hell do you think you are?*

Once or twice she almost stomped into the office to give the arrogant man a few phrases of her own, but the sound of Joe's calm, measured voice held her back. From the moment she'd seen Trevor late that afternoon, she'd wanted to storm Cochran's island and rescue him. Joe had convinced her that for Trevor's safety, they needed to first garner the necessary manpower.

He was right. He would handle this. For once she had complete confidence in a man. When the door finally opened, a stream of orders followed Joe's wake. "I want paperwork, dammit! On my desk ASAP. All the *I*s dotted and every *T* crossed."

Joe stepped out into the hall, a crooked grin on his face and a wink just for her. He popped a stick of peppermint gum into his mouth and offered her the pack.

"Do you hear me, Agent Donati?"

Joe wiped his face clear of all humor as he

turned back around. "Yes, sir. Loud and clear, sir. It's by the book every step of the way from here on out, sir."

"Damn right." The door slammed in front of him.

"Is he going to give you a team of agents?"

"You heard the man. Some paperwork and serious ass kissing, and we'll be ready to go."

"So when do we get Trevor back?"

Joe looked away, clearly unhappy with the answer. "Tomorrow."

She panicked. "And in the meantime?"

"Easy, Evie, easy. They take Trevor anywhere and the agents watching the island will know."

"Promise?"

"Honey, I know you think I could storm that island single-handedly, but we don't want Trevor hurt. There are at least five armed guards out there, and I'm not Mel Gibson."

"I don't want Mel." She leaned her forehead against his. "I want you keeping an eye on the island. And Trevor."

"You got it, *amuri*."

LUCAS STUFFED the worthless sun god in his pocket and chopped his way through the forest, swinging a machete this way and that in an effort to clear a path. To where, he wasn't sure. Nothing seemed in focus. Not his future. Not his past. Nothing. All he could see was the look on Sydney's face when he hadn't been able to come up with the words she'd needed to hear. He'd disappointed her. Again. To top that off, he'd walked away. Again.

He thwacked more violently at a branch. Over and over. Suddenly, the machete was like a deadweight in his hand. His arms lost their momentum and fell to his side. He dropped to the ground and hung his head.

Random, disjointed thoughts ran through his mind, each one darker and bleaker than the next. He couldn't have said how long he sat there. All he knew was that one moment it was dusk and the next full night. All he knew was that last night, because she'd been in his arms, he'd had a solid night's sleep. He'd awakened feeling alive for the first time in too long to remember. All he knew was that when she'd folded into him as though she'd belonged there, murmuring in her sleep, her warm lips against his bare chest, contentment had entered his heart. And joy. Light on his darkness.

Then he'd kissed her, felt her softness, the fullness of her curves, and the world had felt almost right again. It had taken everything he'd had in him to leave that tent.

Oh, afterward, he'd hurt like hell. All day long. Watching her back move so fluidly in front of him in the canoe. The tilt of her head. The lines of her neck. The easy flare of her hips. All day, wanting her. All day, remembering how she had once felt under him and over him, a part of him. God help him, if he let himself, he could still remember her sweet taste on his tongue.

His insides churned, ached at the thought of having to carry on again without her. He closed his eyes for a moment, felt the pressure of the sun god against his leg, and his thoughts cleared. Yes, he'd miss her, but at least what he felt now was real. The pain. The desire. At least it was honest. That honesty felt like heaven after so many years of denial.

He wanted more. More feeling. More of everything. He was sick of the dullness that had coated his existence, sick of the droning white noise of his life. This was it. He didn't know where this would take him. He didn't know what would come next, but the first step was telling Sydney the truth. He had to give her and himself some semblance of closure.

He headed back to camp and found Sydney sitting by the tiny fire, its embers barely glowing. "I need to talk to you."

"Oh, so now you want to talk." She wasn't going to make it easy, and he was glad. He was ready to fight.

"Yeah."

"Well, this isn't a good time for me. I don't want to talk." She dumped a handful of sand onto the fire, her movements choppy and brisk. Angry.

"Look. You wanted answers, and I've got them. Are you going to listen or not?"

She turned around and folded her arms across her chest. Reluctant, but there. Where the hell did he start? "Do you remember after Emily died, right before I left I told you that her death had changed everything?"

"That's not what you said. You said, and I quote, 'I guess we were never meant to be.'"

He swallowed, the memory of that moment drawing his chest tight. "Yes. That's it exactly. What I meant was..." He paused, taking his time, wanting to get it right, needing her to understand. "I meant that if you had never met me, you would never have gotten pregnant, you would have never married me." He took a deep breath. "Emily dying took away the reason for us to be together."

"You married me only because I was pregnant?"

"No!" Damn, this was going to be hard. How could he explain? "I married you because I loved you. Would you have married *me* if you hadn't gotten pregnant?"

"Yes."

"Think about it. Your mother hated me. She thought I'd seduced you, that I'd taken away your dreams. And you? You gave up your master's degree because of me, because of Em."

She closed her eyes. "I might have chosen to take a little more time, but I still would have married you, pregnant or not."

"Well, I wasn't too sure about that back then." He looked away from her, the pain in her face making him falter. "In fact, I was in a very bad place. The sicker Emily got, the deeper my mind went into a tailspin. I couldn't pull out of it. I was Em's dad. I was supposed to protect her. She was just a baby, and I failed her. I failed you."

"I understand you *thinking* those things,"

she said. "God knows I thought them, too. But how could you have *believed* them?"

"Because every day, I spiraled deeper and deeper into a…mental muck. I'd wake up in the morning, look at you and feel as though *I* had caused those dark circles under your eyes. *I* was the reason you couldn't hold down your food. When I touched you, I felt like all I was doing was *taking,* no matter how I tried to give back."

"But—"

"No. Wait." He cut her off. "I have to finish this." He paced back and forth, the urge to run nipping at his heels. "If I hadn't gotten you pregnant, you wouldn't have had Emily, and your life wouldn't have fallen down around you."

He glanced at her, needing to know what she was thinking, yet knowing if he saw the slightest doubt troubling her he might crash and burn. Concern furrowed her brow, but comprehension dawned in her eyes, giving him the courage to go on.

"When she died, I knew, not believed, *knew* with all my heart, your life would be better without me. I had caused all your pain. I didn't deserve your love. Without me in the picture, you could go on. Your future would be bright, brighter than anything I could have imagined at that point in my life."

A deep breath. One final push. "I felt backed into a corner with only one way out. I had to leave you in order to let you get on with your life. With Emily gone, it would be as if you'd never met me."

Like a mirror into his own soul, myriad emotions spun so clearly out of control on her face, in her eyes. She didn't know what to do, what to feel, how to react.

"Sydney." Stopping in front of her, he gently cupped his hands on her cheeks. "Maybe you loved me too much. Maybe I…maybe I didn't love you enough." The moment the words left his mouth, he knew them as untrue. He had always loved her. Still loved her.

"No," she whispered. "You loved me. That's why you leaving never made sense."

"I only meant to set you free."

A tear spilled down her cheek. "Instead you crushed me."

"I'm so sorry." He rubbed the pad of his thumb across her soft skin. "I never, ever, meant to hurt you."

"Why didn't you come *back?*"

"By the time I realized I might have made a

mistake, it was too late. You'd served me with divorce papers. You'd moved on, and I was glad for you. It seemed I'd been right all along."

"You made a decision about us without consulting me," she said, absorbing it, her emotions ricocheting back and forth. Anger, pain, pain, anger. "What else was I supposed to do?"

"You did what was right."

"We deserved more of a chance." Now she was just plain angry.

"You don't understand where I was at. A place so dark, so debilitating that no one could help me. I had let you down on so many levels. Men aren't supposed to be weak. Men aren't supposed to fail. Men aren't supposed to walk away."

"I loved you, Lucas. We could have worked it out."

"Don't romanticize this!" He turned on her, frustration boiling over. "There's nothing—*nothing*—romantic about a man with a gun in his hand and the barrel inside his mouth."

She gasped.

He thought back to that day in Belize, the ugliest day of his life. The divorce papers had been delivered the previous morning. After an all-day drinking binge, he had woken up in an alley, newspapers covering him as though he were already dead. And he knew what he had to do. He'd gone back to his dingy hotel room. He'd picked up that .45 and come so close to squeezing the trigger.

"I never understood how my dad could have killed himself, but, in the end, he saved me. My dad. All it took was a split-second thought of him. What he'd done. What I was about to do. I finally realized I was going through the same thing. A depression. Major clinical depression."

Now that the worst was out, the rest came easier. "That afternoon, I flew back to D.C. and checked myself into a detox center. They put me in a wing for suicide risks, treated me with antidepressants, and little by little, I got better.

"When I checked out, I went back to work. The weeks passed by in a haze of sleeping, working, eating. Before I knew it the weeks turned into months, the months became years, and those blank, foggy years piled up, one on top of another, bringing me here."

"Are you better? Is it over?"

His laugh sounded bitter and hollow even to his own ears. "It's never over." Depression had made him leave Sydney. Shame had kept him away. "Once you've had a depression, you're always at risk. The doctors say I have a genetic propensity toward it. It can run in families."

"Are you depressed now?"

The hardest question to answer. He remained silent for a moment, thinking, listening to his heart, needing to be as honest as possible for her. For himself. Finally, he laid himself bare. "No. Sometimes I can feel it, though, at the fringe, creeping in. Threatening. Gnawing at me. I have hours, sometimes days that are dark, but as long as I keep moving forward, as long as I have hope, I survive."

She let it sink in, every nuance of every word. Defensiveness and anger bubbled to the surface, distorting his words. As she tamped those destructive emotions down, understanding settled over her aching heart. "I failed you, Lucas."

"What?"

"All this time, I believed that you walked out on me at the deepest and darkest moment of my life. I thought I would never be able to forgive you. The truth is…I wasn't there for you. At *your* deepest and darkest moment."

"Syd, don't do this."

"I just whipped that divorce settlement down to you as quick as I could get it drafted. I never even gave you a chance to explain."

"You did what you thought was best with the information I had given you."

"I did what was easiest."

All these years, she'd blamed him and he'd blamed himself. Even when he'd learned of Trevor, he'd forgiven her within a matter of days. Forgiving herself was going to take a lot longer.

"What's done is done," he said.

"What about Trevor?" The kind of father he'd been with Emily, giving, tender, playful, came back to her in Technicolor. "The truth is, Lucas, he could use a father. No, that's not right." She paused, struck by the intensity and sincerity in Lucas's eyes. Trevor's eyes. "He deserves *you* as a father."

He looked as if she'd punched him in the gut.

"We can figure something out," she offered.

"No. We can't."

"We have to try."

"Syd, I didn't tell you these things in order to jump back into your life. You and I both needed closure." He turned his back on her and headed into the tent. "Now we've got it. Case closed."

CHAPTER SEVENTEEN

"ON YOUR LEFT!" Lucas yelled at the sight of a boulder beneath the boiling surface of the brown water. If they tipped the canoe and Sydney got hurt, he'd never forgive himself for making her come along.

"Got it!" Sydney crossbowed at the front while he j-stroked to pivot the stern.

The canoe tilted and water splashed over the gunnels. A precarious second later, and they were through the worst of it. He breathed a deep sigh of relief.

After beating a long steady path down-river that morning, taking only the most necessary of pit stops, they'd spent the last half an hour navigating their way through a particularly difficult stretch of the Urubamba. Several additional minor chutes and they were finally back to the lazy, deep current that had marked the majority of their river passage of the past three days. Using his paddle as a rudder, he steered them to shore for a breather. After that last series of rapids and an afternoon of muggy heat counterposed by intermittent downpours—hot then wet, then hot and wet again—his arms were nearly spent. Hers had to be burning.

"You doing okay?" He caught hold of the root of a tree and tied their boat in place.

"My arms are tired," she said. "But I'll live. Were you able to get a look at the shoreline through any of that?"

"Not really." He turned and scanned the banks of the river, pulled out his plastic bag and studied the map. "Those were some pretty tough rapids. We could have passed the second marker and I wouldn't have even noticed."

"That's it!" she said, holding her hands out to her side. "The spiral!"

"What?"

"The new symbol on the first marker! The lines spiraling inward with small circles surrounding it. It means rapids on the river."

"Do you think the marker is before the rapids or after?"

"Probably before. Now what?"

"Two options. We tie up the canoe here and walk the banks of the river back, which could take us the rest of the day and give Cochran time to catch up with us. Or we keep going." He took a long pull from his water bottle and tossed it back to the floor of the canoe.

"As long as we haven't passed the third marker," she said, "we can probably get by without finding the second. What do you think?"

Cochran catching up to them seemed a bigger risk than missing a clue on the second marker. "We've still got several hours of daylight left. Let's keep going."

After making sure they'd left no sign of their boat scraping along the sandy shoreline, Lucas was about to untie them from shore when the satellite phone rang, a foreign, out-of-place racket in rain forest wilderness.

His stomach pitched at the sound. Evelyn was calling about Trevor. *Finally. Finally!*

"Where is it? Quick!" She shuffled the packs around at the bottom of the canoe, almost losing her balance and tipping them in the process.

"I got it." He yanked a small backpack to his lap. "Relax, or you're going to dump us."

While he unzipped the pack and dug out the satellite phone case, she sat down and gripped her hands together. He handed her the receiver, and she flicked it on.

"Hello." Her hand trembled. "Evelyn?"

"Sydney?" Evelyn's voice came across the line clear enough even for Lucas to hear. "Good. I finally got you."

She grabbed his hand, and he squeezed back, waiting.

"Have you found Trevor?" she asked.

The swift river current jostled the boat, wrenching it free from the tree root tie-down.

"We—"

The boat tilted. The phone slipped from Sydney's hand and splashed into the river.

"No!" she screamed, jumping up and watching it float away on the current.

"Sit down!" Lucas yelled.

She dropped to her seat. He shoved the canoe directly into the river's flow with his paddle and gunned the motor after the phone. Twenty feet. Ten. The receiver sank out of sight into the murky brown water.

"We have to get it back!" she cried.

He mentally aligned the location where it had sunk with a huge tree along the shore.

"How deep is the water here?" she asked.

"At least ten feet." He cut the motor and leaned over the gunnels. As the current carried them past the spot where the receiver had sunk, he plunged his hands into the water. *Please let it be there. Please.* He watched and waited to feel the hard plastic hit his hand.

Seconds later, he leaned back empty-handed, his shoulders sagging in defeat.

Sydney put her head in her hands and sobbed. "No! No! No!"

She was losing it. The hysteria she'd done such a good job of suppressing finally bubbled to the surface, and Lucas couldn't blame her. He felt it, too. Running the boat aground, he hopped ashore, and sloshed through the water. "It's okay." He helped her out of the canoe and rocked her in his arms. "It's going to be okay."

"It's not okay! Nothing's ever going to be okay again!" She pulled away and trudged through the sand, tears pouring down her face. "I asked if they'd found Trevor, and Evie said 'We.' That's all. She didn't say yes. It's been four days and they haven't found him. That's a long time. What if he's hurt? What if they're not feeding him? What if…what if they locked him up somewhere and haven't given him anything to eat or drink?"

He couldn't voice the worst. What if Trevor was already dead? It was Emily all over again, and he felt himself slipping. "Shhh." He stopped her, bracketed her face with his hands, and forced her to look into his eyes. "Listen to me! It's not going to do anyone any good if we fall apart." He moved his hands to her shoulders. "Do you understand that?"

She nodded and swallowed.

"Okay." He sighed, focused for a moment. "Evelyn may not have said yes, but she didn't say no, either. She said *we*. I heard it. Maybe as in 'We know where he is.' Maybe even, 'We found him.'"

She sniffled. "You're jumping to conclusions."

"So were you. Bad ones. The truth is that we can't deduce much of anything, either good or bad, from the word *we*. So instead, let's think about this. Logically." He dropped his hands and looked away, grappling for anything.

"Logically," Sydney murmured. "How 'bout this?" Hope replaced desperation in her eyes. "These people that took Trevor, they're not treating him like he's kidnapped. Remember? At your hotel room? When Cochran let us talk to Trevor? He told Trevor I was away on business. Remember? That means—"

"They want Trevor's cooperation," he added, jumping on the bandwagon. At the time the significance hadn't sunk in, but now he smiled. "And he's a smart kid. He'll figure that out."

"He's going to be okay." She smiled back.

"On top of that, Cochran knows we're here. He probably knows we're ahead of him. All the more reason for him to keep Trevor safe. He's got a bargaining chip."

"And he's not going to mess with a bargaining chip," she nodded, drying her face and her dripping nose with the back of her hand, pulling herself together.

"No. He's not." Lucas brushed his fingertips across her cheek.

"As long as we stay focused."

"As long as we get to the temple before Cochran," he whispered.

"Trevor will be okay." She took a deep, shaky breath and settled. When she looked into his eyes, what he saw there at once comforted and frightened him. "I'm sorry I fell apart," she said. "I know this is hard for you, too."

All day he'd waited for her to have some kind of a reaction to what he'd told her the previous night about his depression and why he'd left her. During the times they weren't busy with river rapids, he'd watched for her judgment, for disdain, scorn or even simply anger. What he'd found, instead, had been a quiet acceptance of him and his explanations. There had been no accusations. No pity. No contempt. She wanted him in Trevor's life. Him.

He should have felt relieved, if not happy. But spilling his guts to her last night had emptied him of more than secrets, done more than drain the bile from his soul. It had left him empty and desolate. Feeling alone again, but curiously lonely for the first time in years. He looked away and swallowed the urge to fall into her arms, to seek the solace he knew he'd find.

"How much...how much farther do we have to go?" she asked.

Grateful for the distraction, he pulled out his map and showed her the positions of the first two markers. "I'm thinking the final marker should be here. Shortly after we merge with the Rio Tambo. By dark we should be hitting the village of Atalaya. Then tomorrow...tomorrow we should find the last marker."

"Did you say village?"

He nodded. "It's not what you think. We're talking a small, extremely isolated river settlement. But they might have a satellite phone."

"Do you think?"

He shrugged. "We should stop there for the night anyway."

"But we just agreed we needed to get to the temple before Cochran."

"We will. I promise. Whether or not we stay in Atalaya for the night isn't going to make a difference," he argued. "By the time we get there it'll be dark. We'd have to pitch the tent anyway. I don't know about you," he continued, "but I've had enough protein bars and trail mix to last a lifetime. A cold drink and a hot meal is sounding pretty good right about now."

"What about Cochran?"

"He's got to sleep, too. Besides, he's probably still a day behind." He sighed. "Look. We need to replenish our gas and food supplies. Call Evelyn. And I'm shot. I could use a break, and you *need* one. We've been pushing it hard for days. We eat a decent meal. Get a good night's sleep. Head off before sunrise in the morning. What could be the harm in a little diversion?"

"SOUNDS LIKE A PARTY," Sydney said.

Lively music floated down the waterway as they approached the outskirts of Atalaya. By the time they spotted the first thatched-roof house the coolness of dusk had fully settled, making the banks of the Urubamba difficult to discern. She was glad to see faint lights illuminating a row of sturdy docks at the forefront of what appeared to be the village center.

Lucas landed the river canoe and Sydney, anxious to find a phone, hopped onto the dock and tied down the boat. While she grabbed their packs, he spoke with a group of young boys playing near the docks. A wedding, they'd answered in response to questions about the music. He flipped each boy ten *soles*. "If the boat stays safe through the night, you'll get twenty more in the morning."

Sydney handed over one of the packs and followed him off the docks. Atalaya was larger and more active than she'd expected for a settlement sitting in the middle of nowhere. There were a few buildings, two lodges, a couple restaurants and several houses. The wedding party spilled out from a large clapboard building at one end of town. Colorful paper lanterns hung from nearby tree branches and a bonfire lit up the dirt street.

They headed in the opposite direction and passed an old weathered structure with a sign claiming, Hostal d'Souza. "This is it. For better or worse."

"A bed and a shower." Her skin and scalp suddenly felt dirty and itchy, and the idea of getting clean revitalized her. "I'm beginning to think Atalaya was a good idea."

"I've stayed here before. Don't get overly excited about the accommodations."

They entered the Hostal d'Souza and found a group of Australian tourists conversing in a rustic lobby. After greeting them, they moved on to the front desk and immediately asked for a satellite phone. Half an hour later, after being unable to reach Evelyn's cell phone, they got her answering machine and listened to her recorded message to them.

"We know where Trevor is," she said in her recording. "He's fine. They're treating him okay, Syd. I've seen him myself. While the FBI is getting warrants and such, we're keeping an eye on him. Joe says we'll have him back tomorrow."

"Good news." Lucas hung up the receiver and smiled.

Sydney swallowed, near tears.

"Hey. What's the problem?"

"Why don't they have him back already if they know his location?"

"They need to be prepared. If Trevor doesn't appear to be in any danger, Joe won't want to take any unnecessary risks."

Only one thing could take away her trepidation. Trevor safe and sound in their own home. But she'd take what she could get.

"In the morning," Lucas said. "We'll head back to Seattle."

"No." She shook her head. "Something could go wrong with the rescue attempt. Just in case, we need to find that temple."

They paid for two rooms, and then lugged their packs to the end of a bare-planked hallway. Sydney unlocked the door and surveyed her sparsely appointed room. With nothing more than a battered table, outdated lamp, and a worn-looking bed and chair, the accommodations seemed better suited to a monastery than a hotel. At least everything was clean.

She crossed the small room, dropped her pack on the floor and tested the mattress. Monasteries probably had more comfortable beds. This one was lumpy and sagged in the middle. The only saving grace was the view. Her room faced a stretch of thick, undisturbed rain forest. A slight breeze through the open windows ruffled the faded curtains and carried in faint music from the wedding party. Lucas checked out the bathroom and closet.

"What are you doing?"

"Making sure you're alone." After checking behind every door, he headed back for the hall. "When I close this door, I want you to lock it and set the chain. Don't leave this hotel without me. Okay?"

"Okay," she absently agreed.

He cupped her chin and gently forced her face toward his. "Sydney, I mean it."

"Okay, okay. I won't go anywhere without you. Promise."

"Keep this with you." He pressed a gun into her hand and walked to his room directly across the hall.

She locked the door, slipped the chain in place and headed for the bathroom. After setting the handgun on the counter, she stripped, pulled the clip out of her hair and stepped into the antiquated, but neatly scrubbed shower stall.

Again, Lucas had been right on target. The

water pressure, if one could actually call it that, was practically nonexistent and a faint fishy odor filled the air. Screw it. She needed this. She lathered herself up with a floral shower gel and ignored the imperfections. After several days of muggy heat, muddy river water and mucky shorelines, it felt like heaven to be relatively clean again. Her reservation about spending the night in Atalaya drained away with the dirty water. And the lumpy bed? Saggy or not, comfort wouldn't matter. Especially if she wasn't alone.

Case closed. His words nagged at her, and her thoughts traveled roads she'd managed to avoid most of the day, rehashing their discussion from the previous night. For all her rantings and ravings, all her tears and sleepless nights through the years, Lucas's intentions in leaving her, however misguided, had been honest and true. She should have known he'd been hurting. Instead, she'd been so wrapped up in her own pain, she'd never noticed.

Remorse thickening her throat, she turned off the shower, dried herself with the only towel the hotel had provided, and then wrapped the thinning terry cloth around her head. Her dingy clothes lay in a pile at her feet. No way was she putting those on again. She rummaged through her pack, found a slightly wrinkled, but clean pair of shorts and shook them out.

A thong dropped to the floor, and the bit of neon pink and orange satin immediately screamed for attention. She dug around for the matching bra. Her heart suddenly racing, she slipped them both on and searched through her bag one more time. No makeup, only lip gloss and a lightly scented lotion. Tossing aside several T-shirts, she came to one and stopped. It wasn't sheer and it wasn't slinky, but the black spandex blend would cling provocatively to her breasts and sported a dipping V-neck.

She slathered on some lotion, pulled the shirt over her head, and, forgoing a ponytail, scrunched up her damp hair and let the curls fall free. Straightening, tugging and squirming, she glanced at her reflection in the old bathroom mirror and adjusted the neckline to show a little cleavage.

She'd messed up in the past by letting Lucas go. No way was she making that same mistake again. This time, if she had anything to say about it, Lucas wasn't getting away.

"HOLY…" LUCAS MUTTERED under his breath. At the sight of Sydney walking down the hall, his throat turned sandpaper dry, no small feat in the heart of a rain forest.

When she entered the hotel lobby every male head in the room turned in her direction. Her loose, curly black hair glistened with moisture from a shower. Her lips looked wet, glossy, and her face shone with freshness. Her tight black shirt was sexy enough to make a man wonder, make his fingers start to itch. And his breath hitch, if he was able to breathe at all. And with those Dakota-freeway legs, she may as well have worn a miniskirt rather than serviceable shorts. She walked toward him. "Ready?"

Too ready, that was the problem. Lucas pushed away from the far wall. "Maybe you should go back to your room. Pull up your hair. Put on a different shirt."

"Why?" Her smile disappeared, and she rested her hands on her hips. The movement stretched the shirt tighter against her breasts, and the itching in his fingers picked up a notch.

"I told you before this can be a dangerous town." He glared back at the men in the lobby, who quickly averted their gazes. "I'm not too excited about the prospect of having to protect you." Not to mention having to look and not touch all night.

"Oh, you're full of it. I'm dressed much less provocatively than they are." She pointed out the front windows toward the view of the village square. "See?"

A group of young men and women walked by the hotel, presumably toward the party. To Lucas's dismay, Sydney was right. The women wore flirty dresses with short hems and thin shoulder straps.

"Come on. Relax." She snagged his arm on her way out the door. "We're here for a diversion, remember?"

They passed by the outdoor wedding celebration on their way to the café and seated themselves at a small table facing the dense forest. Along with a faintly damp, but cool breeze, music from the wedding party filtered through the screen-covered windows lining the entire back wall of the café.

With little to choose from on the menu, the food came quickly to their table. The saucy rice with fish chunks, egg and plantain was served wrapped in a banana leaf, and had been cooked over an open wood fire out back. Though the dish wasn't quite what

Miguel was able to concoct at a moment's notice, it was savory, hot and plentiful. By the time they left the café and stepped onto the covered veranda, Lucas felt more relaxed than he had in months.

Full darkness had settled over the small village, and the wedding party next door had stepped up in intensity. The music was faster, louder. Jungle music. As different from the peaceful sounds of the local musicians they'd heard around Miguel's fire as this rain forest was from the Peruvian highlands. Though the panpipes still sounded prominently, the *charango* guitars and bongos carried the bright, zingy echo of salsa to the rhythm. At times sultry and hot like the rain forest, and at others jubilant and joyous with hands clapping and singers yipping into the night, the sounds made it hard for Lucas to keep his toes from tapping.

Sydney stepped down onto the road, spread her arms wide and stretched. "Now what?"

"We go back to the hotel and get a good night's sleep so we can get back on the river before sunrise." The sparkle in her eyes told him anything more than that would be dangerous.

A group of people passed by and a young

man tugged on Sydney's arm. "Come with us, *señorita!*" He grabbed her waist and tangoed her the short distance to the party.

"*Vengan.* Join us." A woman dragged Lucas toward the bonfire.

"*Gracias.*" He smiled and politely extricated himself from her grasp, all the while keeping his sights on Sydney.

"Lucas!" she yelled, laughing. "Come on!" The young man drew Sydney with him into the heart of the crowd and, without warning, she disappeared.

Lucas shifted and ran ahead. She was gone. Vanished. Alarm washed over him as he pushed through groups of people talking and between rough wooden tables filled with locals eating. Dark heads everywhere. No Sydney. He made it as far back as the musicians and she was still nowhere to be seen.

Had she left? He skimmed the edge of the forest. And stopped at a flash of pale skin and light-colored hair, his heart racing. Cochran? *Damn!*

CHAPTER EIGHTEEN

LUCAS SPUN BACK AROUND, searching for
Cochran, for Sydney, but there was nothing
to be seen in the jungle except green and
darker green. If he lost her. Sweet Jesus, if
he lost Sydney—

Hands wrapped around his waist from
behind—Sydney's hands, soft, warm and
sure—and he knew he must have been
imagining Cochran in the forest. He closed
his eyes, letting the panic blow away on a
long sigh. When he turned in her arms, she
was smiling. "Lost you for a moment," he
said. Her eyes grew serious and he pulled her
closer, never wanting to lose her again,
wanting to make her a part of him, forever.
Wanting the world to go away. And it did.

This moment, the two of them holding
each other in the darkness of a tiny Peruvian
rain forest settlement, was all that existed.
The only sound the trembling rush of his

breath mixing with hers. The only sensations the feel of her body molding to his and that skintight T-shirt beneath his hands. Before he realized what he was doing, he'd backed her toward the outer edge of the party, in the shadows at the side of the building. Now even the music and chatter of the crowd around them drifted away. All he knew was her face and the points where her body touched his.

She glanced up, her lips parted, and all reasonable, rational thought flew from his mind. He groaned and clutched her head between his hands. And kissed her, crushing her lips beneath his mouth. Moving her back against the wall, he covered her cheeks with tender, sweet kisses.

She bent and touched her lips to his neck. "I love you." The words tumbled from her mouth. "I never stopped loving you."

He broke free and stood back, his breath catching in his chest. After all he'd told her? After all his weaknesses and faults? "You don't. You can't."

"I do. I will forever." She splayed her hands against his chest and backed him into a tree.

The painful scratch of bark against his

back took his mind from the warmth seeping from her hands to his heart. When her touch threatened to move lower, he covered her hands and held them. "Don't."

"I made a mistake years ago by letting you walk out of my life," she said. "I won't make that same mistake again."

He nearly lost himself in the unshed tears glistening in her eyes. For one moment, elation thrilled through him. She loved him. After all these years. He'd never fathomed the possibility.

She cupped his face between her hands and whispered, "There's nothing that can tear you away from me again."

Reality crashed down, shattering any illusions he'd oh-so-briefly allowed himself to entertain. "And there's the problem."

"Don't try to say you don't love me."

"Oh, I love you." His voice broke. He pushed away from the tree, gently set her aside and paced in the dirt. "That was never in doubt. But it's not enough. It wasn't enough the first go-round. It'll never be enough. You need to let me go. Get on with your life without me. I'll only bring you pain."

"Let me decide what I need, or don't need."

"Sydney, it's been a long couple of days. You're tired and worried about Trevor. You're not thinking straight."

"I'm thinking straighter than I ever have. I want you. Tonight." She stepped toward him and stopped him with hands to his shoulders. "What does Lucas Rydall want?"

You. My life back. A second chance. What he deserved was a completely different story. "What difference does it make?" he asked. "We find the temple and the Huari bowl, and then you'll go back to Seattle. To Trevor. To your life. I'll go back to mine. Everything goes back to normal."

"That's what you'd like, isn't it?" Her tone suddenly changed. "For everything to go back to the way it was before? For you to go back the way you were before? Dead. Numb. Gone."

"What are you getting at?"

"I've been thinking about what you said last night. Your reasons for leaving me." Her desperation dissipated, and anger simmered to the surface. "I don't think you left for *me*. I think you left for *you*."

Here it was, what he'd been waiting for all day long. "How do you figure?"

"I don't doubt for a second that you're

telling me the truth about your depression, but you were in pain, too. You'd lost Emily. One of the two most important people in your life. I think…just maybe…you couldn't bear to lose me, too. What if *I* suddenly got cancer? What if *I* were killed in a car accident? What if *I* had left you?"

He swallowed hard and looked away.

"So you preempted any possible scenario of me leaving," she said, her voice softening again, "by walking away first."

It wasn't true. He wouldn't let it be true. He would never have hurt her like that.

"I love you, Lucas, and I want you," she went on, her voice now cutting through him like a machete through a whisper-thin leaf. "If you stay away, *this* time it won't be for me." She broke away from him and started slowly back toward the hotel. "I'll be in my room. And I won't be sleeping."

He watched her walk away, feeling weakness and need devour him with her every step, with every swing of her arms and every ripple of the breeze through her long hair. Damn, he was sick of keeping his distance. He was only a man. A man who had been alone for too many years. Her eyes were wide open and she wanted this. There was no doubt what *he* wanted. Deserving or not, tonight they were both going to get what they wanted. It was time to make her remember what he'd never been able to forget.

SYDNEY STOOD BY her hotel room door and put the key in the lock. Lucas's footsteps echoed down the hall, slowed, and then finally stopped behind her. He may have been five feet back, but it made no difference. She could feel his body heat. His need. Swirling in the hot air, intermixing with her own.

She swung open the door, stepped inside and faced him. "Do you want in or out?"

The still night air grew heavy with expectation. The ever-present sounds of party music floated through the open window along with moonlight filtering through the tall wall of rain forest. In three long steps he was beside her. "Definitely in." He kicked the door closed behind them, turned the lock and tossed a box of condoms onto the bed. "Courtesy of the front desk."

For a moment she stood there, her heart racing. Then, as if he'd flipped a switch, her apprehension disappeared. He backed her against the wall, and leaned into her, his arms on either side of her head. He pressed against her, and she wrapped her hand around his neck, pulling him closer.

So many times in the last few days Sydney hadn't a clue what this man had been thinking, hadn't been able to even guess what was going on inside him. But here, in his arms, she could read him. His body beneath her hands, this she knew. With every pulse of his heart she understood his intent, and he was as clear to her as the thoughts in her own mind. He wanted her. He loved her. He would always love her. She would never doubt that again.

"Oh, Lucas!" She shoved away from the wall and backed him into the room. In two swift movements, her T-shirt and shorts were gone, and she was helping him undress.

"You brought this little thing into the jungle?" His fingers dipped under the satin thong. "And this?" His hand cupped the brightly colored bra.

She smiled.

"Neon orange and pink." The sound he made was half laugh, half growl, and then they were naked in front of each other, only milky moonlight shimmering on their skin.

She trailed her hands down him, over tense muscles and tight, wiry hair. After all these years, the hardness of a man, of Lucas, turned her insides to liquid. She pushed him back onto the narrow bed and climbed over him.

"Oh, no, you don't." He rolled her back over, reversing positions. "You wanted tonight? You've got it. Everything." His mouth was on her, over her, in her. "I've never been able to forget how you taste," he whispered against her hot skin, trailing his tongue over one breast and down her belly. "So good. So warm. On my fingers. In my mouth."

She let go a shaky breath. How many times had she dreamed of this over the years? Waiting, teasing, was impossible torture. "Now, Lucas. Now."

When he entered her, she nearly cried out in joy. The feel of him inside her, full, hard, close. Closer. She moaned and angled herself to let him in as far, as deep, as possible. She wanted to be a part of him, to sink inside him. There she would never have to worry about him leaving her again.

How could he leave *this* again?

He moved against her, with her, and all conscious thought escaped her mind. There was only Lucas. His mouth on hers, his breath filling her lungs. His bare skin under her trembling fingertips. All at once the world disintegrated around her only to burst forth again and again. Over and over.

"Sydney!" he moaned and shuddered against her. He took a deep breath and slowed. When he finally collapsed against her, she would've sworn she tasted the salt of his tears on her lips.

He rested his forehead on hers and whispered, "Memories are nothing. This—*this*—is everything."

She was everything. His body released and he took in the soft pink of her face, the texture and sheen of her hair, the curve of her lips. The corners of his mouth curved upward, and contentment seeped into his bones.

She stirred, almost purring beneath him, and her smile widened. As he met her lips in a gentle crush, her words ricocheted through him. *What if I suddenly got cancer? What if I were killed in a car accident? What if I left you?* His breath caught in his throat. He couldn't think of that. Not when he was inside her, not when she was so alive she sparked something dead within him, so gentle and strong she brought his armor crashing down.

She drew back and her smile faded. "Don't tell me you regret this. I don't think I could deal with that."

"Never." He brushed his hand over her cheek. "I could never regret you." He buried his nose in her hair, taking in the fresh, heady scent of her, replacing all those terrible thoughts with all things real, here and now, her skin beneath his hands, her taste on his tongue, her arms enfolding him, claiming him again.

As if he could ever belong to anyone else. He was hers. Always had been. Always would be. Time and distance would change nothing. Death, anger, loss. Failure. They meant nothing to his heart. Nothing to his body.

He found her mouth, open and inviting. Her tongue wrapped around his, drawing him in, and he was lost. Or had he been found?

Hope, pure, alive and bright, surged through him. If they saved Trevor, if he found the temple and that ever-elusive redemption he'd been searching for all these years, then maybe he could stop running. Maybe then he could go home. To Sydney. To his son. A family.

If. If, if, if.

Too soon, the ugly doubts sidled in. He rolled over and turned his face away.

"Lucas," she breathed against his hot skin and nipped at his neck.

She moved over him, spread her legs around him and welcomed him inside her again. The feel of her over him, around him, soothing him, making him whole, if only for a while, overrode all else. He was found again.

"DROP IT DOWN," Joe ordered.

The navigator switched to the nearly silent trolling motor as the boat full of FBI agents approached Cochran's island. Clouds fortunately covered the night sky. There wasn't a single star lighting their way or, more importantly, giving them away.

"This close over water, they'll hear any noise we make," Joe whispered, catching the gaze of each of the agents in turn. "I do *not* want a *sound* on this boat." Evelyn's playful, loves-to-banter guy had been replaced by a calculating, serious, by-the-numbers agent. His gaze stopped at her. "That includes you."

He looked so damned good with his black baseball cap and flak jacket emblazoned boldly across the front and back with the letters FBI. Talk about foreplay. She could have gobbled him up right here. His brows drew down and he gave her the evil eye, telling her clearly she had better not make him regret allowing her to come along on this raid.

She smiled. After several days of searching and a cold night of surveillance on that island, in fifteen minutes, thirty tops, they'd have Trevor back, hopefully not a hair on his head out of place. Another few hours and she'd be in Joe's arms.

The boat silently rounded the far side of Cochran's island and Joe studied the terrain with night-vision binoculars. "I see the three guards. Steer clear of them and run her aground near the point." A hundred feet out, the pilot cut the trolling motor and glided the boat to shore. They landed with a soft crunch against sand and rocks.

Joe glanced carefully around and hopped out. The other agents, each equipped with night-vision goggles, weapons and earpieces linked to Joe's transmitter, filed out behind him. One of the agents helped Evelyn to shore, then anchored the boat beside an outcropping of land, effectively hiding it from view.

Joe led Evelyn to the base of a large ever-
green tree. "Crouch down below those
bushes and stay out of sight," he whispered.
"You come looking for me, and I'm locking
you up when we get back. I mean it. And
leave that flak jacket on."

He turned back to his team. "Brightner,
Dooney, Linhart. You secure the three guards
in back. The rest of you to the main house.
Get in position, wait for my signal. Okay, let's
go." The agents fanned out in a prearranged
pattern, and Joe disappeared into the woods.

One long second after another ticked by
without a sound. The minutes quietly added
up, and Evelyn sat as still as she could. Footsteps sounded from around the point and she
stiffened. Glancing between the branches in
front of her face, she saw one of Cochran's
guards walking the southern perimeter of the
island. Joe had missed this one!

He stopped at the edge of the woods.
Evelyn held her breath and waited for him to
move on. Instead, he pulled out a gun and
walked onto the beach. Crouching down, he
fingered the footprints in the sand. Slowly, he
stood and walked straight toward her. Pa-
nicking, she froze and held her breath. She
could make a run for the woods. He might

shoot, but with the flak jacket, she had a good chance of making it. There was no time. One more step and he would be on her. She tucked her head down and closed her eyes. Nothing happened. She looked up in time to see him following Joe's footsteps into the woods.

She had fully intended to stay behind those bushes. She really had. She trusted Joe implicitly with Trevor's safety, but this was too much. She had to warn Joe. Climbing out from behind the branches, she followed Joe's path through the woods. Soon, she saw the exterior lights from Cochran's mansion. The guard had disappeared. So had Joe. She couldn't see anyone or anything.

A hand gripped her wrist and pulled her down. Before she could yelp, fingers clamped over her mouth and an arm swung around her, cinching her in a viselike grip. She couldn't move, could barely breathe.

"Damn it, Evie," Joe hissed in her ear. "I told you to stay in those bushes."

She jerked away from his hand and whispered, "A guard saw our tracks down at the beach. I came to warn you."

Joe stood backlit by the house's security lights. He motioned to the right with his head. "You mean him?" The guard she'd followed into the woods lay out cold on the ground. "Eat your heart out, Mel Gibson."

Evelyn smiled at the same time as tears of relief welled in her eyes.

He stripped off one of his gloves and handed it to her. "Stuff that in his mouth." Pulling out a set of handcuffs, he secured the guard's arms behind his back. He stood and said, "Now you can get that sweet butt of yours back to the boat."

"No."

"Then watch him." He motioned to the guard and handed her his spare gun. "If he moves, shoot him. I gotta go. Everyone's in position, and they're waiting for me to get into the house." He pointed at her. "Stay here." He ran quietly through the woods and across the yard.

She scooted ten feet away from the guard and pointed the gun at him. Shouting erupted from every direction, "FBI!" and every variation of "put down your weapons!" imaginable. Only two shots were fired before the grounds were lit up and Cochran's guards were handcuffed and lined up in the yard. Where was Trevor? She dashed out of the woods and flagged down an agent. "There's another bad guy in the woods." She pointed behind her and rushed into the house. Joe's voice drew her down the far hall. "FBI!" he yelled. "Put up your hands!"

Evelyn rounded the last corner to find Trevor huddled behind Joe, and Joe training his gun on a man desperately looking for a way out. "Trevor!" she yelled. "Come here!" She bent down and held out her arms.

The terror on Trevor's face instantaneously cleared. "Evie!" He ran straight for her.

"You okay, buddy?"

"Mmm, hmm." Trevor's little arms gripped her tightly.

"Get your hands in the air! Now!" Joe said. "It's over, asshole."

The man slowly raised his arms.

Evelyn drew Trevor into her lap, cradled him and watched Joe through pooling tears. He never took his eyes or his weapon off the guard. And Evie had never found a man more attractive or more lovable. *Why the hell couldn't he be rich?*

CHAPTER NINETEEN

"It's gotta be here." Lucas compared his map once again to the GPS unit, tracing their progress inch by quarter inch. They were right where they should be. Still, there was no sign of the third and final marker. No sign of a column, no sign of stacked rocks, no sign of anything except rain forest as far as the eye could see.

They'd traveled nearly half the day down-river from Atalaya and had gone much farther than he believed the marker would be before finally turning around to take a closer look at the shoreline they'd already covered. Backtracking had been risky with Cochran behind them, and once or twice he thought he'd heard a motor or even voices, but no one had materialized.

They had to find that marker. Soon. Or risk Cochran catching up to them. Edgy now, he unsnapped the strap holding his gun in the shoulder holster, making it more accessible.

"Maybe we need to go farther upriver," Sydney suggested. The boat shifted as she adjusted her grip on the tree branch in an attempt to keep them close to shore.

Most of the river they'd traveled up until now had been lined, at least intermittently, with flat, sandy beaches. Here, the bank dropped some four feet with the jungle refusing to stop until it hit the rushing waters of the Rio Ucayali. Rotting debris clung to the roots and branches jutting out from the sandy bank.

"It's possible the map wasn't carved to scale on the stone wall at Machu Picchu," she continued. "The last marker could be farther out than the other two."

"Possible, but not likely. You've seen the Inca stonework. It's precise. Perfect. There's no reason to believe this map is any different from the everyday walls they constructed around the country."

"Could you have misinterpreted where we are?"

"Once again, possible, but not likely. I've tracked every twist, turn and straightaway since we set off from Timpia." He pointed at a spot on the stained and dirty map. "See this last bend? That's just upriver. It's different from the one before it because it's deeper, sharper. I know this map, and now I know this stretch of river."

"It's been hundreds of years, Lucas." Her shoulder sagged. "Rivers change."

"The marker should still be here."

He couldn't voice the alternative. The mere thought of it churned his stomach. Heavy rains through the years may have weakened the shoreline enough that the marker had fallen into the river. If that had happened, the temple would stay lost. And Trevor? He'd be okay. Joe was seeing to that, but no marker meant Lucas's search would be over. It meant no miracle cures. No cure for cancer.

No, that wasn't possible. He cleared the negative thoughts. The marker had to be near. He could feel it, could almost hear the Inca spirits speaking to him.

"Well, I need to pee," Sydney said, "so hold on for a minute."

Preoccupied, he grabbed the nearest exposed tree root, and she climbed onto shore. He continued looking up and down river, comparing the shoreline with his map and studying the trees for anything abnormal. After a few minutes, the root he'd been holding broke away from shore and he was forced to reach for another. When his hold shifted even more, he glanced absently at the trunk of the small tree. The roots had grown over a large rock, making it difficult for the plant to find solid purchase. The underlying rock seemed natural enough, at first, but as he studied it closer, there seemed to be something unusual about its surface. It was smooth, almost too smoo—

Quickly, he reached out and brushed off the rock surface. Moving farther down, he yanked at a grouping of vines exposing more large, smooth rocks, like the first. All too square. All too perfect. All set too tightly together into the ground and laid out along the shoreline to be natural. Someone had laid them here.

"Lucas!" Sydney yelled. "You need to come and see this. Quick!"

"You gotta see *this!*"

She pushed through the heavy bushes. "I found a bench, or something. Made out of stone. Right here, in the middle of nowhere."

"Take a look at these." He continued down the shore and pushed aside as many branches, vines and roots as he could. More of the same. Large stones, smooth and flat, butted up against each other.

"What is it?"

"Looks like a platform." He caught himself grinning. "A landing platform."

"For boats!"

"Do you know how unbelievable this is?" He shook his head and laughed. "We never should have found this! Several feet of jungle debris would have accumulated over the past five hundred years."

"So what happened to clear it?"

"A flood must have run through here and washed most of it away and it probably caused the marker to fall into the river, too." He drifted to a spot downstream with a lower bank, hopped into the river and tossed their gear onto shore. "Help me get this boat out of the water." Cochran didn't need a written invitation to the doors of the temple.

Once the boat and most of their gear had been stowed out of sight behind a stand of bushes, they searched the landing area and found nothing more than several stone benches in various stages of overgrowth.

Sydney set her hands on her hips. "Not much of a temple, if you ask me."

He shook his head. "This isn't it. The settlement will be inland. In the cloud forests."

"You mean somewhere in there?" She

pointed a thumb toward the seemingly impenetrable wall of green at her back.

"If we're lucky, the hills will be close to the river." If not, he didn't want to think about how many weeks it would take to hack their way through the jungle.

"So how are we supposed to find it? We sure as hell can't just head off through the bush."

"Neither could the Inca. Their home was the mountains. They would have felt like fish out of water way out here. There must be something that indicates a direction." But centuries had passed. It was hard to imagine anything surviving. "Let's find the perimeter of the landing platform. Maybe that will give us some clues."

They moved along the riverbank until they found the right edge of the platform, and then trudged into the forest from there. It was slow going. Though less dense than the main parts of the forest, vegetation had nonetheless completely overrun the ancient boat landing. They were forced to shift around trees, cut back vines and bushes, all the while swatting away ants and swarming mosquitoes.

Eventually, they found the back edge

fifteen feet into the forest. Another twenty or so feet, and she stopped. "What's this?"

He yanked away brush and vegetation, dropped to his hands and knees and dug away the countless decades of dirt and rotting debris over the Inca stonework. The once-straight line of stones had now become quite irregular. Laying his hands flat against them, he tried to imagine building this platform. Why would the line of the platform suddenly change? Why here?

It came to him in a rush. "It's like a sidewalk!" Jubilant, he leaned over and kissed her dirt-stained lips. "You found a damned sidewalk in the middle of the Peruvian rain forest."

She laughed and kissed him again.

He jumped up, held out his hand for her and pulled her to her feet. After slipping on a backpack filled with a GPS unit, some excavating tools and other supplies, he said, "Let's head in as far as we can manage before I start using the machete to clear a path. If Cochran does manage to find the platform, I don't want to make it too easy for him to follow us into the forest."

After several minutes of struggling through the thick branches, bushes and vines, he pulled out his machete and handed her his gun. "I'll clear a path for us. Keep your head up and your ears on the trail behind us."

LUCAS AND SYDNEY barely spoke during the next several hours during which they took turns thrashing their way down the ancient stone path. The sound of the rhythmic swing of the machete cutting through the air, whacking branches, slicing through leaves, was broken only by occasional screeches from packs of spider monkeys swinging through the treetops and a noisy performance from a curious pair of white-fronted nunbirds that seemed to be following them. Finally, they made headway up and out of the river valley on a steep path.

Lucas's arms ached, his shoulder muscles bunched and screamed and sweat poured off his body. Oddly enough, he welcomed the pain. It kept his mind off last night, off the future. It tempered the hope burgeoning as he closed in on his journey's end. Very soon, he would have Manco Capac's bowl or some other *qero*. All they needed was to buy a little time for Joe and his FBI team to rescue Trevor. Then they could take whatever they found back to the States for analysis, and get an ethnobotanist out here to take plant samples. A cure for cancer, a cure for all the Emilys out there, might be only a stone's throw away.

And then what? The question burned in his stomach. Sydney had opened a door for him and all he had to do was walk through. He just couldn't seem to take that last step. He slashed harder and harder at the branches in front of him.

"You need a break." She tapped him on the back and held out her hand. "If you wear yourself out, you won't have the energy to do any excavating at the temple."

He handed over the machete. She handed over the gun.

Her first few swings were awkward and ineffective. Eventually, she found her stride, and he marveled at the strength and purpose driving her arms. On and on she went, nearly straight up the mountain, following their sidewalk into the misty cloud forest terrain. Sweat poured off her face and her arms, and his heart swelled. This was not the same woman he'd met on a college campus. She'd grown in confidence and independence. In truth, he would not have made it this far in his quest for Manco Capac's bowl without her help.

They reached an area where the path leveled out. She made one more slash and pale rock flashed between dark green leaves. "Whoa. Whoa." He grabbed her wrist. "Hold off." He pushed aside several branches to reveal an ancient wall, waist-high and made of more large stones. "I think we found it." He drew his hand reverently over the cool, rough surface.

"It looks Incan."

Large smooth stones had been fitted together so tight, he couldn't force his finger-nail between them. "Definitely," he murmured, adrenaline born of discovery rushing through his archaeologist veins. Though the Temple of the Rain might be monumental for health research, it was also important archaeologically.

"This is big," she whispered.

He glanced into her eyes and warmed with the knowledge that she understood. He followed the line of the gate. It ran the perimeter of a plateau on the side of the mountain and had once most likely served as a pitiful attempt to keep the jungle back. Through the years, without human hands to fight her off, Mother Nature had clearly won the battle. It was now difficult to discern where jungle ended and village began.

Sydney hopped over the gate and smiled. "Well, what are you waiting for? Let's go."

He grinned, glad to share this discovery with her. It felt right. He took a deep breath and followed her over the gate.

As he carefully hacked a path into what remained of a small settlement, he took a cursory inventory of the site. There appeared to be only five stone buildings, their thatched roofs long ago deteriorated. The four nearest them, lined up two on either side and facing each other, and the remaining one stood at the far side of the settlement, built into the side of the mountain. He glanced upward. Misty, wet clouds hung low in the sky, barely above the treetops and, in the distance, he could hear water running, fast. "I was expecting something bigger," he said. "This is a small village."

Filmy tree ferns and bushes had cropped up at the base of every stone structure and in the middle of what had obviously once been a common area at the center of the development. Vines filled in the gaps. Thick, bulging ones hung down from the treetops. Thin, creeping ones climbed along much of the gate and over the surface of the buildings. Bromeliads, air plants, grew on most trees and other surfaces, and orchids, as orange as pumpkins, dangled in the air. The foliage here was as different from what grew along the river as night is from day.

Neither said a word as they pulled up short at one of the first buildings and stood outside the doorway. They were quite likely the first humans to walk upon this sacred ground in hundreds of years, and an expectant hush fell over the forest, as if the birds and monkeys had lined up in the trees to watch and wait. Lucas ran his hand lightly across the stone, the precise craftsmanship unmistakably Incan, then he cleared the vines from the threshold and ducked inside, Sydney close on his heels.

Any wooden furnishings had long ago turned to dust. Only what had been made of rock remained and, if they were lucky, pottery. "These were living quarters."

"How can you tell?"

"Windows. See those stone posts sticking out over there?" He pointed to the far wall. "Those most likely supported some type of bed, maybe even a bunk, of sorts." He brushed aside some of the debris on the floor and tested for density. "This isn't as hard packed as some sites I've encountered, but it's going to take some time to excavate." Centuries of dirt and dust, dead and decaying foliage had accumulated on the ground.

"Did you bring any tools?"

"A few in my pack." They examined the second structure, then the third and fourth. All living quarters. All the same. He pointed to the last building. "That's the temple." Expectantly, they walked toward the arched doorway and the sounds of a waterfall crashing down the mountainside behind grew louder.

They stepped inside what was presumably the Temple of the Rain. Unlike the other buildings, this one had no windows and the roof had never been thatched, causing less decayed matter to accumulate on the ground. Large, flat stone slabs had been positioned on top of the walls, at either end of the building, leaving only a narrow rectangular opening at the center. There, directly below the opening in the roof, sat a stone platform, its surface pitted and marred.

"Is that an altar?" Sydney asked.

"No," Lucas murmured. He stepped toward the stone slab and threw his hand forward, palm facing upward toward the hazy light. Small droplets of water splattered his hand. He looked up and could see nothing but a veil of clouds overhead. "Tears from heaven," he whispered.

"Then this is it," Sydney said. "The Temple of the Rain."

"It would appear so." He glanced around and found other solid stone platforms at each end of the building. One was flat with no adornment whatsoever. The other had a stone box at its center and joists sticking out from the wall that would have once supported wooden shelves. "That must be where they kept the bowl." He placed his hands inside the stone box and felt the edges for any false sides. "There's nothing here. Damn!" He cursed himself for expecting Manco Capac's silver bowl to be sitting out in plain view, waiting for him.

"Could it be somewhere else in the temple?"

"I don't know." He studied the surface of the floor looking for irregularities that might signify something underground. Nothing. They looked in every corner, around every platform, alongside every wall. Nothing. Frustrated, he walked outside and checked the perimeter of the building. Off to the side, he stopped. Several vegetation-covered mounds were lined up against the mountain-side.

"What are those?" Sydney asked, walking toward the closest one. "More stone platforms? For what? Worship?"

He turned in a circle and studied their placement. "There are too many of them." His stomach cramped with apprehension.

"Look at them. Lined up in rows." She made her way toward one and cleared some of the vegetation from the moss-covered stone. She bent to look under the platform. "Lucas, I found something. What are these?"

He knew without looking. The back of his neck prickled, his heartbeat quickened. All of his training and years of fieldwork screamed the truth inside his head, but he didn't want to believe it. He didn't want it to be true.

"They're jars," she said, excited. "Huge ones. Almost as large as me. Maybe these are your *qero.*"

His pulse thundering in his ears, he barely heard her.

"Lucas, what are these? I can't even count all of the jars, there are so many of them." She ran from platform to platform. Finally, she turned toward him. "Are you okay?"

He put his head in his hands.

"What's wrong?"

"Those are mummy platforms," he whispered, his throat suddenly dry as a desert.

"What are the jars?"

He paced, feeling almost claustrophobic. "They'll have human remains inside. Mummified for transport."

"So this isn't the Temple of the Rain?" She grabbed him by the shoulders and held him. "Explain this to me."

He flung his head back. "Oh, it's the Temple of the Rain, all right. But no healing went on here. Tears from heaven? Droplets from the waterfall. And all the Inca who came with Kachi died here. They never made it back."

He watched her sorting through it, watched her confusion pass, and knew he couldn't let her down. "Maybe there's another explanation." He turned away. "I'll find something."

"Lucas." She held him back. "It's okay."

"There has to be something here." He sloughed her hand off his back and went from one table to the next, studying the containers.

"Gonzalo said you'd find a truth, but it

might not be what you're looking for. Remember?"

He didn't *want* to remember.

"And the legend says Kachi's followers, happy and healthy, visited their relatives in their dreams. It was their spirits. Not their bodies," she said.

Tears clogged his throat. He was back to square one, lost, no vision or purpose. Years of research wasted. "I should have known," he whispered. "But I didn't want it to be true." Failure, black, bitter and heavy, weighed on his chest. To absorb it might kill him. He put his head in his hands and tried to let it pass through.

"Lucas." Her arms wrapped around him and her cheek rested against his back. "You don't need to do this alone."

He shrugged away, reached down and pulled the sun god from his pack. "If this is sunshine from this little god, then his storms must be sheer hell." He cocked his hand back to throw it as hard and as far into oblivion as he could manage.

"Wait!" She covered his hand. "I can't hold this without feeling Emily." She peeled away his fingers and held the statue, both palms open. "And when I do feel her, I know she's not a body rotting in a coffin six feet under the ground."

Lucas thought of that impossibly little coffin. Of his baby girl, impossibly dead. He swallowed, his throat constricting, tears burning his eyes.

"Emily wasn't her body." Sydney smiled then, gently, moisture glistening in her eyes. "She was her laugh, her smile, like the smile on this statue. She was light. And sunshine. And freedom. And death wasn't the end of our Emily." She reached up and wiped away the tear spilling down his cheek. "Carry her in your heart, Lucas. Not as a ball and chain around your neck."

He fell into her arms, choking on a sob, shuddering with all the years of unshed tears. He let himself hold on to her, tighter than he'd ever held on to anything in his life. After a long, long while a deep sense of relief settled over him.

He pulled away and studied her face, her eyes. This woman knew exactly what he had gone through with Emily, knew what had transpired afterward, and she still loved him, in spite of it all. He'd been a fool not to lean on her all those years ago. She would have found a way to reach him, the strength to carry him when his legs had crumpled beneath him.

The sound of birds swiftly scattering into the treetops broke them apart. A spider monkey screeched a warning. Too late. A man's voice sounded behind them, filling the pure rain forest air with the foulest of sarcasm. "Well, isn't this touching?"

CHAPTER TWENTY

"Cochran." Lucas spun around, shielding Sydney behind him.

So this was Phillip Cochran. The man who'd kidnapped her little boy. She set her shoulders, shot from behind the protective breadth of Lucas's shoulders and lunged after him. Lucas grabbed hold of her arm. "That jerk came to my gallery," she whispered.

"When?"

"The morning after it was ransacked."

"Figures."

"Professor Rydall." Cochran grinned. He stood near the far side of the village with the butt of a rifle propped against his hip, his finger resting on the trigger. "Thank you for leading the way and so graciously cutting us a path."

The man from the dock at Vashon Island, Jason Kent, stood a few feet behind Cochran.

Four Peruvian men lined themselves up near the gate, nervously looking on. Whether Quechua or not, performing harmful deeds in this mysterious Inca village obviously did not sit well with the group.

"Don't mention it. See you around." Lucas spun and pushed her toward the back of the village and away from Cochran and his motley crew.

One mechanical click and a gunshot tore through the air behind them. Rock exploded, and a bullet lodged in the stone surface of a mortuary platform. Two feet from her arm. Lucas stopped and turned. Fear—quick and merciless—blotted out Sydney's anger at the sight of the rifle pointed directly at Lucas's chest.

"You're not going anywhere," Cochran said. "Until I get what I came for."

"Look," she cried. "This place is all yours. Just let us go—"

"Stay out of this!" Cochran yelled, dismissing her entirely and refocusing on Lucas. "I want Manco Capac's silver bowl, Rydall. Now."

"There's nothing here."

"Oh, no. That won't work." Cochran shook his head. "I've already sold it, and the owner's getting impatient. On his deathbed, barely holding on for those tears from heaven. So where is it, Lucas?"

"Here." Lucas snatched the sun god from Sydney's hand and tossed it toward Cochran. "Keep the sun god. Let us go."

It landed with a thud in the dirt at Cochran's feet. He kicked it aside. "You think I give a rat's ass about that worthless statue?" He raised the rifle and pointed it directly at Lucas's head. He signaled to the men behind him. "Tie them up. We'll deal with them after we find that bowl."

The men surrounded Sydney and Lucas and backed them up against two separate trees in the middle of the village square. Their legs and arms were tied and the ropes cinched tightly around each tree trunk. By the time Cochran's men were done, she could barely breathe. "Sorry about this," Jason said.

"Then let us go," Lucas whispered.

"No can do." Jason shook his head.

"Now all of you," Cochran ordered, pointing at the men. "Excavate the grounds in that temple. Inch by filthy inch."

The Peruvians shuffled their feet and mumbled among themselves. Finally, one of them stepped forward. "The men are not comfortable, *señor*. They wish to leave."

"Well, Luiz." Cochran's smile was tight, controlled. "Tell them to *get* comfortable. We're going to be here awhile."

"But, *señor,* there is *espíritu malo*...very bad presence in this place."

"I agree." Cochran cocked his rifle. "It's me. Now grab a shovel and get to work."

The man Cochran called Luiz, the apparent spokesperson for the Peruvians, turned back to the other three men and spoke in swift, animated Spanish. Jason ushered them on with a gun and the men reluctantly picked up shovels and went into the temple, digging it out, tearing apart the fragile remains, sifting carelessly through the dirt, and finally pounding out blocks of rock.

"I can't believe what they're doing," Sydney said. "They're completely decimating that temple."

"Can you move at all?" Lucas whispered. "Get your hands free? A leg? Anything?"

She struggled, the lines biting into her flesh. "I can't move an inch."

Several hours passed, and they were no closer to freeing themselves. Cochran's men, on the other hand, were coming out of the temple, exhausted, their hands empty.

"We have to get out of here. Quick." He

closed his eyes, clenched his jaw, and pulled against the ropes. Blood oozed from his wrist and dripped down his hand. "They're almost done."

"Stop that," she whispered. "You're hurting yourself."

"And what if there's no bowl, then what?"

Cochran's entire group had gathered outside the temple and were arguing.

"If I can convince him to let me go..." Lucas motioned to his pack five feet away from them on the ground. "I might be able to get to my gun or knife."

"Get into that next building and start digging in there," Cochran yelled at the Peruvians.

More mumbling and head shaking among the men. It appeared as though they'd found something that had upset them. "No pay all right, *señor?*" Luiz yelled back. The Peruvians turned and headed back for the river. "We leave now."

"No one's going anywhere." Cochran lifted his rifle and shot one of the men in the back. Sydney screamed.

"Phillip, stop it!" Jason shouted. "You said no one would be hurt!"

"No, *señor!* No!" Luiz pleaded, holding

out his hands and backing up. The other men were running.

Cochran cocked his rifle again, aimed and shot a second man. Jason lunged for the gun. Cochran sidestepped him and kicked him in the groin. After he fell to the ground, Cochran threw a few more heavy kicks into the man's side.

"Oh, Lucas," she whimpered.

"Don't look."

She closed her eyes, heard Cochran reload and fire once more. When she cracked open her eyes, Jason was still writhing on the ground, but he wasn't bleeding. The only man standing was the Peruvian named Luiz. Cochran took aim, but his rifle misfired. Luiz took off.

"Jason, go get him," Cochran ordered.

"No," mumbled Kent, groaning on the ground. "I'm finished with this. You're on your own."

"I said." Cochran shifted and pointed the rifle at Jason's head. "Bring him back."

Jason grew still, stared straight down the length of the rifle and said softly, "No."

Cochran's trigger finger twitched. After a few tense moments, he lowered the rifle and smiled. "I guess Luiz gets lucky today. Had you going there for a minute, didn't I? Now head back to the river and make sure Luiz doesn't steal our canoe."

Jason staggered to his feet and disappeared into the jungle. Cochran spun around and walked deliberately to Sydney and Lucas, his rifle resting against his shoulder. "Well, Rydall, it appears there's nothing here at your Temple of the Rain, except for a waterfall and a lot of skeletons. Some old. And, unfortunately, a few new ones." He stopped in front of Lucas. "What do you have to say for yourself?"

Lucas's nostrils flared, his jaw clenched and unclenched, and he strained against the ropes.

Cochran tapped his toe in the dirt, oblivious to the cold fury surrounding him. "Then again, maybe you already found the bowl."

He opened Lucas's pack and spilled the contents out onto the ground—Lucas's knife and his gun, along with everything else. "Nothing there." Cochran tossed aside the pack. "Let's see what you have in here." He stood in front of Lucas, dug inside his pockets and pulled out the battered plastic bag with the map inside.

"Amazing. There is a map." Cochran unfolded it and studied the markings. "And it appears we *are* at the Temple of the Rain. What a shame." He refolded the paper and stuffed it into his back pocket. "I was really looking forward to Manco's bowl, or a *qero,* anything I could actually sell."

"I'll find the bowl for you," Lucas said. "Just let Sydney go."

"That could take years, Rydall." Cochran walked to Sydney and circled her. "And I'm not going back to jail. If I let you or your ex-wife out of here, that's exactly where I'll end up."

"Leave her alone," Lucas ground out.

"Very pretty," Cochran murmured. "She wouldn't last a day in the jails down here. Did you know it took four of them to hold me down—"

"It's me you want. Not her."

"Lucas, no!"

"I'm not so sure." Cochran stepped up to Sydney, bent to her neck and drew a sharp breath in through his nose. "You smell like sweat. And fear. I wonder how you taste."

"Keep…your hands…off her." Lucas spoke the words slowly, softly.

Cochran drew back. "What're you going to do to stop me?"

"Untie me, and I'll show you. Then again, maybe you don't have the balls for that."

"Lucas, don't."

Cochran laughed. "Each of you protecting the other. And for what? I'm going to kill you both, anyway. It's simply a question of who goes first."

"I do," Lucas yelled.

"Don't worry, Sydney." Cochran spun toward Lucas. "I'll be back to you in a minute." He grabbed the knife off the ground, slit the ropes binding Lucas to the tree, and jumped back, out of reach.

"You can't use the knife," she cried. "It's not fair."

"Okay." Cochran tossed it to the side. "But don't think for a second that evens the playing field."

And it probably didn't. Cochran had a good thirty pounds of lean, hard muscle on Lucas, and moved with the stealth and control of an animal. Even so, Lucas dived at Cochran, barreling into him with fists flying. Pent-up rage fueled his attack and seemed to throw Cochran off balance. Cochran threw several kicks. Lucas dodged them and landed a few of his own.

Blow after blow to Cochran's face and stomach, his legs and chest. He dropped to the dirt and glanced frantically around. A weapon. Cochran was looking for a weapon.

"Watch out, Luc—"

Cochran grasped a thick branch from the ground and came up swinging it in a wide arc.

"No!" she screamed.

He struck Lucas in the chest. Lucas crumpled, gasping, to the dirt. Like that, the tables turned. While Lucas lay on the ground wheezing for breath, bloodlust bloomed on Cochran's beaten face. For several long, agonizing minutes, he went after Lucas slowly, methodically, picking his targets. One after another. Shoulder. Kneecap. Groin. Jaw.

"Stop it!" she cried. "You're going to kill him."

Another well-placed kick and Lucas flopped on his back, unmoving.

"You're a maniac! And a coward!" Sobbing, she strained against the ropes. "Give me a knife, and I'll kill you myself." She could have done it, too, without a twinge of remorse. Stabbed him over and over and over.

"All right." Cochran straightened and gulped a deep breath. He swiped at the blood covering his eyes as he crossed the square toward her. "It's your turn." He picked up the knife and dangled it in front of her. "Is this what you want?"

He dragged the cold, blunt edge of the blade down her cheek. The razor-sharp tip of the blade cut into her neck. "If you were one-tenth the man Lucas is," she choked out through clenched teeth, "you'd cut me loose and give me the chance to kill you. With my bare hands."

He ran his free hand through her hair, took a step closer and buried his nose in her neck. She jerked on the ropes, wishing she had the knife, wishing she could fight. Finally, she turned her head and bit down on his ear.

"Sonofabitch!" He backhanded her and jumped away. "You tore my ear!"

Tasting his blood on her tongue, she screamed, "Give me the chance and I'll tear your head off!"

With one swipe of the blade, he cut through the ropes and yanked her free. "You want me, you got me." He stood back, tossed the knife onto the ground between them and grinned. "Go ahead. Grab it."

Without taking her eyes off him, she lunged for it. He didn't move, only studied her with eyes more animal than human. She steadied her breath. Moved back and around him. Looking for a way in. If she could just… She charged. Jabbed. He sidestepped.

She missed his chest and managed to slice his arm, but he seized her wrist and forced the knife to the ground.

She twisted in his grasp, grappling for the knife. She kicked, scratched, punched, pulled hair, bit hands, and all of it had as much effect as David in hand-to-hand combat with Goliath. She was on the ground and he was on top of her, and all she could think of was Lucas. And Trevor.

"Are you ready," Cochran said, breathing hard, "to die?"

She grappled in the dirt. For something. Anything. Her fingers closed tightly around the sun god, and she swung her hand up, hitting him on the side of the head. The blow held little force, weak as she was, but it was enough to make him loosen his hold. She sucked in a breath and scooted away.

"Bitch." No heavier than a rag doll to him, he drop-kicked her ten feet away.

She landed, her body slamming on top of her leg. She heard the crack of bone a split second before pain shot through her body. She caught sight of Jason Kent standing at the edge of the jungle and screamed, "Do something! Please!"

"Phillip!" Jason yelled across the clearing. "Leave her alone."

Cochran's blood-covered fist stalled in midair. "What did you say?" His lips curled back in a wolflike snarl.

"You must be getting bored with this one-sided match. Isn't it time for more of a challenge?"

Phillip turned toward Jason, and Jason pulled out his .38 and took aim. "Stop right there."

"Shoot him!" Sydney screamed. "Just shoot him."

LUCAS SLOWLY CAME TO and blinked to clear the blood from his eyes. A sickening wave of nausea passed through him and he coughed, trying to clear his throat. His head pounded, his body throbbed as though Cochran had stuffed him into a meat grinder, and his bruised—probably broken—ribs made it hard to suck in enough air to stay alive. None of it mattered. Sydney. Oh, God, he had to find her. If Cochran had killed her… Anger and fear battled for control. First Emily. Now Sydney. No. He couldn't give in yet. If she was alive, he had to do something. She had to be alive.

Cochran and Jason argued behind him as Lucas struggled to lift his head, to move at all, but his body was having none of it. Finally, he saw her face, moving toward him, on the ground, her eyes open. She was bloodied and bruised, but he'd never seen anything more beautiful. Relief swept through him along with something else he couldn't name, something so intense it infused energy to his broken body. He would get them out of this. Some way, he would keep her alive.

"Are you okay?" he whispered.

"I think my leg is broken, but I'll make it." He shifted toward the voices. Cochran stood thirty feet away and Jason Kent was pointing a gun at him. Good. Lucas could think of no better solution than the two of them killing each other. "You don't have the balls," Cochran yelled. Jason's hand went limp and the gun he was holding nearly dropped to the ground.

"Shoot him!" Sydney shouted.

"He's not going to shoot *me*." Cochran didn't even bother to turn in her direction. "Are you, Jason? You know I'm right, don't you?" He laughed and threw Jason a patronizing glance.

"Sydney," Lucas whispered. "Where's the other gun?"

"I don't know." She shook her head. "It was behind you, but I can't see it." Tears gathered in her red-rimmed eyes as she finally reached him and clenched her outstretched fingers around his hand. The side of her face swelled an angry, puffy red and a dark purple bruise was already forming around her neck. Fear, cold and deep, clawed at his heart. "I love you." She said the words as if neither of them would see that evening's sunset. If he didn't find that gun, they wouldn't.

Desperate, he summoned the strength to get his left arm under him and lever himself up. There it was. The gun. Only three feet away, but every inch seemed like a quarter mile. He dragged himself across the dirt and strained to reach it.

"Gonna shoot me, Jason?" Cochran taunted. "In cold blood?" Jason stood there, staring at him. "I didn't think so." Cochran laughed. He turned and saw Lucas had moved. "Ready for some more, I see."

"Leave them alone," Jason shouted and raised his gun.

"No!" Sydney cried, crawling in front of Cochran's path to Lucas. "Don't you touch him!"

Cochran flung her aside. He grabbed

Lucas by the back of his shirt and flipped him over.

"Don't do it, Phillip," Jason warned.

"And who's going to stop me?" Cochran sneered back at Jason. "You?"

"No." Lucas pulled the trigger. "Me."

The shot pierced Cochran's chest and blood spread across his shirt. Stunned, he stared down at Lucas. Time stood deathly still, and then his knees collapsed. He crashed to the ground. Jason went to Cochran's limp frame and pushed him over. Blood gushed from the hole in his chest.

As the adrenaline rush subsided, a gray fog of unconsciousness threatened Lucas's vision. He turned the gun on Jason and fought to hold his shaking arm steady, fought for each and every shallow breath.

"I'm sorry, Lucas," Jason said. "Shoot me and with the shape you two are in, you'll never make it out of this jungle alive."

"Syd," Lucas mumbled. "Take the gu—"

All went black.

CHAPTER TWENTY-ONE

EVELYN HAD HOPED it would be mediocre. That Joe Donati would be, as he'd said of so many women, a prettily wrapped package type of a man. All frilly paper and shiny bows disguising an ordinary iron or popcorn bowl.

How wrong could one woman be?

With Trevor sound asleep for hours in his own bed, she flopped onto her back in Sydney's guest bedroom and stared at the ceiling, a little flabbergasted by the talent Joe had demonstrated so excellently on her. Not only had he taken the time to discover exactly where she liked to be touched—how hard, how soft, how long—but he'd also talked with her, laughed with her, treated her like a person, not an object. It hadn't been just great sex. It had been fantastic sex. The best she'd had.

Chocolate? Who needed it? She had man-candy lying next to her, and he licked back.

He rolled them both together onto their sides, folded his arm under his head and sighed, lazy and deep. The sound sent an answering purr of contentment thrumming through her. Then he sat up and looked at her, taking his time, his gaze lingering while she lay there, not a scrap of sheet or blanket covering an inch of her skin. Despite his scrutiny, she didn't feel exposed or vulnerable. She liked this man. *Really* liked him.

He opened his mouth to speak.

Please don't say anything stupid. Please don't ruin what is perhaps the most perfect moment in my life. Please. Please. Please.

"*Mai fattu annamurari,*" he whispered. "*Emi burcia lu cori.*"

"What did you say?" she said, almost afraid to ask.

"You burn me, Evie. Burn me right to the bone." He brought her fingers to his lips. "Burn my heart. Burn my soul."

Now *that* was what a man said to a woman after great sex.

"You are one beautiful woman. I swear, I could sit here and look at you all night long."

A tad clichéd, but that wasn't too bad, either.

"Marry me."

Two words too far. Her head snapped up

and she felt her mouth gape open. "We met only a few days ago."

"I know." He chuckled.

"Don't you think it's a little soon to be talking about the rest of our lives? Because that is what marriage means to me. What does it mean to you?"

He propped himself up onto one elbow and looked her in the face. "It means growing old with one woman. Sharing a bed with only one woman. It might mean children. It might not. I'm open on that point. But I won't give on this, it means being friends and lovers through good times and bad."

She looked away.

He cupped her chin and urged her back. "Evie, I'm thirty-eight years old, and I have never once come even close to proposing. I've dated more women than I care to remember. But enough to know exactly what I want. And I want you."

"It's too soon," she whispered, her thoughts spinning.

"I'm okay if you want to take some time and think about it. I'll wait." He grinned as if it was only a matter of time before she gave him the answer he wanted to hear.

That smile. She could soak it up the rest of her life. She did know exactly what she wanted, and he happened to check out on every item but one. "How much does an FBI agent make?"

He didn't seem at all put out by her question. Chock up one more point.

"I'm on special forces, so I bring in over a hundred thousand. I doubt I'll ever earn more than two."

Comfortable. Not nearly enough.

"Money's important to everyone." He sighed. "How important is it to you?"

"Number one on my checklist."

"Why?" He showed not one speck of judgment or defensiveness. He simply wanted to understand. Make that one more point for Mr. Making This Very Difficult.

"I grew up on a farm, if that's what you could call those ten flat and barren acres in eastern Montana. My father's a worthless drunk who never held down a job for more than three months at a time. My mother's a worthless drunk's wife. I guess you could say that my sister and I were lucky. The old man never beat on us quite as much as my two older brothers."

She sat up, wrapped a sheet around herself

and walked to the window. She hated talking about this. The last thing she wanted was anyone's sympathy, but if she owed Joe anything, it was an explanation before she broke his heart. Broke both of their hearts.

"We were so poor we scrounged berries and roots from the woods, stole potatoes and chickens from the neighbors. Bet you've never been so hungry that you sized up a stray dog for a barbecue." She looked over her shoulder, hoping to find pity welling up in those dark Sicilian eyes. Finding at least one crack in that perfect armor would make what she had to do easier.

"No. I haven't."

Damn. He was still only listening.

She turned back to the window. "I guess that's all I have to say." If he didn't get it, the rest of her story would fall on deaf ears.

He wrapped his arms around her from behind. "I think you're trying to say no, and I'm trying to understand. But, Evie, there isn't enough money in this world to wipe out those memories."

She turned within his arms, her hands shaking. "There has to be. Somewhere."

"Is that your answer?"

"Joe—"

"Shh." He put two fingers over her mouth, silencing her. "Don't say anything. Not yet." He took a step back and paced the room as if to gather his thoughts. When he came back, he stood directly in front of her, his eyes earnest and fair.

"*Ti vuoggiu beni.* I love you, Evie, and I'd do almost anything for you, but you're a stubborn woman. You get your mind set on something, and that's the way it's going to be. I'm not stupid enough to think I could hang around and change your mind. This isn't a threat or an attempt at manipulation. It's simply the way things are."

"But—"

"Shh." He reached up and drew his thumb over her mouth. "You say no right now, and I'll be gone and out of your life within the hour. I won't come back. So think long and hard before you give me your answer."

THE DRIVE to the Lima airport in the dead of night seemed surreal with the city whizzing by Sydney's window like a DVD on fast-forward. The atmosphere inside Pepe's truck was quiet, tense, suffocating. While Lucas and Pepe sat in the front, she sat as comfortably as possible in the back, her broken leg stretched across the seat. How strange that a day and a half ago she'd been deep in the Peruvian rain forest, a madman threatening to kill her and Lucas.

The ordeal was over, she reminded herself. The bad guys were either dead, in jail, or, in the case of Jason Kent, long gone by now. Although he'd disappeared the moment the Peruvian authorities showed up, the fact that he'd dragged Lucas and Sydney back to the river one by one on a makeshift stretcher proved he'd meant them no harm.

Most importantly, Trevor was safe, and she and Lucas were finally going home.

Probably, she would have felt better had she and Lucas had time to talk and resolve things. But during the flurry of the last thirty-six hours—helicopters, airplanes, police officers, doctors and nurses—they hadn't had a moment alone.

Pepe parked at the airport curb, and Lucas got out and held open her door. With four cracked ribs and a torn shoulder ligament, not to mention numerous bruises and cuts, he was moving a little slower than normal, but he would heal. They would both heal. She swung her casted leg out and reached for his hand. After she steadied herself, he held out her crutches. "Pepe, can you please take care of the luggage?" he asked.

"*Sí, señor.*"

Lucas had arranged their flights at the hotel. Now they only had to make their way through customs and security. She hobbled toward the terminal, but sensed him hanging back. "What's up?" she asked, turning.

He glanced away.

After several days with him in the jungle, he looked out of place dressed in faded blue jeans and a clean, white T-shirt standing next to an ordinary car parked on the street. He needed a canoe paddle in his hand or at least a backpack slung over one shoulder.

The only thing about him reminding her of the rain forest was his expression, preoccupied and serious, the one he'd worn since they'd gotten on that first helicopter from Atalaya to Lima. His brow was furrowed, eyes alert, lips tight. She could lie and tell herself that he was simply still in pain, but that wasn't the problem. "Lucas?"

He pushed away from the side of the car. "Coming."

She felt for the sun god in her front pocket,

and its presence reassured her. Everything was going to be okay. They just needed time to decompress.

After trudging through long lines in both security and customs, they made it to the gate. The Lima airport didn't smell any better this time around than the last. Jet fuel, drug dogs, sweat. For 11:30 p.m. it was amazingly hot and stuffy.

"I will see when they'll begin boarding the plane," Pepe said, jostling his way through the crowd.

Sydney found a quiet corner to wait. She turned to find Lucas studying her, and all the distractions of the airport—the noise, the people, the smells—disappeared.

After so many years, they were finally alone with nothing between them except love. They'd made amends for past wrongs. They should be the happiest two people on earth. Instead, a veil of uncertainty hung between them, and she couldn't put a finger on why.

"You're going home." He closed the short distance between them, reached out and smoothed a curl from her face. "It's over."

For a moment, she closed her eyes and let herself believe that. Let herself lean into his hand and forget the world in the feel of his touch. All that mattered was right here, right now. When she looked into his face and saw the questions shredding him, bit by bit, her chest tightened. Finally, after all these years, she could read him. His mask was gone. "You're not coming with me, are you?"

"This isn't going to work. You. Me. Trevor." Desperation fired from his eyes and determination set his jaw in a hard line. "I feel like I'm in a car speeding forward on a collision course with a brick wall. I don't want you in it. Seat belted or not."

Disbelieving, she shook her head. "You never even bought an airline ticket? You've known all along?"

His silence said it all.

"Don't I have a say in this?" she cried. "Don't I get to decide what's right for me?"

He dragged a hand through his hair. "You don't understand what you'd be getting yourself into."

"That's not fair." She couldn't go through this again. She might understand his leaving better this time, but it only made the thought of living without him all the more unbearable. There would be no anger to help her face each day, only the heart-wrenching truth. "I'm a different woman today. I know I would be there for you in a way I wasn't there for you with Emily."

"That's exactly my point. You shouldn't have to be."

"So you're going to give up?"

Pepe returned, holding up both hands with fingers spread, as if to say ten minutes until boarding, and then he took a position twenty feet away, guarding them from onlookers.

"What am I supposed to do?" Lucas said. "Bring you and Trevor down with me?"

"You're not bringing anyone down. You just think you are."

He stared into her eyes for one breath-stopping minute, and she tried to forget about his words, tried to listen to him with her heart. That's when she felt it, saw it, the barest glimmer of doubt. He wasn't positive this time that separating was the answer. They still had a chance.

"I love you." She reached out to him, but he backed away. "We can make this work."

"You feel that way today," he said. "What about tomorrow? What about the day when I wake up and everything is black? And I won't talk. And I won't let you in. And you'll start wondering if we have any guns in our house and whether or not they're loaded." He took a deep breath and shook his head. "When I don't answer the phone, you'll worry. When I don't get home on time, you'll worry. In the back of your mind it'll always be there. Between us. What kind of life is that, Syd?"

With his every word, she watched his doubt fade, only to be replaced by an even stronger determination. "So you can't make any guarantees," she cried. "Neither can I. There could be a truck out there right now with my name written all over its grill."

"That's different."

"No, it isn't. Look, I'm not fool enough to believe our future is going to be all red roses and sparkling champagne. Hell, I don't even want that. But there has to be a way we can work this out." She looked around her, grasping for reasons. "Depression has warning signs, right?"

"Sometimes."

"Well, then, it might not blindside you like it did the first time. Right?"

He didn't answer.

She moved in front of him, wanting to reach out and touch him, yet frightened it might send him right out of her life. "Years ago I took the easy way out in filing for a divorce." She spoke softly. "I would do anything to take it back, Lucas. Anything. Please. Come home. Give us some time."

She wasn't getting through. He'd made up his mind, and she couldn't do a damn thing about it. "Staying here is not the answer," she cried, frantically trying to make a dent in his thick skull. "It's just another easy way out. Don't you see that? Dammit, fight for us! Fight for Trevor. He needs you." Her voice cracked. "You think Emily was a daddy's girl, you've never seen a boy who's grown up without a father suddenly find one. You will be everything he's ever dreamed of and more."

"Except for the walking away part. You and I both know he won't be able to count on me."

"No, I *don't* know that." She shook her head, listening to his pain. "I *do* know that you'll love him. I *do* know that you'll be the best father you can be, and that's all anyone can ask."

Lucas watched her eyes pool, her lips quiver, and her shoulders slump as if she would crumble to the ground and disintegrate. Hell, by the time he was done there'd be nothing left of her. He had to make this easier. Quicker. "Goodbye, Sydney." He clenched his teeth and forced himself to turn away and head for the exit.

"Lucas?" Her voice was barely a whisper behind him. "Do you love me?"

He stopped, his knees nearly buckling at the sound of her voice, her vulnerability, her desperation. "More than life," he whispered, keeping his back toward her.

"Then know this, if you walk away, you take my life, my breath with you. I will spend each day knowing there is a love out there so perfect for me, so right, and it's out of my reach, gone forever."

She was killing him. "You'll move on like you did before," he said, his voice stronger as if he could make himself believe it. "You'll forget about me."

"Forget about you?" A half laugh, half whimper issued from her throat, and his gut clenched at the sound. "Forget about what we shared in the hotel room in Atalaya? Forget about your smile, your touch, your walk, your voice? Your legends?"

Behind him, he heard her take two steps toward him. *Don't touch me. Please, don't touch me.*

As if reading his mind, she stopped. "I

tried forgetting about you once. It didn't work then. It won't work now."

"You're strong. Stronger than I ever gave you credit for. You'll be all right."

"Oh, I'll survive. For Trevor. I'll even try to be happy for him. But at night, when it's dark and quiet, after he's asleep and I'm alone, I'll be thinking of you. The warm heaviness of you against my back. The way you smell. The feel of you inside me. I'll be aching to talk to you, to hear your voice. To look at you. To touch you."

He hung his head and she was behind him, her cheek resting against his back, her arms around his waist. He let himself feel her. One last time.

"I belong to you," she whispered. In her hand she held their sun god. She unclenched her fingers, pressed the statue against his heart and made him take it. "And you belong to me."

Over the intercom, an attendant announced, "Flight 163 to Houston now boarding."

"Lucas," she urged. *"Please."*

Sydney's heat emanated from the little gold statue filling his chest with the bittersweet ache of her warmth. But he knew what he had to do. She was safe. Trevor was safe. It had to be enough. Cauterizing his emotions, he pushed her arms away. "I have to leave. Now."

"Lucas!"

He stopped, turned slowly and committed the sight of her to memory. Eyes red-rimmed. Tears streaming down her face. Her glorious hair in wild disarray. This was what he did to her. This was why he had to leave.

He held the statue tight, as if he might forever hold her warmth in his hand, and made himself turn away. "Pepe, make sure she gets on that plane."

CHAPTER TWENTY-TWO

"Mom!" Trevor's voice infused Sydney with relief the moment she shifted her leg cast out the door and climbed awkwardly out of Joe Donati's car. He ran from the back of their small Victorian in Queen Anne Hill and into her arms, almost knocking her into a row of rhododendrons.

It felt like months since she'd last seen him, held him. Now they were both home. Her baby was safe. After a long, tight embrace and a few joyful tears, she held Trevor away from her, examining him, every inch of his skin, his hair, his eyes. "Honey, did they hurt you?"

"I'm fine, Mom. Honest."

She took another long, hard look at him, ascertaining for herself that he was, indeed, in one piece both physically and mentally. Finally satisfied, she leaned back. "I missed you sooo much."

"I missed you, too," Trevor said. "But what happened to your leg?"

"I was in a car accident." She avoided looking him in the eye. He was bound to ask questions about his trauma for the next several days, maybe even weeks, but the less he knew about what had happened to her in Peru, the better.

Trevor's worried brown eyes took in the deep purple bruises on her neck and face. "Are *you* okay?"

"I'm home. Can't ask for more than that."

Joe hauled Sydney's luggage out of his trunk and set it on the grass by the driveway. "Sorry, Sydney, for shanghaiing you downtown before bringing you home. If there hadn't been a hearing scheduled for the morning, I could have waited a few hours for your statement."

"That's okay, Joe. I'm glad the whole business is done and out of the way."

Trevor screwed up the side of his mouth. "I wanted to come down to FBI headquarters, too, but Evie wouldn't let me."

"Sorry, buddy," Joe said.

"They just had a lot of questions, Trev." Sydney ruffled his hair, and her heart constricted at its texture. So much like Lucas's. "You would've been bored silly."

"I'll tell you what." Joe crossed his arms over his chest. "If it's okay with your mom, I'll take you down another day and show you the detention cells. That's our jail."

"Tight! Can I go, Mom?"

Sydney chuckled. "Sure."

The back door slammed. "Hey, stranger." Evelyn walked across the yard and slung her arm over Sydney's shoulder. "You look terrible, but I'm glad you're home."

"Thanks, Evelyn, for taking care of things up here." Sydney turned into her friend for a hug.

"It was my pleasure. Really." Evelyn pulled away and winked at a grinning Joe. Preoccupied as she was, even Sydney could tell there was something going on between those two.

"Where's Lucas?" Evelyn asked.

Sydney swallowed. After crying most of the flight home, tears would no longer come. "He stayed in Peru."

"Good," she said. "He can rot there for all I care."

Sydney's reaction must have shown on her face. Evelyn narrowed her eyes in concern, but Sydney shook her head. Even if she could find the words to tell her friend what had happened, this wasn't the right time.

"Something happened while I was in Peru." Sydney pointed back and forth between Evelyn and Joe, changing the subject. "What's going on with you two?"

They grinned at each other and laughed in unison.

"They're getting married," Trevor said.

"What?"

Evelyn wrapped her arm around Joe's waist. "Can you believe it? And he's not even rich!"

"Oh, Evelyn! That's wonderful!" Sydney hugged her tight, and then stepped back. "How did this happen?"

They made their way to the house as Evelyn recounted their last week. "In the end, it was pretty simple," Evelyn said. "I figured out that I can make my *own* million. Why wait around for a man to do it for me?" She tapped a pink lacquered fingertip against her cheek. "I'm thinking corporate art acquisitions. Could lead to some pretty hefty executive clients."

"I'm marrying me a sugar-mama." Joe winked.

"Be my maid of honor?" Evelyn asked.

"Absolutely." Sydney pushed open the back door and peered inside. The last time she'd been in this exact position, the entire contents of her house had been in ruins from Cochran's ransacking. It seemed like a lifetime ago. "You cleaned everything up. That must have been a chore."

"We weren't able to save a few things, but Joe and I did the best we could." Evelyn brushed her hand back and forth across Sydney's back.

"Thank you. Both." She stepped inside and into the kitchen and took a deep breath. Home. She thought she'd be glad to finally be on safe ground, surrounded by all the familiar sights, sounds and smells. Instead, a terrible sense of loss struck her full in the face. This place would never feel complete again. Everything seemed wrong. Empty. She would forever see Lucas at the table, in the kitchen or up in Trevor's room.

"Hey." The smile died on Evelyn's face. "You're home."

Joe carried her luggage through the kitchen. "Where do you want these?"

"Upstairs if you don't mind."

"No problem." Joe tossed a backpack to Trevor, obviously sensing a problem. "Help me carry this stuff upstairs? Then you can show me how you're doing on that new Harry Potter game."

"I'm on the third level!" Trevor exclaimed, already on his way.

"Awesome, dude." Joe closed the kitchen door behind him.

"Spill it." Evelyn put her hands on her hips. "What happened in Peru?"

For the next half an hour, Sydney talked and talked, and for once in her life, Evelyn didn't say a word until Sydney was finished. "So he stays in Peru?" Evelyn crossed her arms and leaned into the counter. "You come to Seattle. Life goes on like before and that's it?"

"No, that's not it," she whispered. "Lucas belongs in this house. He belongs with Trevor and me."

"What are you going to do about it?"

Several possible actions crossed Sydney's mind, before the one that made sense settled at her core. This was small and big at the same time, but it was no easy way out. "I have to talk to Trevor." She went through the kitchen door and found Joe and Trevor hanging on the couch playing video games. "Trevor, how 'bout you shut that off for a few minutes so we can talk."

"One sec. I need to save the game."

Evelyn motioned toward the kitchen, and

she and Joe disappeared. A few minutes later, Sydney heard the back door close and Joe's car heading down the drive.

"What's up, Mom?"

Sydney nestled next to Trevor on the couch and smiled, the rightness of her decision lifting her heart. "Do you remember that guy, Lucas Rydall, who came to our house?"

"We had spaghetti, and I think I talked to him on the phone when I was with Jason."

"Yeah, that's him. There's something I need to tell you, but it's hard to know where to begin." She fidgeted with her hands, searching for the right words. "Lucas...well, he's more than an old friend of mine. He was...my husband. We were married. He's... Emily's dad."

"Emily's dad?" First confusion and then comprehension slowly dawned on Trevor's face. "That means he's..."

"That's right." Sydney nodded. She was fighting for Lucas, jumping in with both feet. "Lucas is your dad, too...."

THREE DAYS, FIFTEEN HOURS, thirty-some-odd minutes and counting.

The solid thud of hammer against nail reverberated over and over in Lucas's head, drowning out thoughts of Sydney. Taking care to not reinjure his broken ribs and sore shoulder, he pounded in another nail and another, faster and faster, forcing himself to concentrate on the wooden plank beneath his hands or risk flattening a thumb. Two more sections and this fence would be fully repaired. One more rooftop to fix and it would be late enough to safely return to Miguel's, eat dinner and crash in bed.

The bed he'd shared with Sydney.

Damn. There she was again.

He set aside the hammer and closed his eyes against the late-afternoon sun, allowing himself a few moments to remember her eyes, the feel of her lips, her taste, her voice. She felt as solid to him as the hammer in his hand and he smiled. A cold mountain breeze cut through his jacket, chilling the sweat on his skin and urging him back to the task at hand.

"*Señor* Lucas?"

Lucas twisted around. The son of Miguel's neighbor stood behind him. "*Sí?*"

"Don Miguel. He wishes you home."

"*Gracias.*"

The little boy took off running, and a sense of resignation settled in Lucas's gut. So far

Miguel had left Lucas to his own devices, and Lucas had known it wouldn't last. He finished repairing the fence, put away his tools and headed back. Miguel was sitting at the table, his eyes closed in prayer or meditation. "What's up?" he asked.

Miguel opened his eyes. "Come. Join me."

Lucas crossed the room and glanced down at the table. Two *kintus,* one for each of them, were fanned out on the rough wooden surface. "I don't need to go through the motions of a *kintu,* Miguel."

Miguel remained quiet for a moment and then said, "Sit. Just talk then."

He didn't want to sit. He wanted to get back to work. He wanted to keep busy. "I'm fine, Miguel. Don't worry."

In truth, Lucas was doing okay, maintaining a rigid schedule of sleeping, eating and working on any number of odd jobs for Miguel's friends and neighbors, giving him little time to despair. He'd been sleeping through every night, he was hungry at meal times and he felt no urge to isolate himself. If anything, Miguel's presence eased his mind.

"This afternoon," Miguel said. "I went to the shed for some equipment. I thought about the gun. You. I'm worried."

Lucas paced beside the table. This was exactly why he couldn't be with Sydney. He couldn't do that to her. "I'm okay, Miguel. Really."

"How do you know?"

He just did. He didn't have it in him to go back to the Temple of the Rain with an ethnobotanist just yet, but that would come after his ribs and shoulder were fully healed.

"What has changed, Lucas?"

"Changed?" He stopped behind the chair. Maybe Miguel was right, something had happened in the rain forest. There was a moment, one snapshot in time, he woke up thinking about every morning. It was the look of Sydney's face, dirty, bloody and bruised, as she crawled toward him, wanting to help him, while Jason tried to make up his mind about killing Cochran. More than anything else, Lucas had wanted to make sure Sydney made it out of there alive. But there was more to it than that.

"It was Cochran." Lucas pulled out the chair and sat down, suddenly exhausted. "And getting beaten to within an inch of my life." Then he understood. He glanced up at his friend. "I want to live, Miguel. For the first time in six long years, I not only don't want to die, I want to live." Something powerful, beautiful suffused him. He wasn't done with this life yet. There was more he wanted to do, more he wanted to see.

"How do you want to live, Lucas? How?"

Lucas bent his head and a tear dropped onto the battered wooden tabletop. "With Sydney and Trevor."

"And the *kintu*, Lucas?" Miguel passed his hands over the coca leaves. "Do you now understand its meaning?"

"I'm not sure."

"What of *ayni?* Taking care of each other, living in a state of reciprocity?"

"I thought I was taking care of her. And Trevor. By keeping away."

"No, Lucas. You have only half of the equation because you are scared. And in fear we are all stupid. All of us."

"I might be confused, but I'm not scared, Miguel."

"Do me a favor and pretend this is your first *kintu* ever."

Reluctantly, Lucas sat back and waited for his friend to begin. First the *ayni*. Miguel spoke in Quechua, an ancient blessing. Lucas followed him in the *ayni* by gently blowing on the *kintu,* breathing his life force into the sacred coca. Miguel offered their *kintus* to the four winds, the north, south, east and west and to the *Apus,* the holy mountain peaks. Then he lifted the coca leaves to Lucas. Lucas had done this a hundred times before, but this time felt different. This time he finally understood. *Ayni,* taking care of each other. Now he knew exactly what it meant.

Lucas turned to Miguel, offered the leaves to his friend, and then closed his eyes. A change washed over him, more of a feeling than anything, subtle but potent. Finally, his heart taught him what his head hadn't grasped about the blessing Miguel had first shown him so many years ago. "I feed Sydney. She feeds me."

"Yes, Lucas." Miguel nodded. "That is life."

Lucas swallowed. "I need to go home."

"TREV, DID YOU GET everything on your list packed?" Sydney yelled up the stairs.

"Almost!" Trevor shouted. "One sec."

"When you're finished, bring your suitcase down." Sydney walked back into her kitchen, mentally checking off the items tucked away in the bags lined up against the wall. Passports, clothing, snacks for the plane, electronics, books—

A knock interrupted her mental note-taking. Without thinking, she crossed the room and opened the back door. *Lucas!* He stood on the steps, a suitcase in each hand and a pack slung over his shoulder as an airport cab left her driveway. He looked travel weary and hesitant, and Sydney had never seen a more wonderful sight. The urge to catapult herself into his arms over-whelmed her.

Wait. She calmed herself. *Wait.*

"Hey," he said.

"Hey, yourself."

"Can I come in? These bags are getting a little heavy."

She jumped back, awkward and unsure. "Please. Put your stuff down."

Two steps into the house and he dropped his bags off to the side. "That's everything I own." He half smiled, his hands out to his sides.

"Everything?" *Wait.*

He nodded, studying her face. "I came to stay." The look in his eyes was part hope-ful, part vulnerable and all love. "If you'll have me."

Now! She stumbled into his open arms and pressed her lips to his mouth for a long, quiet moment. Then she slid her cheek against his, breathing in his scent, feeling the roughness of the stubble on his skin. "You're here. You're really here." She laid her head on his chest, listened to his heart beating fast and faster still. "Why?" she finally whispered. "What changed your mind?"

"A lot of things." He rested his chin on her head. "A big part of it was finally figuring out what happened to me in the rain forest." He sighed and tightened his grip around her shoulders. "When I was lying on the ground where Cochran had left me for dead, dirt and blood in my mouth, pain racking every muscle and bone, I lifted my head and saw you crawling toward me. And I had the most terribly wonderful sensation."

He pulled his head back and tilted her face to his. "I didn't understand what it meant because it was such a new and different feeling for me. But the other day, I figured it out. I didn't want you to die. I wanted you to live. More than anything else. But *I* wanted to live, too. With you." He cupped her face in his hands. "I'm finished running, Syd. My life is here. With you and Trevor. If you haven't changed your mind."

She laughed, let out her joy, loud and full, and kissed him again. Gradually, they softened against each other, opening, believing, trusting. His hold loosened around her back, caressing her gently.

"If you ever leave me again," she murmured, "there won't be a corner on this earth you'll be able to hide. I'll hunt you down, and I *will* find you."

Tenderly, he wiped her face dry. "Is that a promise?"

"Damn right."

"I've got a promise of my own." He buried his fingers in her thick curls. "I promise, I won't ever leave Trevor. I won't ever leave *you* again." He smiled over her head and nodded toward the suitcases piled by the door. "And speaking of leaving, were you going somewhere?"

"To Peru. With Trevor. To get you back."

"With Trevor?"

"I told him everything. He can't wait to meet you. All over again."

"Mom?" Their son stood in the doorway, a small suitcase in one hand and a questioning look on his face. There was little doubt he'd never seen his mother in a man's arms, and the room grew still with expectation. "Hi…Mr. Ryd…" He faltered and then grinned broadly. "Hi…Dad."

Lucas sucked in a breath. Trevor took two slow steps and then ran into his arms. Lucas lifted him, tears pooling in his eyes, and wrapped one arm around Sydney, drawing her into their warm circle. "A life worth living." He pressed his lips to her temple. "And worth living well."

* * * * *

The Sheriff's Daughter

by

Tara Taylor Quinn

May 24

1:00—Lunch

2:00—Interview (It's the retired cop. Credentials in folder.)

2:20—Meeting with Rodney Pace. (Presentation schedule included in red folder on desk.)

6:30—Dinner with partners from Mr. Calhoun's firm. Hanrahan's.

Note: Proof Sheriff Lindsay's book. Sign checks and contracts before leaving. (In blue folder.)

Further note: Don't forget to eat.

SARA CALHOUN SMILED as she read the final line Donna had jotted on the daily agenda, which sat atop a newly readied pile of folders on her desk at the National Organization for Internet Safety and Education early Thursday morning. The red-eye she'd taken from a PTA conference in Anaheim had just landed at Port Columbus International Airport half an hour before. She couldn't remember the last time she'd eaten.

If she'd gone straight home to shower without stopping at the office first to review the day's materials, she could have had breakfast with Brent.

Glancing at the plain gold watch on her wrist—a college graduation present from her parents—Sara sat, pulled the pile of folders onto her lap and started to read.

THE DOORBELL RANG just as she was finishing her makeup. Stroking a couple of coats of mascara onto her lashes, Sara quickly dropped the tube in the sectioned container on her dressing table and raced to the stairs. Maybe it was just a salesperson, but she couldn't stand to not answer.

She never let the phone ring, either.

It was five to nine. She'd spent so long at the office already that she was now late for work. But the sun was shining, May flowers were in bloom and an entire lovely summer stretched ahead.

Sara slowed at the bottom of the stairs, taking a deep breath to compose herself as she smoothed a hand down her slim brown skirt and brushed the pockets of her jacket. Dignity and class were her mantras. Always.

Brent expected this from her.

"Can I help—" The ready smile froze on her lips. A cop was standing on her doorstep.

Something had happened to her dad. Or Brent.

The young man's mouth moved, but at this moment Sara couldn't concentrate sufficiently to make out his words. "What?" she asked, willing herself to hear what he was saying. "What happened?"

"Are you Mrs. Sara Calhoun?"

"Yes." She wished she weren't. Law enforcement officials never came to deliver good news. She ought to know. She'd grown up with one.

"You are." The young man's gaze deepened, studying her.

"Yes," she managed to say, bracing herself.

And nothing happened. Officer Mercedes, according to the thin nameplate above his left pocket, just stood there, apparently at a loss for words.

"Can I help you?" she finally prompted, mystified. She was the one getting the bad news—wasn't she?

"I...uh...I've been planning this moment for a long time and I thought I was completely prepared. But now I have no idea what to say."

Planning this moment? One didn't usually plan to deliver bad news.

He looked so lost, so young, Sara's heart caught. "You're sure it's me you want to see? I'm Sara Calhoun, formerly Sara Lindsay. I'm married to Brent Calhoun. He's an attorney…."

Relief made her talkative.

"Antitrust. Yes, I know," the tall, well-built officer said with a rueful grin. And a nervous twitch at the left corner of his mouth.

He ran his hand through his short sandy-colored hair, his raised arm drawing her attention to the belt at his waist—and all the defensive paraphernalia strapped there. That gun looked heavy.

"And, yes, you're the one I'm looking for."

The kid was young, his green eyes switching back and forth between innocent and knowing as he stood there, shifting his weight. He couldn't be much more than twenty-one, which made her thirty-seven seem ancient.

"What'd I do? Forget to signal a turn? I have a habit of doing that, though I'm working on it," she said, brushing a strand of hair back over her shoulder. This had to be his first house call.

He frowned and then, glancing down, his face cleared. "Oh, the uniform," he said. "I'm not here on official business. I work the night shift in Westerville—just got off duty and finished my paperwork."

Westerville, a north Columbus suburb a bit west of the New Albany home she and Brent had purchased six years before. There was a park within walking distance of every home in their area. Barely thirty when they bought it, she'd still believed that her workaholic husband was going to agree to have the children they'd always said they were going to have.

"Speaking of work, I'm late," Sara said now, suddenly anxious to be on her way.

"I can come back another time."

"No." She shook her head. What could a young cop possibly have to do with her that would justify a second trip out? Or any trip? "I'm listening."

"And I'm finding that there's just no way to say this except outright."

She waited.

"I'm your son."

Queens of Romance

Uncertain Summer

Serena gave up hope of getting married when her fiancé
jilted her. Then Gijs suggested that she marry him instead.
She liked Gijs very much, and she knew he was fond of her –
that seemed as good a basis as any for marriage. But it
turned out Gijs was in love…

Small Slice of Summer

Letitia Marsden had decided that men were not to be trusted,
until she met Doctor Jason Mourik van Nie. This time, Letitia
vowed, there would be a happy ending. Then Jason got the
wrong idea about one of her male friends. Surely a simple
misunderstanding couldn't stand in the way of true love?

Available 1st August 2008

Collect all 10 superb books in the collection!

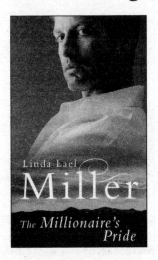

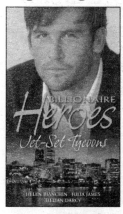 

Two men have vowed to protect the women they love…

New York Times bestselling author

DIANA PALMER

Hard to Handle

Hunter

On a top secret operation in the desert, chief of security Hunter knew Jennifer Marist needed his protection. Soon he discovered the lure of Jenny's wild, sweet passion – and a love he'd never dreamed possible.

Man in Control

Eight years after DEA agent Alexander Cobb had turned Jodie Clayburn down, Alexander could hardly believe the beauty that Jodie had become… or that she'd helped him crack a dangerous drug-smuggling case. Would the man in control finally surrender to his desires?

Available 20th June 2008

Celebrate 100 years of pure reading pleasure with Mills & Boon®

To mark our centenary, each month we're publishing a special 100th Birthday Edition. These celebratory editions are packed with extra features and include a FREE bonus story.

Plus, you have the chance to enter a fabulous monthly prize draw. See 100th Birthday Edition books for details.

Now that's worth celebrating!

July 2008

**The Man Who Had Everything
by Christine Rimmer**
Includes FREE bonus story *Marrying Molly*

August 2008

Their Miracle Baby by Caroline Anderson
Includes FREE bonus story *Making Memories*

September 2008

Crazy About Her Spanish Boss by Rebecca Winters
Includes FREE bonus story
Rafael's Convenient Proposal

Look for Mills & Boon® 100th Birthday Editions at your favourite bookseller or visit
www.millsandboon.co.uk

2 FREE

BOOKS AND A SURPRISE GIFT!

We would like to take this opportunity to thank you for reading this Mills & Boon® book by offering you the chance to take TWO more specially selected titles from the Superromance series absolutely FREE! We're also making this offer to introduce you to the benefits of the Mills & Boon® Reader Service™—

- ★ **FREE home delivery**
- ★ **FREE gifts and competitions**
- ★ **FREE monthly Newsletter**
- ★ **Exclusive Reader Service offers**
- ★ **Books available before they're in the shops**

Accepting these FREE books and gift places you under no obligation to buy, you may cancel at any time, even after receiving your free shipment. Simply complete your details below and return the entire page to the address below. You don't even need a stamp!

YES! Please send me 2 free Superromance books and a surprise gift. I understand that unless you hear from me. I will receive 4 superb new titles every month for just £3.69 each, postage and packing free. I am under no obligation to purchase any books and may cancel my subscription at any time. The free books and gift will be mine to keep in any case.

U8ZED

Ms/Mrs/Miss/Mr ....Initials ....
BLOCK CAPITALS PLEASE

Surname ....

Address ....

....

....Postcode....................................

Send this whole page to:
UK: FREEPOST CN81, Croydon, CR9 3WZ